After Siege

AS THE WORLD DIES, BOOK 4

Rhiannon Frater

After Siege
As the World Dies, Book 4
by Rhiannon Frater
Copyright © 2020
All Rights Reserved.

ISBN: 9798660092374

Edited by Felicia A. Sullivan
Interior formatting by Kody Boye Publishing Services
Cover Artwork and Layout by Corey Hollins
Interior graphics by Terence-Jaiden Wray

http://rhiannonfrater.com/

This book is a work of fiction. People, places, events and situation are the product of the author's imagination. Any resemblance to actual persons, living or dead, or historical events, is purely coincidental.

Also by Rhiannon Frater

As The World Dies
The First Days
Fighting to Survive
A Very Fort Christmas
Siege
The Untold Tales
After Siege

The Bastion Series
Escape to the Last Bastion
The Last Bastion of the Living
The Mission of the Living

The Hidden Necromancer Series
The Unblessed Dead
The Accused Dead
The Cursed Dead

The Living Dead Boy Series
The Living Dead Boy
Lost in Texas
Journey Across Zombie Texas

Short Story Collections
Zombie Tales from Dead Worlds

Dedicated with much love to my husband.

For all the readers who encouraged me to return to the Fort.

Somewhere in Texas

PROLOGUE

There was once a princess who lived in a metal castle with her little boy, a prince with magical light up shoes and a naughty smile. She loved him very much and they were very happy, even though the metal castle was old and starting to fall apart and the princess didn't have much money left in the castle's treasure room.

Although the prince's father was the court jester, he did not live in the metal castle. He lived somewhere else with a new wife and baby. The princess didn't like him much. The jester could be funny and nice, but he could also be cruel. He'd broken her heart once and she vowed to never let him do it again.

One day, the jester came and claimed the little prince for a fun weekend across the village at his house. The princess always missed the little prince when he had to visit the jester, but she knew his father loved him very much. So she waved goodbye as the jester carried him away in a big fancy carriage.

What she didn't know was that it was her final goodbye.

The monsters came that day. Monsters that were terrible and cruel. They turned the good people of the village into monsters before the princess even knew what was happening. By the time she understood that evil had taken over her land, it was too late. The little prince and the jester were lost.

The princess made a solemn vow to find the little prince in his new monster form and free him from the evil spell. She learned how to become a hunter and killed the monsters one by one.

Finally, one day, the princess found the jester and the prince. They were monsters now too. Her heart broke all over again when she saw the little prince's magical light up shoes. She freed their souls with an arrow of love and sat down and cried until she had no more tears to shed.

In the night, she dreamed of an angel who told her to travel to a fortress on a hill. The angel told her that she would find good people there who would help her fight the monsters. So the next morning the princess packed up all her possessions and left her metal castle.

As she traveled, she started to worry she'd imagined the angel. That maybe she was foolish to follow the dream. And then she saw it. The fortress on a hill. And she knew the angel had told the truth.

The princess was met by a mighty knight who helped her onto his horse and carried her through the gates into the fortress. Once inside, she saw all the good people who were valiantly fighting the monsters and knew that she had found a sanctuary.

The princess - who would now be a monster hunter - had found a place to call home.

CHAPTER 1

Paperwork of the Dead

"Zombies might rule the Earth, but there's still paperwork to be done."

"I guess things aren't as different as I thought," Emma answered while watching the middle-aged black woman shuffle folders around on the big desk. "Can I help?"

"No, no. Give me a second. Everything is a mess since I'm just moving in." Dressed all in black from a long skirt to the scarf draped over her shoulders, the other woman looked far different from the dirty and sweaty jeans-and-t-shirt-wearing crews outside. Though her eyes were a little bloodshot and there were dark circles under her eyes, the woman had taken care to apply a tiny bit of eyeliner on her eyelids and a touch of dark lipstick on her lips. Her thick salt-and-pepper curls were pulled up into a poufy bun with a few tendrils clinging to her forehead. Emma couldn't help but stare at her. It had been so long since she'd seen another woman that wasn't a zombie.

The old building smelled of mildew, fresh coffee, the woman's flowery perfume, and a whiff of stale body odor lingering from days past. Light poured through the tall windows into the large office that was filled with banker boxes loaded with more files. The walls were bare except for two maps - one of Texas and another of the town of Ashley Oaks - a portrait of an older black man, and a very old Texas flag in a frame. Picking up a name placard, the woman set it down at the edge of the desk for Emma to see. A fresh label was taped over the previous name. It read: Yolanda Williams, City Secretary.

Emma rocked on her heels, her leather cowboy boots creaking. The fan in the corner did little to cool the room and beads of perspiration ran down her spine, soaking the bottom of her red t-shirt. A little nervous in her new environment, she braided her chestnut-brown hair with trembling fingers just to give her something to do while waiting.

After living an entire year on her own, Emma was overwhelmed by this new world she'd discovered. While the high walls surrounding several blocks of downtown Ashley Oaks were impressive enough, the carefully-controlled chaos happening within them was even more so. In the shadow of the ten-story hotel, people bustled about doing various chores while sentries walked the high walls. The place was called The Fort, and Emma could definitely see why. She hadn't been this safe in over a year. It was hard to imagine the zombies breaching these walls.

"Found it!" Yolanda held up a ledger with a faded green cover. It looked like a relic of another era. "Peggy had everything set up on the computer, but I have my paper backups. If we ever lose power, we'll need them."

"How *do* you have power?" Emma asked, her eyes flicking up to the sputtering fluorescent lights overhead.

"Hydro-electric plant. Some military personnel are up there with engineers keeping it going. We have a ton of generators outside in case we do lose power. Travis, Juan and Eric have got all the bases covered."

"I met Juan coming in."

The tall, green-eyed cowboy with the thick West Texas accent had ridden in on a horse to save her from a zombie as she'd approached the wall. His entrance had been impressive. Handsome, kind, and somehow fragile, she had to admit she found him more than a little attractive. The fact he'd adopted orphaned children impressed her even more. She'd met his son, Troy, when she'd arrived. The sweet child had reminded her painfully of her own lost boy.

"Juan is the head of construction. He's the one who got people to start building walls on the first day. Travis is our mayor. Nice city guy who is doing an okay job. Eric is an engineer from Austin. Sweet as pie, that one. The three of them have The Fort feeling almost like the old world except for the phones. Apparently some poles went down the first day. But we have a ham radio, CBs, and walkie-talkies. That's something." Yolanda settled behind her desk and flipped the ledger open. Picking up a pen, she appeared even more flustered than Emma. "Move that box and take a seat. I should have told you that before. I'm just a little rattled after yesterday and so damn tired. We're all running on hardly any sleep around here. I'm sure you know how it is."

"Absolutely."

Emma heaved the box onto the floor and perched on the edge of an old metal and vinyl chair. It looked like the type of chair that inhabited every government building in existence. It made her strangely nostalgic.

"I'm sorry we're so disorganized right now. That zombie horde coming through gave us a fright and we're still cleaning up."

"I heard it. Felt it. It went right by my Airstream," Emma answered.

"You're so blessed they didn't know you were in there. There were thousands. I've never been so scared in my life."

"I was drunk when they passed by. I had no idea there were so many." After putting down the zombified body of her little boy, she'd drunk herself into a stupor and passed out. The zombie herd had knocked aside her Airstream on their way through the area.

"Well, God was looking out for you. Now, let me get you registered. What is your name?"

"I'm Emma Valdez," she answered, opting for her maiden name instead of her ex-husband's last name of Russell.

"Oh, are you Hispanic like Juan? Do you speak Spanish?"

"A quarter Lipan-Apache, actually. That's where I get my name. My grandfather's people are from on the border with Mexico. The rest of me is German stock from the Texas Hill Country with a big dose of basic redneck. I can speak a tiny bit of Spanish, but I'm not fluent."

"Ah, okay. We have some former migrant workers who don't speak a lot of English. I try to find them work partners that can communicate with them."

"Juan said that everyone has assigned jobs."

"That's right. Everyone contributes."

"I can hunt," Emma offered. "My grandfather taught me how. I'm a good shot."

"Oh, that's good! We lost several of our good hunters recently." Yolanda hesitated, a shadow of pain flitting over her face.

"You lost a lot of people to the horde?"

"No, no. They left before the horde got here. There was a... disagreement."

Emma lifted her eyebrows, curious, but not comfortable with pushing to find out the details.

"Have you had a lot of interaction with the zombies, Emma? Know how to kill them?"

Emma couldn't help but give her a sad smile that was tinged with bittersweet pride. "I killed an entire town of zombies."

Yolanda's eyes grew wide. "Oh, so you might be good on a rescue squad."

"Rescue squad?"

"We go out and help people get here. There's less now, sadly, but we sometimes get calls for help." Yolanda bent over the ledger, making notations.

The scratch of the pen against paper reminded Emma of her days taking online courses after she had decided to improve her lot in life. She'd spent hours on coursework, writing everything by hand before transferring it to her laptop. After being derailed by pregnancy, her life had been dictated by Billy's needs. Finally, she'd decided to take charge of her life. She'd only finished part of a semester when the dead began to walk and she'd lost her son. Her daydreams had devolved into nightmares.

Sitting in the office watching Yolanda work, it felt like the last year and a half wasn't real. All that death and gore, the endless sorrow, the burning rage, was fading to a dark memory in the light of hope. She could take charge of her life again and maybe find a sliver of happiness. It made her dizzy just thinking about the possibility of finding a new role to fulfill other than grieving mother and vengeful zombie killer.

"I'm not sure when I'll be able to assign you to a patrol. I have to dig through all these boxes and get the schedules sorted out. I can assign you a hotel room now. I'll get someone to take you to where we keep our inventory so you can select toiletries and find more clothes. There are three meals a day and we all eat in the hotel dining room."

Yolanda continued to talk, explaining the ins and outs of the fort, and Emma gripped the metal armrests of her chair to keep the room from spinning. Again, she was dazed by the abrupt change in her life. To go from being alone, scavenging for food, and relentlessly killing zombies while searching for her dead son to a place filled with life and people was too much to process.

"Yolanda!" Juan called out from the doorway.

The woman stopped speaking and looked up.

"I think you need a better introduction speech," he said with a wink. "I think you're overwhelming her."

Emma tried to force a smile, but was certain it looked fake. She was feeling slightly lightheaded. Perhaps it was the heat, though most likely it was her mind attempting to drink in every new bit of information flowing her way.

"Dammit. I am. Peggy had this down to a science." Yolanda shook her head, looking annoyed. "Damn her for leaving us."

Leaning against the door frame, cowboy hat in hand, Juan gave Yolanda an encouraging smile. "You're doing a good job though, you know. You got this."

"I hope so." Rummaging around in a box, Yolanda wagged her head disapprovingly. "If only she had said something."

"We were all freakin' out. None of us noticed Peggy was panicking more than the rest of us. It's not your fault."

"I keep telling myself that, but I don't believe it. When I think of how scared she was and little Cody..." Yolanda closed her mouth, tears welling. "How could she? He was a baby!"

"No one knew she'd do that," Juan said gently. "If we'd suspected, we would've done somethin'. You know that."

"It's like losing Tobias all over again." Yolanda's gaze

flicked to the portrait of the gentleman on the wall. "I didn't see that coming either."

Emma rubbed her hands against her thighs, her fingers lightly grazing over the holes in the knees. It wasn't too hard to piece together what had happened. Apparently Peggy had been the former city secretary and had taken her life and that of her child prior to the horde arriving, leaving a vacuum that Yolanda was trying to fill. People didn't always die in this world by natural causes or a zombie bite. Sometimes they chose to check out. She'd found two of her neighbors hanging in their living room. Another had taken an exit via shotgun.

"Life ain't kind," Juan muttered. "And can be fragile."

The sound of keys jangling filled the office. The conversation paused while Yolanda searched for the correct key. The weight of personal loss created a heavy atmosphere in the office.

"Boss," a voice said from the doorway.

Juan pivoted around. "What's up, Enrique?"

A small-statured man with deeply tanned skin and dark eyes leaned against the doorjamb. Drenched in sweat, filthy with dirt and what looked like cement dust, he wiped his face with a kerchief. "We're working on that new wall, but we got zombies coming in from those warehouses along the train tracks. I pulled the crew back in."

Juan pulled his walkie-talkie off his belt. "I'll let Nerit know."

"Let her know they're runners."

"Is that what you call them? The fresh ones?" Emma asked.

"Yeah. The new ones are scary fast."

Enrique nodded and disappeared down the hallway.

While Juan radioed in the situation, Yolanda approached Emma with a key with a post-it note wrapped around it. "This is your room. Feel free to change it around however you want. If you wait a few minutes, I'll find someone to take you up there."

Juan interrupted his conversation to say, "Don't worry about it, Yolanda. I'll make sure she's settled in."

"Oh, okay," Yolanda said with surprise but also a knowing look in her eyes.

Emma knew that expression. It was the one the ladies at church got when they happened upon a new bit of gossip to spread around.

"Nerit is going to check out the situation. I'm gonna join her. Want to tag along and see how we do things around here?"

Though she'd had her fill of zombies, Emma nodded. "Yeah. That sounds good."

"You don't have to, you know," Juan said, suddenly seeming nervous. "I know you're new here."

"No, no. If this is going to be my home that entails learning how things function here."

Juan grinned. "You're going to do fine here. I feel it in my bones."

That smile made her a little fluttery and she blushed, much to her dismay. Under his cowboy hat, his face reddened too, much to Yolanda's obvious amusement.

"What about my stuff?" Emma asked, pointing to her bag and weapons.

"Bring the rifle, machete, and pistol. Yolanda, she can leave the bag here, right?"

"No problem."

"Thank you," Emma said, slinging her rifle over her shoulder.

Juan waved her through the door. "Okay, let's go see what those fuckin' zombies are up to. Nerit's going to meet us out on the wall."

Strolling through the old City Hall building, Emma took a deep breath and rubbed her sweaty palms against her jeans. When they reached the door to the outside, Juan skittered ahead of her to open the door. The sunlight poured through the exit, nearly blinding her.

Pulling on her sunglasses, Emma stepped out into the Fort.

CHAPTER 2

Welcome to Badassery

The glare of the sun was blinding. The shadow cast by the hotel had moved away, leaving the busiest area of the Fort in direct sunlight. Juan tucked his cowboy hat onto his curls and gestured for Emma to follow him down the back steps of City Hall and into the heart of the complex.

Strolling past the Fort occupants, Emma noted they were all ages, genders, and from different racial and ethnic backgrounds. The Fort clearly was a place for everyone as long as they were willing to get along and do some hard work. All looked exhausted and sweaty as they stood around in small groups watching Juan and Emma pass by.

Dust stirred in a faint breeze and the smell of hard-working bodies was pungent. That hard work had come to a halt and everyone was eerily quiet. There was a smattering of hushed conversations, but the loudest noise was the wind blowing in through the gap in the hills to the east. It was a little unsettling until Emma observed the yellow flags erected over the sentry posts. On them was written SILENCE/SILENCIO. That explained the work shutdown.

People were taking advantage of the time out to drink from frosty water bottles handed out by some teenagers dragging an ice chest on wheels.

"What's up, Dad?" a teenage boy whispered to Juan while handing him a bottle of water. He had messy brown hair that fell over his eyes and partially hid his freckled nose.

"Zombies are causing trouble, Jason. We're on our way to check it out," Juan said in a voice so soft Emma could barely hear it.

The boy's gaze shifted to Emma. The intensity of the teenager's stare made her feel like an interloper, and she resisted the urge to apologize for an offense she didn't know she had committed.

Jason nodded solemnly and moved on to the next group with two other teens following.

Juan leaned over to say in her ear, "My oldest. Jason."

Jason appeared to be about fifteen. Juan looked like he was a little older than her in his late twenties or maybe early thirties. The math didn't exactly add up unless Juan had been a really young father.

Emma mouthed, *Adopted?*

With a grin, Juan cracked the water bottle open. He took a swig, then leaned over again to answer, his breath frosty against her ear. "All my kids are adopted. All four of them."

"Oh. Wow."

Emma's approval of the Latino man climbed upward.

A tall, striking older woman with silvery-blonde hair and fine lines on her tanned face emerged from the hotel entrance. She wore her jeans, cowboy boots, and a short-sleeved plaid cotton shirt over a black tank top like a uniform. Dark sunglasses covered her eyes, and there was a distinct military bearing to her stride. Emma noticed people straightened their spines and looked attentive the second she appeared. Motioning to Jason, the woman held one hand out. The teenager tossed her a water bottle. Barely glancing at it, she plucked it out of the air.

Leaning over again, Juan said, "That's Nerit."

The woman walking toward them exuded strength like no one Emma had ever met before. She suspected she'd experienced things that would shake most people.

Keeping her tone low, Nerit addressed her. "Emma, welcome to the Fort. Rune told me you had arrived and what he said about your history was impressive. You'll be a great asset to our community."

The accent Nerit spoke with sounded familiar, but Emma couldn't place it.

Emma was bewildered. "How does he know about me?"

With a hint of a smile, Nerit replied, "He has inside information."

Emma gave Juan a questioning look. "The ghost thing?"

"Yup. The ghost thing."

Juan had told her that Rune was a medium, a man who could see and speak to the dead. In a zombie-infested world, he would definitely have unique access to information most people wouldn't have. Emma completely believed in ghosts. She was convinced one had told her to come to the Fort. She vividly remembered the beautiful woman with the long black hair and soulful dark eyes urging her not to kill herself, but live. Of course, the dream had occurred while Emma was drunk as a skunk, but the Fort did exist right where the woman said it would.

Gesturing for Juan and Emma to follow, Nerit strode toward the collapsible stairs that led over the inner wall. Falling into step behind Juan, Emma shivered despite the heat. The eyes of the people of the Fort were trained on her, probably curious about her after hearing Rune's stories. She fought the impulse to respond to the inquiring looks and explain that she was no one, just a young woman who killed all the zombies in her town while seeking to put her baby to rest. In this horrible new world, those actions couldn't be too unusual, she surmised. Everyone surviving had to have similar stories.

The wooden steps led to a platform encased in camouflage netting. Nerit slipped under the entrance flap with Juan at her heels. Emma took a second to observe the view of Main Street. The town blocks in either direction ended with a concrete wall. The street was dotted with piles of lumber, bags of soil and fertilizer. Groups of people were huddled in the shade alongside one building, taking a break. It appeared they'd been making planter boxes before the call to stop working.

Emma stepped into the sentry outpost and the netting fell behind her.

Two people stood with Nerit. One was a man with a reddish-brown complexion and indigenous Mexican features. The other was a redheaded white woman slathered in sunscreen to protect her freckled face and the bare bony shoulders sticking out of her army green tank top.

Emma shrugged beneath her red top to alleviate some of the tension in her shoulders, the fabric clinging wetly to her skin. Tendrils of her chestnut brown hair stuck to her cheeks and she tucked them behind her ears to keep them out of the way.

Keeping her voice at a low volume, Nerit said, "Enrique says we have runners. What's the status, Katarina?"

"I've spotted maybe a dozen runners down at the end of Second Street. They're definitely hunting us, but haven't spotted anyone living yet. They're doing that jerky back and forth dance they do when they suspect the living are around, but can't spot 'em. Martin," Katarina pointed to the man next to her, "has the lowdown on what happened when they first appeared."

If Nerit was scared or worried about the brewing, she didn't show it.

Emma was impressed.

"Juan, ask Martin for details, please," Nerit instructed.

Juan turned to the shorter man and asked him a question in Spanish laced with a West Texan accent. It was a combination that Emma found amusing. The twang didn't faze the shorter man, who nodded, and answered. Martin explained to Juan in Spanish what he'd witnessed on the far end of the Fort. Gesturing as he spoke, the construction worker was surprisingly calm considering he'd just eluded the undead. His white T-shirt was drenched with perspiration and he was covered in the ruddy dirt native to the area. Emma caught a few words here and there, but her high school Spanish had faded from memory soon after she graduated. She did capture the gist of what was being said. The zombies had appeared abruptly, sprinting at top speed toward the tracks.

With a nod, Juan patted the man on the shoulder, then conveyed the story to Nerit. "His crew was clearing the traps and doing zombie body removal when they saw the runners coming out of the tree line." Juan pointed to the nearby foothills that bordered the west side of town. "The zombies hit the tracks and headed straight for them. I don't like it. Fresh dead means we missed survivors heading our way probably needing help."

Martin spoke up again. Emma picked up more than half of what he said this time, her old Spanish lessons sparking to life. The news sounded bad and Juan's reaction was a confirmation.

Visibly pale, he swore in Spanish then dismissed the other man.

After Martin left, Nerit asked, "What is it? What's wrong."

"This is bad, Nerit. Martin recognized the zombie that chased them to the ladder. He says it was Ed's oldest, Eddie."

"Shit," Katarina moaned.

Emma felt distinctly out of place as this news rocked the people gathered around her.

Nerit squared her shoulders and lifted her chin. "It was Ed's choice to leave. We couldn't have made him or the others stay if we wanted to."

"Belinda," Juan said, pain and grief infusing the name. "She went with them."

Recognizing that Emma was out of the loop, Nerit turned to her. Taking off her sunglasses, she revealed keen gray eyes with a hint of green at the center. "Before the horde came through, there was an incident where one of the main entrances was opened to let people inside. This was after the order had been given that we were locked in. No one in or out. Our lead hunter, Ed, was upset by this development. So were a few others. They banded together and demanded that they be given vehicles and weapons so they could take their lives into their own hands and not depend on the Fort for safety."

"Damn fool idea," Katarina muttered.

"They left here? This is a fortress. Literally. I can't..." Emma faltered seeing Juan's devastated expression.

"In times of war, people make choices we may not always agree with. They decided to leave, and it looks like they ran into trouble," Nerit said.

"We need to send out a rescue team right away," Juan said with great urgency. "We need to act now."

Katarina and Nerit glanced at each other with troubled expressions, but it was Nerit who spoke up.

"If Eddie is a runner, chances are it won't be a rescue."

Juan whipped off his cowboy hat and anxiously ran his fingers through his damp curls. "Nerit, we can't know that until we see the runners and verify it's Ed's people. Even if some of the runners are from his group, that doesn't mean there aren't survivors of whatever shit went down out there. We have to make sure."

"*After* we deal with the runners and save *our* people, Juan."

The following stare down was one Emma already knew Juan was going to lose in spite of his desperation. In the short time she'd been around Nerit, it was abundantly obvious that she was respected and a strong leader.

Juan was the first to break. He averted his eyes, tucked his hat back on his head, and resignedly asked, "So what do we do?"

Katarina pulled out a tattered hand-drawn map of the fort, cleared some half-full water bottles from a folding tray, and spread it out on flat surface. "Maybe we should lift the order for quiet. Noise might draw the runners to the wall on our north side since that area is closest to where Martin's people were when attacked. There aren't any traps there, so we'll have to shoot or spear 'em."

Nerit studied Katarina's map, her forehead furrowed with concentration. A thoughtful silence followed for a few seconds. "I don't want to put our people in unnecessary danger. The sound of gunfire might pull zombies to our location. If we have any vestiges of the horde in the city limits, we have to be careful since we have so many teams outside the wall. That would complicate everything."

"So spears then," Katarina said. "Pike them from above."

Juan shook his head. "Spears aren't going to work on the northern wall. We built it higher because it's on a hill, remember? We didn't want the zombies bunching up at the base of the wall and building a ramp, so we added a few feet to the top. Spears won't reach. Plus, we got two crews in that area. None of those buildings are secured and aren't safe. We don't want to put them in more danger."

Emma peeked at the map. There was a lot more to the Fort

than she'd realized.

"We can send out a pied piper," Katarina suggested. "Pull the runners away from where we have our people hiding and lure the zombies out of town."

Nerit crossed her arms and wedged the knuckles of one hand under her chin, clearly giving Katarina's recommendation some thought before answering. "I would say at any other time that might be viable, but the horde could have stragglers. Venturing close to the city limits could be deadly for anyone we send out that far."

"That fuckin' zombie horde is screwin' up everything," Katarina groused.

Nerit glanced at Juan. "What do you suggest?"

"We got some defenses set up that weren't triggered when the horde passed through. I say take the running zombies out with what we've already got rigged. That way we won't use ammo and attract any stragglers in our direction." Juan pointed to a spot on the map. "Right there is our best shot. That area was totally missed by the horde."

"The west end of Main Street," Nerit said.

"That's where a lot of our traps are untouched by the horde. We have several fire and razor wire traps that weren't tripped. They won't make a lot of noise."

Katarina shuddered. "Only one zombie was dumb enough to go through there. Jason's razor wire traps are brutal. She was legit in pieces."

Juan took off his cowboy hat to wipe the sweat from his brow. "My boy is thorough in his designs. We could eliminate quite a few of them-if not all-with the traps."

"Slower zombies are easier to deal with one on one," Nerit said. "Since our best driver is on maternity leave, I'll be the lure. Any suggestions on a vehicle, Katarina?"

"Greta says that sweet Mustang the scavengers brought in a month ago is noisy and fast."

"Then I'll take that one."

Juan nervously chuckled while tucking his hat back on his head. "Admit it, Nerit."

"Admit what?"

"You're a sniper, the equivalent of a stunt driver, a military strategist, and hard as nails. Basically, an all-around badass. You were Mossad, weren't you?"

Nerit tilted her head to regard Juan with a stare that sent chills down Emma's spine. A second later a bright smile lit up Nerit's face. "Don't be silly, Juan. I was simply an IDF sharpshooter. I served like all the other Israelis do. Nothing more than that."

"Bull-fuckin'-shit," Juan replied, shaking his head.

Ignoring him, Nerit pivoted away. Emma automatically straightened as the imposing woman's gaze settled on her.

"Emma, are you ready for a first assignment?"

"I'm ready and willing to do whatever," Emma said.

"In case something goes wrong and we have to resort to bullets, I'll need people covering for me. Let's see how good a shot you are *if* you're needed. Katarina, take her to the West Main Street sentry post."

Nerit gave Emma a brief, warm smile, before focusing on Juan and becoming stoic again. "Juan, get the elevator ready. I'll stop at the corner of Main Street and Elm and run for it."

"You know, someone else could do this, Nerit. You're recovering from your illness."

"It's fine, Juan. As you pointed out, I'm a badass."

"Don't throw my words back at me, for fuck's sake," Juan grumbled. "Let someone else do this."

"Just do as I say, Juan."

Emma knew that tone from years of living with her grandparents. She gave Juan a furtive look to see how he'd respond.

With a grunt, he bobbed his chin, relenting. "Fine, but I don't like it."

"You don't have to." Nerit departed by sliding under the netting, which had the finality of someone slamming a door shut.

"Don't worry. As you said. She's a badass," Katarina said, nudging Juan with her elbow. "Follow me, Emma. Let's see what *your* badass rating is."

CHAPTER 3

Time to Kill Zombies

Emma hurried along Main Street with Katarina toward the wall located down the block. The pretty red brick road was so scorching hot she could feel the heat radiating through the soles of her boots. Sweat trailed down her neck and back while the strap on her rifle dug into her sore shoulder. Discomfort was an old friend. Since the zombie rising, her body was constantly covered in bruises and scratches from her long days killing zombies. The only time she hadn't experienced pain was when she chugged liquor and passed out in her Airstream.

The vintage trailer was a far departure from the Fort. The old buildings lining the street were constructed from red brick with pretty decorative details like white pillars, decorative scrollwork, and hand-painted tile insets. It was easy to imagine the town bustling with activity during its heyday, but Emma doubted that time period had been in recent decades. Some of the structures were in good condition, while others looked like they'd been abandoned for a long time. In one store filled with gardening equipment, she caught a glimpse of people hunkered behind a counter peeking out at her.

"Is it always this exciting?" Emma asked in a hushed voice.

"Nah. Sometimes it's so boring you wish something exciting would happen. Lately, though, it's been one helluva rollercoaster ride. One where the cars go sailing off the track and leave you beat up something awful. Or dead." The inflection in the redhead's words revealed so much. It was the sound of loss and anger.

"The horde coming through must have scared the shit out of everyone."

"That's putting it lightly. But even before that happened we were dealing with a shit-ton of bad stuff. If we can handle what we've gone through in the last year, we can deal with anything that comes our way. I'm sure of that."

Boots pounding against the concrete, Emma jogged behind Katarina toward the concrete brick structure cutting off Main Street. It was about ten feet high. A sentry post was built flush against the wall and spanned the entire width of the street. The wooden structure appeared sturdy and several sentries were clustered behind one of the three olive-green hunting blinds erected on the platform.

When they arrived, Katarina scaled the ladder straightaway. It wobbled a little beneath Emma as she climbed up after the other woman since it was rigged to be easily retracted. She was careful to keep her rifle flipped onto her back and out of her way. The last thing she wanted to do was to catch it on one of the rungs and make a damn fool of herself in front of the others.

Reaching the top, she joined the three other people gathered behind the blind along with Katrina. They were a diverse group: a man probably in his late twenties with dark skin and jet black hair; a blonde white woman around Emma's age with a deep tan and athletic physique; and a scrawny older white man who looked every inch the redneck stereotype.

"Emma, this is Rashmi, Stacey, and Ennis."

"It's a pleasure to meet all three of you."

The three nodded at her in welcome and she returned the gesture.

"What's going on, Kat?" Rashmi asked.

His accent was British, not Indian, which surprised Emma. Then again, she'd never met anyone who was Indian.

"We've got runners wandering around and Nerit is going to lure them into the traps."

Rashmi frowned. "Shouldn't someone else do it? She's still recovering." "Have *you* tried to tell Nerit not to do somethin'?" Katarina chuckled. "Like that's going to work."

Stacey laughed. "She *is* stubborn. I wouldn't dare try to boss her around. Nerit is scary in a lovable way."

With a scowl, Ennis leaned against the wall at his back. "I ain't scared of her. I can handle her just fine. But that being said, what does the scary old bitch want us to do?"

Stacey clearly took offense at his comment. "Don't call her a bitch!"

"I meant it as a compliment!"

Ignoring the squabble, Rashmi focused on Katarina. "What are we supposed to do?"

"Give her cover if anything goes wrong. Otherwise, we hold our fire," Katarina replied.

Stacey looked mystified by the order. "Hold our fire? Why?"

"We don't want to drag more zombies our way. Nerit wants the traps to take care of them. It's quieter."

"Aw, shit, Kat! We're going to have zombie bodies piling up and stinkin' to high heaven. The one we have out there right ain't cleaned up yet. She's smelling up the whole area! Makes guard duty miserable out here."

Katarina didn't appear impressed by his woes and dismissively shrugged. "Since most of the traps didn't go off over here and there is only *one* body, priority clean-up was elsewhere."

"Which is why she should have gotten picked up first. She's the *only* one on this end," Ennis argued.

Emma raised one finger. "Excuse me, but after the horde came through why is there only one dead zombie in this area? How did that happen?"

"The rest bypassed the town after the main firewall was set off. She's the only zombie that ventured close enough to this section to set off the razor wire trap," Rashmi said.

Emma flinched. "Ugh. That sounds messy."

Rashmi nodded. "She's in pieces."

"Well, in pieces or not, she's giving me the creeps. Got one eye staring right at us." Ennis shuddered. "I can feel it right now, all-accusing like. I could always feel that hag's evil eye on me."

Stacey leaned toward Emma and said, "He's convinced the zombie is his ex-wife."

"I *know* it is."

Rashmi's annoyance with Ennis was evident. "How could it

be your ex? Be logical, Ennis. You said she was in Beaumont when the z-poc started. How could she possibly be here?"

"You have no idea how damn ornery she could be when she got in a mood. She always threatened to haunt my ass. I'm tellin' ya, her zombie would hunt me down. I could see her trackin' me down just to make me miserable."

"She's dressed in Chanel. I swear it's Hilary Clinton," Stacey insisted.

"That's even more ludicrous," Rashmi protested. "How could she possibly travel here all the way from the East Coast?"

Ennis sniffed loudly, glaring at Rashmi. "My ex probably stole a nice outfit. I'm telling you it's her. With all these damn ghosts running around, I bet she possessed her zombie body so she could track me down! I know what she's capable of!"

Emma suspected this was a recurring argument. Ennis was definitely the stubborn type.

"We're off track," Katarina cut in.

"Sorry," Rashmi said, obviously annoyed. "Please, continue."

"As I said, our job is to give Nerit cover if anything goes wrong. We'll split up along the wall to make sure we cover the whole area. Don't open fire unless she's in direct harm. Once the runners are dead, we'll clear out any of the slow ones that follow with the spears." Katarina tapped a pile of makeshift spears with her foot. The weapons were made out of long pipes with trowels, knives, and screwdrivers secured to the end. "Firearms are a last resort. We don't want to attract more zombies after we got rid of the horde."

Thrusting his hands into the pockets of his jeans, Ennis rocked on his heels while twisting his mouth into odd shapes. "This plan don't make sense. How the hell is she going to make it over the wall? We got razor wire traps all along this side."

"Juan is rigging up the elevator."

Ennis snorted. "Like that'll be safe."

"What's the elevator?" Emma asked curiously. The Fort was much better equipped to deal with the zombie threat than her home had ever been. The ingenuity of the layout and the defenses impressed her. Despite all that, she couldn't imagine them building an elevator.

"It's not an actual elevator," Stacey explained. "It's some sort of crane."

Katarina gestured vaguely at the horizon. "There was a crew doing work on a highway overpass when it all went to shit, so we acquired a crawler crane. Juan rigged it up so we can either lower heavy items over the wall or bring something in," Katarina answered. "Take a peek out there and you'll see why she needs it."

Emma looked through one of the windows cut into the hunting blind at the rest of the street stretching out in front of her. Some areas of the road bore graffiti warnings.

"The spray painted areas are fire traps," Ennis explained.

"Isn't setting the zombies on fire dangerous?" Emma asked.

"They're afraid of fire. They'll either retreat or evade the flames, hopefully stumbling into the razor wire traps," Katarina replied.

Ennis pushed his hand past her face to point. It reeked of gun powder and tobacco. "She'll have to drive between the traps and catch the elevator on that yonder corner."

Emma was a little skeptical. "Will that work?"

"Don't know. First time we're bringing anyone in that way." Ennis shrugged. "Gonna be interesting."

"It sounds risky," Emma said. "But I guess there isn't an easy way over the wall, huh?"

Tucking her unruly red hair back from her freckled face, Katarina turned toward Emma. "Sometimes we have to get imaginative. They used to bring people over the inner wall in an excavator. It'll work."

"We should have sent a kill team out to take out the runners," Rashmi mumbled.

Stacey shook her head, disagreeing. "There are too many crews out beyond the wall. If the gunshots bring in any stragglers from the horde, we'd be risking everyone. Nerit rounding up the runners near the fort and bringing them here is a solid plan. Especially since we don't know how many there are."

"Playing Pied Piper didn't go so well last time," Ennis pointed out.

Katarina's back stiffened, her expression hardening. "Yes, it did! We redirected a good chunk of the horde! Our people gave their lives leading them away and did a damn good job doing it!"

"Just shut up, Ennis," Stacy whispered. "She's hurting."

"I didn't mean no offense about Bill," Ennis said, raising his hands defensively.

Blinking away tears, Katarina pointed at the various points along the wall. "Pick a spot and get ready."

Rashmi lightly touched her arm, clearly meaning to comfort her, but Katarina pulled away.

Understanding that a line had been crossed, the three guards moved away from the two women. Emma remained at Katarina's side offering silent emotional support, but not making any moves to soothe her. Everyone mourned differently. It was best to respect their boundaries.

A loud beeping noise drew her attention to the north side of the road. Over the tops of the buildings, a crane was visible, moving slowly into position.

Swallowing hard, Katarina composed herself. "The wall stretches down one more block. That's a new section where we keep all the construction equipment. We built it before the horde arrived."

"You have a lot of territory to protect," Emma noted.

"Yeah, but we can abandon some of these sections if we need to retreat to the hotel."

"It really is a fort."

"Exactly." Yanking her walkie-talkie off her belt, Katarina turned it on. "I need to call in to the dispatcher."

Emma nodded, focusing on the road and its many traps.

"Julie, this is Katarina. We're in position."

"How is your situation?"

"There's no sign of zombies on this side."

"The runners are hunting on the north side. One of our teams

had to get on the roof of that old gas station to avoid them. They reported at least a dozen runners."

There was a burst of static, then Nerit said, "*I'm in the paddock waiting for Juan to report he's in position.*"

"I can see the crane now. It's almost there," Katarina said.

"*You'll be happy to know that I'm not alone. Kevin is with me.*"

In the background, a man said, "*Damn straight I'm with you.*"

Though Emma didn't know the owner of the voice, she was glad someone was accompanying Nerit. Like everyone else, she was uncomfortable with Nerit's attempt to handle the situation on her own. Apparently, she had been ill for a while. There was a certain aura about Nerit that was intimidating, but also charismatic. It made sense that she wanted to maintain her image as a badass in the eyes of the people who fought alongside her. Maybe like Emma, she wanted to prove herself to the others. Emma understood that sentiment.

"*I'm getting in reports of runner activity near one of our teams in the alley near Ash Street, Nerit,*" Julie said.

"*We'll handle them.*"

Katarina dropped the hand holding the walkie-talkie to her side. The voices of the others on the frequency occasionally updated each other. After an explosive sigh, she said, "I'm so sick of zombies."

"Me too."

"I don't doubt it since according to Rune you killed a whole town of them on your own."

Emma laughed. "He appears to be spreading my legend far and wide."

"He knows we all need a good story to lift our spirits."

Nearby, the crane came to a halt and Juan's voice over the airwaves saying he was in position.

"I cleared a town, but you defeated an enormous horde of zombies. I would think that would be enough to lift everyone's spirits."

Katarina leaned one hip against the wood rail and shrugged. "Well, yeah, but we lost people. So it's a mixed bag."

The walkie-talkie sprung to life. It was Nerit.
"We've got runners following us. Get ready."
Katarina swung her rifle off her shoulder. "Did ya hear that?"
"Yup. I'm ready."
It was time to kill zombies.

CHAPTER 4

This Was a Bad Plan

Emma knew things were going to go wrong.

Though safe behind a high wall, hidden from view by the hunter's blind, and armed with her grandfather's rifle, her gut told her that shit was about to hit the fan. Without a doubt, Nerit and the others thought they had a good plan. Technically, she could see where it would probably work, but something felt off.

After diverting the massive horde of zombies, the people of the Fort looked exhausted and tensions were high. It was the type of emotional and physical state that resulted in mistakes. It was not an ideal atmosphere in which to make hurried decisions about how to obliterate yet another threat.

Listening to the constant stream of updates over the walkie-talkie, Emma leaned against the rail inside the hunting blind and peered out the open window cut into the fabric. The road ahead appeared clear except for the traps that were covered in cloth painted to look like the road from a distance. The layout was clever, designed to herd the zombies into the razor wire traps by setting off strategically placed fire traps.

Ingenious.

Still...

Over the walkie-talkie, a man's voice said, *"We have around twenty runners in pursuit. There are some slower ones scattered in the streets, but they're not an issue. We're about three blocks away from the traps."*

Emma rested her rifle butt on her hip while she listened. That many runners was a concern no matter how calm the man sounded.

"Runners are kinda smart," she said, working through her concerns aloud.

In her periphery, she saw Katarina glance toward her. "Yeah. Sometimes."

"In the early days of the z-poc, they were smart enough to open car doors. That's when I learned to always lock them. They used tools too. One threw a brick through the window of a building I was hiding in. If these runners are new, they might not fall for the traps once the first one goes off."

Katarina grunted. "Shit. You got a point."

"I might be wrong."

"Yeah, but if you're right this might not be as easy as we thought. Let me call in." Katarina tugged the walkie-talkie off her belt. "These last few weeks have got us burned out. We don't need to be making stupid mistakes."

Emma was uneasy expressing her concerns. Being known as the zombie killer of an entire town was not something she was comfortable with at all. People could get the wrong impression about her and assume that she was some kind of know-it-all. She hoped she wasn't coming across as arrogant or condescending.

While Katarina urgently spoke with the others with a grim expression stamped on her face, Emma studied the area. Since she wasn't familiar with the town, she memorized every bit of the road in front of her. Even as the possibility of the plan going awry was discussed beside her, the noise of the Mustang's approach reverberated through the streets. It was definitely loud enough to keep the runners' focus and draw out any of the slower zombies lingering in the town.

"If they avoid the traps, open fire. It's as simple as that," Nerit said through the crackling of the airwaves. *"If we pull more slow zombies to the wall, we'll deal with them."*

Again, Emma experienced a twinge of unease. Maybe it was because she wasn't used to working with other people. Being responsible for only her life was vastly more comfortable than worrying about others. At the same time, it would be foolish to dismiss the longevity of the Fort in a dangerous new world. It was formidable, an impressive testament to the tenacity of the inhabitants and the effectiveness of the leadership.

Still...

Emma caught movement down the block near the mouth of an alley. A tree or bush was casting shade against the brick wall, but some of the shadows were too compact to be foliage. Hoisting her rifle into position, she aimed toward the silhouettes that had caught her attention. The rippling shadows constantly changed shape. The longer Emma stared at them, the more certain she was that they were cast by something moving through the alley.

More runners?

Before she could share her concerns with Katarina, the Mustang roared around the corner two blocks away from the wall. It was an older model, a bit battered by time. A few seconds later, the runners appeared. Alarmingly fast, they sprinted after the car, howling. Keeping a tiny lead on the small herd charging after it, the sports car headed toward the traps.

Flicking her gaze to the alley, Emma regarded the spot where it intersected with the road. The shadows were deepening. Maybe some of the runners were attempting to intercept the car by cutting through the narrow passage between buildings.

The Mustang was nearly to the first trap when a balding white man darted out into the road, waving his arms. Even from where she was perched up on the wall, Emma could see that he was alive and terrified.

Nerit must have realized the man wasn't a threat for the brakes squealed. The sports car shimmied and left streaks of rubber on the road behind it as it jolted to a stop. Not too far behind, the runners howled as they closed in.

Emma witnessed the moment the man grasped the error of his ways. He must not have realized the purpose of the sports car roaring through the streets of Ashley Oaks and assumed he was about to be rescued. The sight of the runners sent him into a blind panic and he bolted toward the wall. The razor wire trap sprung so fast, Emma didn't even see it strike the man. The flying pieces of his legs and arms announced his awful end.

"Shit," she gasped.

A woman's shrill screams immediately followed. Emma

caught sight of several people emerging from the alley. There were at least ten, including a black woman holding a small child wrapped in a blanket with only dark curly hair showing over the fabric.

"We've got survivors!" Rashmi shouted.

The scene below devolved within seconds. The runners altered their path and headed straight toward the easy prey on foot. The Mustang roared forward, cutting off the runners, sending a few hurtling through the air. A few struck a nearby store front, shattering the display window. Undeterred, several runners clambered over the hood and dove onto the dismembered man and tore into his torso.

Zombies didn't eat the dead.

"He was still alive. Oh my god!" Katarina wailed.

Emma fought the sudden need to vomit.

The rest of the runners were closing in on the frightened people on the road at such a fast speed it was hard to track them. Another trap went off, fire pluming into the air. A runner, engulfed in flames, thrashed about wildly. The sight of fire panicked the rest of the zombie pack and they fled toward the Mustang.

The runners' retreat bought the people on foot valuable time. Unfortunately, the freaked survivors splintered apart, some foolishly running toward the Mustang, while others scampered toward the wall.

"Give them cover! Give them cover!" Katarina yelled.

Emma wasn't sure who fired the first shot, but she took the second. She sent a bullet through the head of the runner closing in on the mother and child. She immediately searched for another clear target, but smoke billowing off the corpse and the frantic chaos below made it difficult. The survivors and runners rushed in different directions, making it even harder to tell them apart.

Another fire trap exploded near the location of the Mustang. This time a living man shrieked in pain and terror as he was engulfed in flames. Nerit and a tall black man, who must be Kevin, emerged from the sports car. Nerit immediately fired a bullet into the head of the burning man, putting him out of his misery.

"Avoid the marked sections on the road!" a voice shouted over a loudspeaker. *"Those are traps! Avoid-"*

The thick smoke from the burning zombie and dead survivor was foul and made visibility difficult. Emma concentrated on tracking the woman holding the child. So far she'd managed to avoid the traps and the zombies. The immolated corpses soon became smoldering ruins, the flames dying out on their blackened flesh. Drawn by the cries of fear and frenzied movements of their prey, the runner pack doubled back and split apart to pursue the panicked people.

A frightened young black man in an Atlanta Braves baseball cap rushed toward the Mustang with runners rapidly closing in on him. As he darted past Nerit and Kevin, they opened fire with pistols, providing cover.

"Stay close," Kevin barked.

Instead, the survivor dove into the car.

Nerit shouted after him, "Don't!" but the car door slammed shut.

A second later, the car engine roared to life. Yelling, Nerit kicked the side of the sports car as Kevin dragged her aside. The Mustang barreled forward, knocking away the runners trying to scramble onto the hood. The car hit a fire trap a second later, flames licking over the hood. The driver realized his folly and tried to course correct only to hit a razor wire trap. The front tires blew out instantly. Again, it was Nerit and Kevin that saved him when he scrambled out of the car. Resorting to machetes, probably to avoid friendly fire, they hacked through a throng of slower zombies that had arrived from one of the side roads.

Losing track of the mother in the smoke, Emma swore and barreled out of the hunter's blind. It was worthless now that the zombies were on a rampage. She ran along the catwalk, the wooden structure trembling beneath her feet, and found a better location. Spotting the screaming woman clutching the small child, relief washed over her. They were nearly past the traps.

"Stay away from the spray painted areas!" Emma shouted at the frightened woman.

Sighting a zombie right behind the fleeing survivor, Emma fired. The bullet struck it square in the forehead and it tumbled back into a razor-wire trap. It was instantly sliced apart, pieces of it skittering across the road. Screaming, the woman wrapped her arms tighter around the child.

"Don't move!"

Emma's shout was subsumed by the screams of both the living and dead. Nerit and Kevin held their ground while the people on the wall attempted to pick off the zombies. The festering bodies on the road threw up black smoke, making visibility difficult. Many of the shots missed their intended targets.

Another fire trap went off, the heat washing over Emma. It was closer to the wall, and the body engulfed in flames went down in cries that could either be those of the living or undead. Frantic, Emma scanned the area for the woman and child. She spotted them through the haze dangerously close to the razor traps.

"Don't move! Stop right there!"

Constant weapon fire culled the number of runners along with the slower zombies stumbling into the chaos. Emma again lost sight of the woman when another fire trap exploded. Several runners darted away only to be hacked apart by a razor trap. Blood and viscera sprayed the area. Over the noisy mayhem, Emma heard a female voice screaming. Setting one hand on the top of the wall between rods of rebar, she leaned forward to see how far the drop to the road would be if she tried to jump down.

"Help me! Help me!"

The woman stumbled out of the haze, her grip tenuous on the struggling child wrapped in the blanket. The thick coils of her hair blew around her head in a dark halo. Twisting around in the woman's arms, the small child gazed up at Emma.

"Oh, shit."

The little boy was definitely dead. A catcher's mask secured on his head with duct tape was the only thing keeping him from sinking his teeth into the flesh of the woman clutching him close.

"Help us!" the woman cried out again.

A slower zombie emerged from the smoke, its form so emaciated it resembled a walking skeleton. Aiming with her rifle, Emma concentrated on eliminating one threat at a time. Her mind was racing despite her determination to focus. How the hell were they going to deal with a mother desperate to keep her dead son with her?

Juan emerged from the smoke, swinging a machete to neatly decapitate a slower zombie. "I got them! I got them!" Gripping the woman's arm, he jerked her past a trap and toward the corner where the makeshift elevator waited. Nerit and Kevin were already on the move with three remaining survivors.

"Give them cover," Katarina ordered from nearby.

Reloading, Emma tried to blot out the dead boy's eyes peering up at her. He was a little older than Billy, a child who should have a long life in front of him. Instead, he was a zombie, snarling behind a mask.

"Fuck, fuck, fuck," she whispered.

Dizzy, her stomach a tight knot, Emma fought the urge to vomit.

Instead, she concentrated on killing the risen dead.

CHAPTER 5

All Clear on the Zombie Front

A few minutes later, the last bleats of the all-clear horn echoed into the hills then fell silent. The zombies were dead and the crane was lifting the survivors into the Fort.

"You did good," Katarina said.

Listening to the whine of the crane, Emma glanced up at the redhead. "I did what I had to."

"You pulled through for those survivors."

"It's the first time I've saved people. Usually I was putting down zombies. I can't believe we saved anyone in all that chaos. It went to shit so fast."

Katarina hoisted her rifle over one shoulder with a weary sigh. "That's the reality of the world now."

Sitting down on the catwalk, her rifle resting on her knees, Emma stared at the towering hotel. The air smelled like burned flesh and smoke obscured the glaring sunlight overhead. She concentrated on steadying her breathing, her trembling fingers brushing over the warm metal of her weapon. The little boy's dead gaze haunted her.

"Did you see the kid's face?"

Katarina shook her head. "No. Why?"

"He's not alive. They had a mask on him to keep him from biting."

The color washing out of her ruddy face, Katarina muttered, "Shit."

"He can't be let inside."

"I'm sure he won't be. Nerit would never let that happen." After a tense moment, Katarina added, "I'll check in and see what's up."

The catwalk trembled as Katarina strode away. When she started talking over the walkie-talkie, asking for the status of the mother and child, Emma wasn't surprised. Paranoia was the standard of the world.

Emma closed her eyes, leaning her head back against the wall. Though the little boy had dark skin and eyes, he'd reminded her so much of Billy. He was at that sweet age where children had chubby arms and a round tummy that felt so soft and warm when you held them close.

"That was intense."

Rashmi dropped into a squat next to her and Emma opened her eyes. Ennis and Stacy were down on the other end of the catwalk.

"To put it mildly," she replied with a weak smile.

"You okay?"

She shrugged. "Just a little PTSD."

With a somber nod, Rashmi said, "We all have it. Undiagnosed, but...the nightmares are bloody awful, aren't they?"

"I have new content for them now. Those razor-wire traps are scary as fuck, but I gotta say those fire traps being set so close to the wall were a bad idea."

"I agree. The smoke was worse than expected," Rashmi admitted. "I'll put that in my report when I'm off duty."

"Report?" Emma chuckled. "Everything here is so organized. It's so strange."

"Paperwork. It exists even now." Rashmi flashed a grin at her. "It's damn annoying."

Katarina returned, the walkie-talkie clutched in her hand at her side. "I got word from Juan about that kid. They aren't letting the mother bring him in."

"I can't believe she thought we'd allow him inside the walls," Rashmi said.

Katarina glanced down at the walkie-talkie, her freckled face tense. "Apparently someone told her we have the cure to the zombie virus. She's been traveling this way for months. All the way from fuckin' Georgia."

Rashmi stood, an incredulous look on his face. "Georgia! Seriously? All that way?"

"They started with a group of nearly one hundred. They thought the Fort was held by the military and that a lab here had the cure. Altogether, we rescued four. Only *four*!" Katarina shook her head in disbelief. "They came all this way for nothing."

Emma was sick to her stomach. If she'd thought there was a cure for Billy, she also would have lugged him across the country wearing a catcher's mask. "Why would they think y'all had the cure?"

Katrina shrugged. "Who the hell knows?" "Disinformation travels faster than you'd expect. Especially when it carries a seed of hope," Rashmi said. "I heard about the Fort through a ham radio transmission. I only caught it once, but it was the worth the risk trying to get here. Hope is a great motivator."

"Hope can get you killed," Katarina grumbled.

Emma got to her feet. Holding her rifle with one hand, she gazed at the destruction in the street below. There were so many bodies and the stench of fresh death assailed her. "What now?"

"We head back and leave the others to finish their scheduled duty," Katarina answered.

Somehow, that felt wrong. Like they were abandoning the others.

"Nice meeting you, Emma," Rashmi said with a firm handshake.

It was a small comfort that his hand was trembling. If he hadn't been affected by the battle, Emma would have been worried.

Following Katarina back down the ladder, Emma noticed the noise level within the Fort was rising. Workers were trickling out of the buildings and machinery started up in a street nearby. The crane was silent again, having delivered its cargo to safety within the walls.

As abruptly as the battle had started, it was over.

The walk back to the inner wall was in silence. Emma didn't feel like talking and Katarina seemed to be in the same state of mind. When Juan appeared at the end of the block, cowboy hat tilted back on his head, Emma wasn't surprised. He acted like she was his responsibility. Hands on his narrow hips, he waited.

She didn't quicken her stride, for she needed a few more moments to herself. The child in the mask had shaken her to the core. It was only a few days ago she'd seen her sweet little boy's face twisted into that of a snarling monster and put a bullet through his undead brain.

"Y'all did good," Juan called out as they approached.

Katarina grunted. "That was all sorts of fucked."

Juan lifted one shoulder and winced. "Agreed, but we saved some folks."

Katarina stopped in front of Juan, her fingers tightening on the strap connected to her rifle. "None of them were Ed's people, huh?"

Emma joined them because she had no idea where to go next. It was strange to be out in the open and not fear the undead. The high wall was something that would take getting used to.

Juan's jaw set in a hard line and he shook his head. "Nah. The runners weren't either according to Nerit."

"So how did Eddie end up a zombie and at the wall?"

"That's a mystery." Juan shrugged, his gaze forlorn. "At least for now."

"I hate mysteries," Katarina mumbled.

"Well, we got one on our hands."

"How the fuck did Eddie get turned?" Katarina wiped her brow and stared toward the hotel. "We can't catch a break."

"It's the z-poc." Juan directed his gaze to the wall.

"That's what everyone keeps sayin'. Doesn't make it any easier."

Emma wanted to speak up, but hesitated. It was strange to be part of something bigger than herself. Her voice was just one of many.

"Once we've got our people inside the walls and things settle down, maybe we can send a team out to look for Ed and his people."

"That sounds like a fool's errand to me, Juan. If they ran into the horde, they're gone."

Juan lowered his head so his hat hid his face. "We can hope for the best."

"But plan for the worst." Katarina patted Emma's shoulder. "I'll catch you later. I need to get back to my post."

With a small wave, Emma said, "'Later."

Silence followed Katarina's departure.

The world around Emma didn't feel real. It was hard to believe she'd woken up this morning in her destroyed Airstream. She'd made a harrowing journey here only to be engaged in a battle against the undead within hours of arriving. Maybe she was passed out in her trailer, dreaming. It would explain just how fucked up everything felt, especially the child in the mask.

"I want to say that things aren't usually this fucked up, but I'd be lying," Juan said after a few seconds.

Emma shrugged, repeating what he'd said. "It's the zombie apocalypse."

Juan let out a bitter grunt. "Yeah. Still, you just got here and shit has already hit the fan."

"I'm used to it. Sadly."

"I feel bad about you ending up on the frontlines right away."

"Don't. It's just how things are now."

Juan scuffed the toe of his boot against the asphalt and jerked his cowboy hat off to run a hand through his hair. This was clearly a nervous tick. "It's got to get better at some point, right?"

"If we're lucky." Emma hesitated then asked, "What happened to that woman and the kid?"

Juan averted his pretty green eyes, his long lashes casting shadows over his cheeks. "*That* situation is fucked."

Anxious to know what had happened, Emma stepped toward him to catch his gaze. "Clearly. What did you do? What did you say to her?"

Juan rubbed his bicep. The topic of conversation was unsettling and he appeared to struggle with answering. She suspected the look in his eyes was guilt. It was strangely comforting that he looked as upset as she was over the gruesome situation. "We couldn't let her bring him inside the wall, you know."

Emma cocked her head to gaze up at him. "Right. So...where is she?"

Sighing heavily, he said, "Outside the wall."

"You didn't let her in?"

"No, no. I begged her to come inside the walls, but she wouldn't. Not without her kid."

"You're shitting me." The words slipped out before she realized it made perfect sense that the mother wouldn't abandon her child.

"I can't say I blame her. She traveled all this way only to find out we don't have a cure. I don't know if she believes us when we tell her we don't have one."

Again, Emma thought of Billy and his light-up shoes. When she'd seen those shoes glowing in the darkness of the grocery store, she would have done everything in her power to save him. Instead, she had fired her rifle and put him to rest. "That makes sense. Hope is hard to give up."

"We aren't complete assholes. Nerit gave her a weapon and one of the bugout bags we keep along the wall. The mom is holing up across the street from the Fort in one of the office buildings."

"So what are you going to do about her?"

Juan sighed wearily and shrugged again. "Leave her be until she comes to her senses."

Emma pondered the last year of her life and let out a bitter chuckle. "That might not happen. Hope is hard to give up if you're lucky—or unlucky—enough to still have it. I hoped for months that I would find Billy alive. The night I accepted I wouldn't have a happy ending, I was inconsolable. It took days for me to sober up."

With a weary look, Juan adjusted his cowboy hat on his curls. "We can't force her inside, Emma."

"I agree."

"There's a big 'but' hanging on the end of your comment."

"Not really. I agree with you. You can't force her inside. It's just that the thought of her holed up in an abandoned building with her dead child is heartbreaking. Coming all this way hoping for a cure and there's not one. Shit. That would have destroyed me."

Juan pressed his lips together, nodded, and gazed off past Emma.

"This world is shit," Emma declared. "Absolute shit."

"I can't argue with you, but we are trying to make things better for everyone within these walls."

Emma understood the complexity of the situation. "Why did she think there's a cure here? Did she say?"

"No. She freaked out when we told her we couldn't save her kid."

"I can imagine."

"Nerit is talking with the others we saved. She wants to find out where the disinformation came from. That group was nearly a hundred people when they started out from outside of Atlanta. They split apart on the way here, but a lot of them died."

"I can't even imagine."

"It's got me worried that maybe there are more on the way from other locations."

Emma thought this was a definite possibility if word of the Fort had spread as far as Atlanta. "What if there are?"

Perplexed, Juan lifted his shoulders, hands splayed. "Hell, I don't know. We got resources for the people we got now in the Fort. Those will last us for a while. We don't mind taking in people, but..." With a sigh, Juan fell silent.

"You can't save everyone."

"Maybe we can. I don't fuckin' know. We might be the best chance for people out there."

"We have to save ourselves in the end. You can't feel responsible for everyone stuck out there."

"You're probably right, Em."

"Juan, I kept waiting for the military to swoop in and rescue me, or show up with a cure. Of course, that never happened. I eventually realized I had to save myself. Hell, the U.S. government probably isn't even around anymore."

Juan glanced off to one side as though measuring his next words. "Did you know that what's left of the federal government is in Galveston, Texas?"

"No shit?"

"The vice president, who is now president, is holed up on the island with what remains of the cabinet and some surviving military higher ups. They blew the bridges up and secured the island."

For a moment hope erupted in Emma's chest. Maybe somehow the United States government could yet come through for the citizens of the country. Those thoughts were quashed by Juan's downcast expression. It wasn't comforting.

Noticing her questioning look, Juan continued. "We heard through the apocalypse grapevine that they're dependent on survivor encampments on the coast for supplies. ."

As quickly as she'd felt hopeful, Emma was despondent. "We really are on our own then. Which proves my point."

Juan grinned.

Emma arched an eyebrow. "What?"

"You said 'we.' I take it you're starting to feel at home here."

Despite her trauma and weariness, she grinned back at him. "Well, I haven't been here *too* long. I've already had to kill a bunch of zombies, which is normal for me. So I guess I *do* fit in here."

Juan nudged her shoulder with his fist. "I told you that you did. By the way, Nerit wants me to show you around before you head up to your room. She feels you're a valuable resource and that you should get a lay of the land. That okay? You up for a tour?"

Though she was exhausted, Emma nodded. She would be more comfortable after learning the ins and outs of the Fort. It would be good to know the layout of her environment, especially where to hide if things went south.

CHAPTER 6

Tours and News

The sun and humidity created a sweltering heat inside the garage where the Fort's vehicles were housed and maintained. It was hotter than hell and reeked of grease, mold, and gasoline. Emma's nose wrinkled at the stench. The walls were covered in old newspapers yellowed by time. The name of the extinct daily newspaper was painted over the garage entrance and an old punch clock hung by a door leading deeper into the building.

Juan was obviously proud of the cordoned off area where the Fort's vehicles were stored, which was a center of activity as the crews from outside returned. While he chatted with a woman named Greta, who ran the garage, Emma drifted over to a hand-drawn map of the Fort. The people of the town had used available resources to quickly create a safe haven for themselves utilizing the arrangement of the buildings. The central hub was the big area blocked off by the ten-story-tall hotel and the newspaper building. Since those two buildings touched corners, the construction crew had only had to wall in two sides of the large space. The City Hall building was also included in the perimeter. Emma had noticed the bottom floor windows and doors were covered in burglar bars providing a barrier to the outside.

"Checking out the layout?" Juan asked, joining her.

"It's pretty impressive. I take it you built this wall first?" She pointed to a place on the map.

"Yeah, but we used semi-trucks and sandbags to close off the area while we built it," Juan replied.

Emma raised an eyebrow. "I'm surprised the city officials let you do that. Doesn't that type of thing have to go through a committee? Even in the zombie apocalypse?" Though her tone was joking, she was curious. Small town politics could get nasty.

"When the city leaders see people torn apart in front of City Hall, it makes it a little easier to convince them to build a wall. But I gotta admit:, they put up a fuss. I argued at the time we could always tear it down later. I'm not going to lie. It was fuckin' hard as hell to get the city manager to sign off on it. The mayor ignored him and gave us the go ahead. The city manager-"

"Tobias," Emma said, remembering the picture on the wall in City Hall. There had been a label under it. "Yolanda's husband, right?"

"How did you figure that out?"

Emma explained about the photo.

Juan nodded sadly. "Tobias couldn't deal with what was happening. His kids and grandkids all died at the school where people had been told to go for shelter. He convinced himself they were just sick. In need of help. He had a breakdown and tried to save them. You know how that went."

"Poor Yolanda."

"I honestly don't know how she does it, Em. Lost everyone, but she's a godsend. Peggy and her..." Juan faltered, tears welling in his eyes. Setting his hat on his head, he sucked in a deep breath, then explosively let it out. "Damn. I keep forgetting she's gone."

"Yolanda and you both get this look that says her death wasn't expected. She took her life, didn't she?"

"And her boy's. Cody. That kid was skittish about everything." Juan sighed. "You couldn't even say 'boo!' to the kid without him losing it. I always thought it was weird that such a strong woman had a kid like that, but now I see she was just hiding her own fears. She kept askin' for reassurances that the Fort wouldn't fall when the horde came through. We were all scared. We had contingencies, escape plans, and all that. She was a part of all the planning, but it must have been too much for her. She poisoned her kid and did herself in."

"I'm so sorry to hear that," Emma said and meant it.

It was definitely easy to understand the disappointment and anger in Juan's expression, but a part of her sympathized and understood why Peggy had made her decision. If Billy had been alive with her the last year, the choices Emma made would've probably been quite different. She was furious with her ex-husband, Stan, for not somehow saving Billy, or giving him a better exit from the world. Tears welled in her eyes at the memory of the horrific wounds that had covered her son's body. What would she have done to spare her son that death?

"This isn't an easy world to live in sometimes," Juan muttered. "But you know that."

"All survivors know that." Needing a change of topic before she started to cry, Emma said, "So you said you used semi-trucks as a barrier first?"

"And the construction trucks. We also had chain-link panels as a barrier inside the truck line. Anything we could use to put a barrier between the zombies and us, we used. Added rebar spikes later on. The next section we built was this area we're in now, so we could go in and out with our vehicles without risking zombies getting into the main area."

"I like the double paddock."

"That was my idea," Juan said, puffing his chest a little. "We had to build fast and anticipate what might be coming our way."

"What I said earlier about us saving ourselves, I can see clearly you did that. I like how you didn't just wait around for someone to save you. You just kept building what you needed."

Looking surprisingly bashful, Juan shrugged. "We couldn't wait for the Army or FEMA or whoever to show up. The town survivors were all crammed inside the walls and ready to fight for their lives. Then the city folk started arriving and we needed more room. Taking over the hotel was one of our first victories."

"You should be proud of what you accomplished here."

"We are. I am. It's just...we did what we had to."

"I understand."

"I know you do."

They shared an awkward moment where neither one knew what to say next. It was Juan who pointed to the buildings across from the garage. Horses drank from a trough set near a stable while several teenagers put up some saddles. "We added that recently. When we found the horses, we needed to make them a stable. So we renovated those old abandoned buildings. It's temporary until we can take another block and build them a proper stable."

"Isn't walling in more areas risky? More to defend."

"Yeah, to a degree. We got the people to guard the walls. We also needed barriers between the main area and the zombies or banditos."

"Fallback positions."

"Yeah. It's designed like an old medieval fortress for a reason."

Staring at the map, Emma recognized the similarity. "Whose idea?"

"Me and Travis.'"

"The mayor, right?"

Juan nodded. "The new mayor. Architect in his old life. Leader in this one."

"And you?"

"Construction worker in the old life. Same in this one," he replied.

"I think you're more than that here."

"I just help get shit done."

"And you're the father of four adopted kids."

His smile widening, Juan cocked an eyebrow at her. "That I am. And I'm good at it too. Which was surprising to me. What about you?"

"Mom and student in my old life. Fearless zombie killer in this one."

"Shit, Em. I shouldn't have asked."

"It's okay. We all got our burdens to carry."

"I'm sorry about your kid."

"Me too."

Juan hesitated. "The mom with the boy in the mask must have shaken you up a little."

Emma was a little surprised by how intense his gaze was, as if he was trying to read her inner workings. "I can't help but think about what I would have done for Billy. I would've traveled a thousand miles on foot if I thought I could somehow bring him back. But I couldn't. That's reality."

In the beginning, she had wondered if one day there would be a cure for the zombies. That maybe somewhere out in the world in a secret lab there was a miraculous remedy. During her darkest days, when she had come to accept that Billy was one of the undead, she'd hoped that this was the truth. It was only after months of culling zombies that she had accepted that there was nothing left of their human selves inside their slowly decaying bodies. After the apocalypse started, her grandfather had instilled in her the belief that the purpose of her survival was to deliver peace to the dead.

Juan's expression altered from curious to despondent. "It's hard to accept reality when you lose someone you love. I still struggle with it."

"That makes you human."

"I suppose."

"I'll be honest. I didn't want to live after I put Billy to rest. I came here because a ghost told me to in a dream." She giggled at the outrageousness of that statement. "That sounds ridiculous."

"Nah. Not after what I've seen. Trust me. Around here, we've all seen our share of ghosts." Leaning against the wall near the map, Juan folded his arms across his chest. "This is a good place to make a new life, Em."

Emma glanced out the garage door toward the sunlit courtyard. Nerit was out there talking to Kevin. The woman embodied strength that Emma envied, and hoped she could discover inside herself.

"Em?"

"I wasn't even sure this place existed, but I'm here now and it feels right."

Juan nodded in agreement. "Yeah, it does."

A Hispanic woman, dressed similarly to Emma, approached them with a welcoming smile on her face. Her dark hair was in a tight French braid under a cowboy hat and she had a passing resemblance to Juan. When he spotted the newcomer, he swept her up into a tight hug and she grinned up at him.

"You're back! And in one piece!"

"Lucky for me! Those damn runners had us trapped on the roof of that old gas station."

"We took care of them for ya."

"Took you long enough," the woman cracked, poking his chest.

"Hey, Em, this is my cousin Monica," Juan said. "Monica, Emma. She's new."

The woman's handshake was firm and quick. "Nice to meet you. You're already the hot gossip in the hotel. News travels super-fast here."

Emma widened her eyes, not sure what to say.

Monica set a hand on her hip and cocked her head to regard Emma. "Don't worry. It's all good. Rune says you're some sort of kick-ass zombie killer that took out an entire town of them. You're already a legend."

"I-I just did what I h-had to," Emma stuttered, embarrassed to be exalted for a task that was sacred and necessary.

"My cuz is right about the gossip, Em. Wildfire."

"It's those old biddies who hang out when the hair salon is open. They see *everything*. I'd barely kissed my girlfriend when they'd already told everyone Bette and I were a thing."

Emma absorbed this information with surprise. "Girlfriend? Things are a little more progressive here than in my town."

"Trust me. We've had our share of homophobia." Monica's expression darkened. "Had a whole group of Baptists leave because our sinnin' was going to bring hell down on the Fort."

"Damn." Emma regarded the dour expressions on the faces of the cousins and realized things weren't as idyllic as she'd assumed. "That was recent, wasn't it?"

"The approaching horde did bring out the worst in people,"

Juan admitted.

Monica pointed at Emma and then herself. "We're cool, right?"

"I am all for people lovin' whoever they want. Back home folks called the only lesbians in town the spinster sisters to keep the scandal from delicate ears. Frankly, the spinster sisters gave the impression of being a lot happier than most of the married couples in my old church."

Monica's shoulders relaxed. "I knew you looked like a cool chick."

"She's going to fit right in. I feel it," Juan said with an approving look in Emma's direction.

Tilting her head, Monica regarded him thoughtfully. "Oh really?"

Leaning toward his cousin, a defiant look in his eye, Juan said, "Yeah. Really."

"I *see*."

Emma could see the wheels spinning about in Monica's head. Matchmaking was apparently alive and well even in the zombie apocalypse.

Emma directed her gaze away from the cousins, watching the activity outside the garage. Again, she was struck by the bustle of the Fort inhabitants. Everyone was always on the move, hurrying to some task. The SILENCE flags were gone and the hum of activity permeated the humid afternoon air. There was a long line of people outside the portable building that served as a medical center. Emma had been cleared through there when she'd first arrived. It was disconcerting to realize how many people had been stuck outside the gates.

"Everyone gets checked in when they come from outside." Monica wiped her face with a Harley-Davidson bandana. "It's annoying, but it prevents anyone with a zombie bite from entering the main area of the Fort."

"I thought people who got bitten turned right away," Emma said, her gaze flicking to Juan. "How could someone get in with a bite?"

Monica gave Emma a befuddled look. "Seriously?"

Juan shuffled his weight from one foot to the other, a little uncomfortable with the topic. "Haven't you noticed that not everyone turns the same way, Em?"

"Honestly, no. I lived on the outskirts of town. I was busy taking care of my grandparents when the outbreak happened. I've never seen someone turn."

"That explains it," Monica said.

"Shit. You've been lucky then, Em."

"It's obvious I've got a lot to learn yet about what happened to the world outside my town. We were cut off immediately when the cable went out. I did piece together what happened to the townsfolk in the months after the outbreak."

"When you were killing them off?"

"Yeah. When I was giving them peace."

As Emma had systematically put down the zombies the town residents had become, she'd seen clues about their demise. She suspected that people attempting to flee the outbreak in the larger cities had only managed to bring it to rural Texas. A car with out-of-state plates had crashed into a gas station and had been slathered inside with blood. She'd bet all her worthless money that car was the start of the death of her town. The bits and pieces of news she'd heard through the snowy reception on her grandfather's old black-and-white television before the stations had gone silent reported that it was a fast-spreading virus wiping out the citizens of America bite by bite.

Stepping slightly in front of her cousin, Monica said, "I can tell you what I know about the zombies, Emma. Some turn faster than others. It depends on several factors: like how healthy you are, your immune system, genetics, that sort of thing. At least that's what Bette says. She was a medic in the Army." Monica pointed to a young woman with short, cropped blonde hair slowly working her way down the line with two somber looking armed young men behind her. It appeared that in order to speed things up, Bette was performing examinations on the spot.

"So if someone's been bitten, then what happens?"

"They have a choice to do themselves in, or have someone do

it for them." Again, there was a hint of guilt in Juan's tone. "Usually a loved one. If they're around."

He started out of the building and gestured for the women to follow. Emma fell into step with Monica.

"Once in a while the bitten ask to be put outside the gates so they can turn." Monica scowled with disgust. "That third option is one I don't understand. Why anyone would choose to turn zombie confuses the hell out of me. I don't ever want to be one of those things. I'd rather eat a bullet."

Emma now understood why the two armed men were with the medic. It sent a chill down her spine. "Seems like a harsh way to deal with someone in that situation."

Monica shrugged. "When you see what happens when someone's bitten, it changes you inside, Emma. It kicks in a survival instinct you didn't even know you had and it gives you the ability to do shit you never thought you could. Trust me on that."

Gazing at the two people walking with her, Emma wondered what it'd be like to face one of them if they were bitten and give them the three options. It was a heartbreaking scenario she didn't even want to consider.

"We're not assholes, you know. We're just trying to stay alive. You've been on your own, Em, so our rules might sound brutal to you." Juan was slightly defensive, as though ready for her to disapprove of their methods.

"I'm trying not to judge, Juan. Especially since I never had to deal with that situation. At first, I worried that whoever died, even naturally, would come back, but my grandparents passed away peacefully and remained dead."

"It's the bite that does it, Em. Something in the saliva. Blood doesn't carry it. That is what we've observed so far."

Having been splattered with zombie blood, Emma suspected Juan was right. "Everyone I put down always had at least one bite. Though a lot of times they were chewed up and mangled." Emma shivered, remembering Billy's horrific wounds.

"I can't imagine what you went through," Monica said with a sad shake of her head. "I hope it gives you some peace that you saved lives today."

"It was a change from what I've been doing the last year. Definitely something I could get used to." Emma didn't want her thoughts to drift to the woman with the little boy in the mask, but they did. She didn't feel like she'd saved them, especially since the mother was outside the wall. It was time for a change in the conversation. "Is it always like this? Crazy busy?"

"We've had some lulls in zombie activity where we got a shit-ton done around the Fort," Juan replied. "That's when we got a majority of the exterior walls up. But once we knew that massive herd was heading our way, things got pretty intense. We're cleaning up from them coming through. The zombie bodies are disease carriers. We have to bury them in mass graves."

Monica frowned. "It would be great not to deal with zombies or banditos or any of that kind of bullshit for a while."

"Banditos. Y'all keep mentioning them, Monica. Who are they?"

"The Boyds. They got busted out of prison and went back to making meth, killing, kidnapping, and raping."

With a sour look, Juan started up the collapsible wooden steps that led over the interior wall. "You're lucky you didn't run into those assholes. We took out the majority of the gang, including the leader. We haven't heard or seen anything from them since last year, but some might be out there."

Emma hesitated on the stairs. "Wow. I missed so much. I was so convinced that most of us were gone, that I was one of the last, that I didn't even bother trying to leave town. I'm kinda glad. Apparently, the whole world went insane."

Monica gently took her arm to guide her over the wall. "You're lucky. You didn't have to deal with a lot of bullshit. Not to say that what you went through wasn't awful, don't get me wrong. But there's been some stuff that's happened around here that I wish I could forget."

"Don't we all," Juan muttered. "Hey, Monica, could you help Em get settled in? I need to go check in with Travis."

"Sure."

"I'll catch you later, Em." Juan lightly touched her arm then dashed off on his long legs.

"Is he okay?" Emma asked.

Monica shrugged. "No. None of us are. Anyway, I'll take you to our Fort storage. We keep a stockpile of clothing, shoes, toiletries, and that sort of thing that we gather on salvage missions. You can get some clothes and supplies. One of the salvage teams made it as far as a Walmart superstore and returned with a bunch of Levi and Wrangler jeans. I'm sure there will be some in your size. Sound good?"

Emma couldn't help but smile. "Does it ever."

"Good. Just let me know if you need anything else."

"I could use a drink later," Emma replied. "Please tell me the Fort's not a dry community."

"Oh, hell no!" Monica laughed. "We have a ridiculous amount of liquor. After dinner tonight, I'll grab my girl and we'll hook you up with a nice icy cold one."

Emma grinned. "I'd like that."

CHAPTER 7

Starlight and Dog Farts

The air conditioning unit hummed beneath the window, obliterating the sounds coming from outside. The room was nice, tidy, and suited Emma's needs. It was far fancier than anything she had owned in her previous life. It was easy to see herself living in the small space and making it her own as time went on. She would have to find some frames for Billy's pictures. In the meantime, she had them propped up against the lamp on the bed stand.

Spread out on the soft gray and white comforter on the bed was a collection of brand-new clothing, most of it salvaged from a Walmart superstore in a nearby town. There were tank tops, sports bras, two packages of colorful panties, two pairs of jeans, three sweaters, and a secondhand leather coat that would help her survive the colder weather in the winter.

Emma's new jeans were a little snug, but they were comfortable after the tattered clothing she'd been wearing since the beginning of the zombie apocalypse. To actually be wearing a brand-new pair of Levi jeans was a luxury that was difficult to wrap her head around. She hadn't had a new pair of jeans since she was in high school. Emma had grown up on the lower end of middle class. After the birth of her son, she'd sunk into poverty, struggling to make ends meet as a single mom. Her paychecks had gone into making sure Billy had decent clothing, medical care, and healthy meals. She'd settled on a wardrobe from the secondhand store, went to the doctor if over the counter remedies didn't work, and ate cheaply. Her needs were insignificant compared to her son's. Now that he was gone she had to look after herself.

Tearing open a package of socks, Emma was surprised to find her eyes welling with tears. She struggled to understand the sudden wave of emotions filling her. Gripping the package with both hands, she sat down on the edge of the bed. She wasn't even sure exactly what she was feeling. The need to cry was overwhelming. Perhaps it was simply the shock of finding herself in a safe, clean environment with people who genuinely were interested in befriending her. The Fort was everything she had given up hope of finding. To be surrounded by a community determined to rebuild in the dead world was too much to comprehend.

She dabbed at her eyes with one of the new socks and sniffled again.

It was also difficult to see intact families within the walls of the Fort, especially those with small children. It was easy to imagine a scenario where Billy was with her. Though she kept him firmly in her heart at all times, it was not the same as having him in her arms. She would have done anything to save him, even travel hundreds of miles with a catcher's mask duct taped to his head in hopes of a cure. Now that she was in a safe place, the guilt of survival was more potent. Why had she survived when so many others had died? Even if she didn't have an answer, she couldn't ignore the feeling that as a survivor she had a role to play in rebuilding the world. It was time to learn to live again. She'd have to learn to exist with the guilt.

Shoving her freshly washed hair out of her face, Emma drew in a deep breath, held it for a few seconds, then exhaled. She repeated it a few times until she was more in control. It was a trick her grandfather had taught her and it helped quell anxiety.

Earlier, when Emma had sat down in the dining room for a dinner of macaroni and cheese and homemade biscuits, she'd discovered her legend had grown significantly. It was a little daunting to have so many people gathering at her table asking questions about her past and how she'd found the Fort.

Luckily, Monica and Bette had arrived to save her. Emma had been grateful. She'd enjoyed the dinner and conversation with the two women even though she'd been keenly aware of being observed by others. The couple seemed to understand her discomfort. Both had made an effort to divert the attention of the people who attempted to approach Emma. She greatly appreciated their consideration.

Emma had briefly glimpsed Juan and his children at the far end of the hotel dining room, but hadn't dared leave the comfort of Monica and Bette's company. Seeing Juan with four kids of varying ages and a German Shepard had made her heart ache for Billy. At least some people were able to be parents despite the horrors of the apocalypse. If humanity was to survive, it would need a new generation raised with an understanding of the new world.

Sadly, she didn't get that chance.

Neither had that mother outside the wall.

That thought was sobering and she patted away more tears.

She had an invitation to join Bette and Monica downstairs for some beers and conversation. It would be easier to hide in her new room. Did she really want to go down and be social? She didn't want to talk about being a fearless zombie killer or discuss the scene outside the wall. Additionally, there were a lot of rumors about what had happened to Ed's group after they had left the Fort. Eddie showing up at the wall as a member of the undead had upset plenty of people and speculation was running rampant. Emma's cursory understanding of the situation made it difficult to discern what was based in fact or the concoction of someone's wild imagination.

Picking up the hand-drawn map Monica had given her earlier, Emma tried to memorize the layout of the Fort. Juan was right. It definitely resembled a medieval fortress with its rings of walls centered around the towering hotel. Monica had been considerate enough to mark the area where they were meeting for beers and conversation.

Emma sighed heavily, surrendering. "Aw, shit."

She had to keep living.

No more hiding.

Folding the paper and tucking it into her jeans, she took another calming breath while pulling out a new pair of colorful and wildly patterned socks from the package. She slipped them on then reached for her battered boots. They were still comfortable, so she hadn't picked up a new pair. Besides, they'd been a graduation gift from her grandfather. They made her feel connected to the good parts of her past.

Once she was done making herself presentable, she headed out of the hotel room. The hallway and the elevator were empty, giving her a few more moments to herself. But when the elevator doors opened on the lobby, she was immediately overcome with the sound of conversation echoing through the vast room. Again, overwhelmed, she nearly ducked back into the elevator.

Glancing up at a sign taped far up on the wall that read "New plan. Fuck it," Emma steeled herself and strode into the surprisingly busy lobby. Though a few people glanced her way, most appeared intent on observing a white knuckle match between two elderly gentlemen playing chess. A quick look around the vast room revealed that it was in use as a common area. People were playing board games, knitting, quilting, or just sitting and chatting. Most of the people were older and the atmosphere was comforting. It reminded Emma of her grandparents' living room.

She skirted past the group and followed the signs pointing to the hotel exit. What appeared to be a janitor's closet had been converted into an entrance. Faded safety posters remained on the wall, but were covered in graffiti. Emma found some of the notations a little amusing. Someone had even drawn zombies in some of the illustrations.

Outside the air was humid, though cooler. Standing near the entrance of the hotel, she stared out over the spacious area that she had been told was the first walled in section of the Fort. It was the size of a city block, yet claustrophobic with the cement block wall enclosing it. She couldn't imagine what it had been like in those first days when the Fort had been being built while zombies destroyed the world.

The lights in City Hall were on, as were the lights in the portable building tucked up against the back side of the old newspaper establishment. The memorial area appeared to be empty. She walked along a well-worn pathway that cut between City Hall and the flourishing garden.

Near the far end of the enclosed block, beside the wall bordering a street lined with small stores, was an area set up with picnic tables, old lawn furniture, and several large barbecue pits and smokers. It was here that Bette and Monica were sipping beers and chatting. Arnold and Lenore, the couple she'd seen when she'd first arrived at the Fort, were seated on top of a nearby picnic table arguing passionately about Snape from the *Harry Potter* books. A few other people Emma didn't recognize were gathered around a cooler filled with ice and bottles of beer.

"There you are!" Monica called out. "Grab a beer and take a seat."

Emma squeezed past a few people discussing the successes of the day. She picked up a frosty bottle of beer and pulled a battered lawn chair over to the couple. Taking her seat, she twisted off the cap and took a swig. It was light beer and tasted awful. She was a whiskey lover, but the alcohol would help her relax.

"How's it going?" Bette asked.

"Better. Got a nap earlier."

"I would have killed for a nap today," Bette admitted. "We were swamped until nearly dinner. I wish I could take one day and just sleep! It would be nice to have a break from zombies."

Emma understood that desire oh-too-well and how often that sort of wish wasn't fulfilled. She would never recover from the sleep she'd lost since Billy was born. The zombie apocalypse hadn't helped her sleep deprivation either.

"Today got pretty borked," Monica said with the shake of her head. "All those damn runners sprinting around made our job hard today."

Bette focused on Emma. "Is it true about the woman with the zombie kid? She had him in a mask?"

Emma took another sip of her beer. It didn't taste any better. "Sadly, yes."

"For real? That's fucked up." Monica winced. "Where'd you

hear about that, babe?"

"I overheard Katarina talking to Nerit about a lady with a zombie kid in a mask. I wanted to ask about what happened, but they took off before I could. Is it true the mom thought there was a lab with a cure here?"

Emma wasn't sure how much she could or should tell them. Since no one had told her not to share what she'd seen, she went ahead and nodded. "Her whole group believed we had the cure. That's why they came here from Georgia. A lot died along the way."

"Wow. That's horrible. I wish I had a cure to give her. That sucks." Bette frowned, rubbing the label on her beer bottle with her thumb.

"I wonder if there is a cure. Somewhere out there in some secret lab. And if there is, how do we find it?" Monica sighed. "When I think of all the people we lost and how a cure could change everything, it's so frustrating that no one found a way to stop it."

"If there is a lab out there, babe, chances are it's the one where the outbreak started. Which means the scientists who could've stopped the outbreak are dead."

"I hate that we don't have a cure. I miss Jenni a lot. She shouldn't have had to die just because of a bite on her hand."

"To Loca," Bette said, tapping her girlfriend's beer with her own. "May she rest in peace."

"She's some kind of a legend around here, isn't she?" Emma asked.

"Why do you ask?" Bette cocked her head, curious.

"I've heard of her."

"Not surprised," Bette said somberly. "I only met her briefly and she left an impression on me, that's for sure."

"She was...somethin' special. Loca, but special."

Bette nodded in agreement with her girlfriend's declaration. "Without a doubt."

"Did Juan tell you about her?" Monica asked.

"Juan's little boy was showing me around and pointed out her picture to me."

A sad smile pressed onto Bette's lips. "Troy is a sweetheart. He reveres her since she saved his life."

Emma was reluctant to share with Bette and Monica that Jenni's ghost had directed her to the Fort and that Troy had somehow been aware of Jenni's influence. Though she was convinced that Jenni had guided her, it was difficult to admit that a ghost had intervened in her life in such a profound way. Apparently, belief in ghosts was not a big deal anymore, but Emma didn't want to be seen as using Jenni's name to impress anyone.

"It was like he could sense my grief and he wanted to share his own loss."

"Or maybe he thinks you're a little like her," Bette suggested.

"Loca?" Emma grimaced. "I hope not. I may have killed a town of zombies, but I ain't crazy."

"I meant a hero."

"It's not an insult to be called loca, you two," Monica explained. "It's a term of endearment in Hispanic culture. Jenni was a grieving mom who went through a whole lot before and after the zombies. She was also a badass zombie killer and saved a lot of survivors. People liked her and the nickname was a loving one."

"It sounds like we could've been friends. We have a lot in common when it comes to loss and killing zombies. I just hope people aren't expecting me to be like her."

Monica settled back in her chair and set her hand on Bette's. Their fingers intertwined and the two women exchanged furtive looks.

"A few might," Bette started tentatively. "I didn't know Jenni, but I do know people depended on her a lot. It's normal to look for new heroes when we lose one."

"I liked her a lot, Emma, but there was something about Jenni that scared me. Sometimes she was like an untamed force of nature. I wouldn't call it a death wish, but she lived her life without guardrails. She was haunted by the death of her kids. It affected her a lot, but she'd never admit it. She wouldn't even talk about them to my cousin and they were together. It was like there was all this pain and sadness just below the surface and she was ignoring it as hard as she could. I knew her, and yet I feel I didn't *know* her. She was brave, but it was scary how far she would go to save others. I suspect she was willing to risk herself because she couldn't save her kids on that first day. It was like she was trying to pay off that debt, whether it was by saving others or sacrificing her life."

Bette stared at her bottle of beer, wiping away the condensation with her fingers. "She gave her life so that a bunch of us could make it here safely."

Again came the pinch of guilt. "I couldn't save the people of my town, but I could give them final peace. They didn't deserve to become those damn things."

"You did right by them. I respect you for doing that."

Nervously, Emma lowered her eyes at Monica's comment and flexed her fingers around the beer resting on her thigh. "It wasn't a big deal."

Monica leaned forward and tapped her knee to get her attention. "Emma, we need heroes, but not another Jenni. She was one-of-a-kind. She was running from her demons and lived her life in a way I wouldn't wish on anyone else. We're not expecting you to be a second Jenni. We're just glad you're here to help us rebuild."

"Am I looking like a deer in headlights?" Emma asked with the nervous giggle.

The other two women exchanged amused looks and grinned.

"Maybe just a little," Bette replied. "I mean, the whole Fort is talking about you killing an *entire town* of zombies. You've definitely been granted legendary hero is status right off the bat. We know that can be pretty intimidating."

"Don't get me wrong. Everyone's been great. It's just they all keep *staring* at me."

Monica sneered at the hotel. "People around here are good, decent folk, but they can be a real pain in the ass. And speaking of pains in asses..."

Juan appeared in Emma's periphery, beer and chair in hand. He set the lawn chair next to Emma and collapsed onto the frayed blue and white plastic seat. Like Emma, he was dressed in fresh clothing and his curly hair was tucked behind his ears in a short ponytail. Taking a long swig of his beer, he leaned back in the chair, his long legs stretching out to nearly touch his cousin's feet. Jack, the German Shepherd she'd met earlier in the day, settled down beneath his legs and yawned with contentment.

"Kids in bed already?" Monica asked.

Juan laughed, shaking his head. "Nah. I left them with my mom. They're pretty hyper after being cooped up in the hotel room all this time. I'm going to be glad when we get those bodies cleared away so they can get some fresh air."

"Do you let them past the wall?" Emma glanced at him, curious. She had no idea what it was like to be a parent in the z-poc.

"No. Absolutely not. But we do let them into the Main Street area to play and hang out with their friends. With all the corpses remaining outside the walls, I don't want to take a chance with disease. There are a lot of bugs swarming the bodies."

"When are you clearing those out, cuz?"

"Bulldozers tomorrow. After that, the powers that be say that we get a few days off to recover," Juan replied. "Just going to keep the sentry and housekeeping shifts running."

"We do need a break," Bette said, looking pleased.

"Think those fuckers out there will give us one?" Monica waved toward the hills. "Gawddamn zombies."

"They're on the move away from us," Rune said, joining them. The biker set a lawn chair beside Emma and settled on it with a beer in both hands. His snowy white hair fell over one shoulder in a braid.

"How do you know?" Monica asked.

"I got word from one of my friends," Rune answered.

"Why didn't this friend tell you about the runners?"

"Because the friend only shares what it wants to share."

Staring intently at his beer, Juan said, "It's not Jenni, right?"

"No, compadre, it is not the loca."

Juan nodded and took a sip of his beer.

Obviously curious, Bette leaned toward Rune. "So who? Anyone we know?"

"Nah. It's a ghost following the horde because his wife is a part of it. I knew him back in the day, old biker friend, so he dropped by to say hello before moving on after her."

"Ghosts stop by to say hello?" Emma scrunched up her face in disbelief. "Seriously?"

Rune shrugged. "Sometimes."

"You're a very interesting person, Rune."

"I can be. But most of the time I'm just ornery."

Emma wanted to ask him if he saw ghosts around her, but thought better of it. The older man stared at her with his keen blue eyes and she got the impression he was waiting for her to ask. She took another swig of beer and held her tongue.

"Your ghost friends should be a little more helpful with the info," Monica said, her tone a bit bitter. "Like why Eddie showed back up as a zombie.

"The dead got their own agenda. I can't make them do my bidding. Hell, I'm doing *their* bidding most of the time. If they don't want to talk, I ain't got nothing."

Flicking his gaze toward Rune, Juan straightened in his chair, the tension in his shoulders revealing his anxiousness. "So you don't know about Ed, Belinda, and the others at all, right?"

"Sorry. I ain't got nothin' on what happened to Old Ed. I wish I did. He was a good guy until he got a case of the stupids and took off."

Bette stared at her beer as though contemplating how much more to drink. "This is a weird, weird world."

The conversation lapsed into silence. Emma tilted her head so she could observe the night in all its brilliance. Despite the huge spotlights illuminating the area around the Fort, the stars were visible overhead. The vast firmament of the heavens was breathtaking. It had been a long time since she'd felt safe outside, longer still since she had last admired the stars. Back at the old Airstream she'd hidden inside its metal walls, too afraid to venture outside in the dark for fear of the undead. It was surreal to feel safe enough behind the high concrete walls to sit back and relax.

"Shit! What's that smell?" Monica abruptly exclaimed, covering her nose.

Emma caught a whiff and choked. "Oh my God!"

"Did a zombie get in the gates? Because damn!" Bette jumped to her feet and took a few steps back.

"It's not me!" Rune exclaimed defensively. "I've blasted some good ones, but that ain't me!"

Emma eyed the dog next to Juan. "I think he's the guilty culprit."

Chuckling, Juan petted the dog's head. "The kids gave Jack some macaroni and cheese. Not the best idea. Jack, those are some impressive dog farts."

It amused Emma to see a smidgen of guilt in the dog's eyes. It didn't last long, because the dog let out another one and gave everyone a big doggie grin.

"Glad you're here, Em?" The twinkle in Juan's eye and smile were a little naughty, the tension from earlier draining out of him.

Emma wasn't sure he was talking about being in the range of the reek, or being at the Fort. Covering her nose and mouth with the collar of her shirt, she gave him a thumbs up.

"Then we're ending the day on a high note. And that I'll drink to."

Juan tapped her bottle with his and winked.

Again, she was reminded of just how handsome he was.

Emma took another long swig to hide her blushing face and wide grin.

It would be hours until she retired to her hotel room, happy with the promise of new possibilities.

CHAPTER 8

Tamale Interrogation

A knock on the door startled Emma from a deep slumber. The room was dark except for a line of bright sunlight peeking through a gap in the curtains. Her hand instantly closed on the pistol under the mattress and she rapidly rolled over beneath the covers, pointing at the trailer's front door, only to discover she was aiming at a window. Disoriented, she flailed about until she located the actual door to the hotel room.

Another knock.

It took her a few seconds to remember that she was on the sixth floor of a tall building behind high concrete walls.

Zombies wouldn't be banging on the door.

With a sigh of relief, she sagged back onto the pillows.

A glance at the clock revealed it was early afternoon. She'd slept close to fourteen hours straight.

A third knock, this one a little harder, demanded to be answered.

Sliding her legs out from under the comforter, Emma shivered. The air conditioner had made the room icebox cold. It would take some getting used to after the heat she'd endured in the trailer.

A fourth knock, this one hard and sharp, sent a stabbing pain through her skull. She wasn't hungover from the light beer. She'd only drunk one bottle, but she'd slept too long, resulting in a throbbing headache.

"I'm coming!" she shouted at whoever was so impatient.

Dragging on her new jeans, she zipped them as she padded over to the door. She combed her fingers through her hair and tugged her t-shirt down over her stomach. Stifling a yawn, she opened the door.

An older Hispanic woman stood on her doorstep. Dark hair shot through with silver, she smiled brightly at Emma and presented her with a covered tray. "I brought you some food since you hadn't come down to eat," she announced.

"Oh, thanks." Emma's stomach gurgled as the rich smell of Mexican food hit her.

"Venison tamales, ranchero beans, and rice," the woman ticked off, digging a diet soda out of the pocket of a cheery, colorful, flower-print apron.

"I just realized how hungry I am. Thank you...uh...err..."

"I'm Rosie, Juan's mother. I run the kitchen."

"This smells amazing. Thank you." Unsure of what to do next, Emma stood in the doorway.

Rosie stepped into the room, brushing past her, and strode over to the small table near the window. Setting the soda down, she said, "Juan was worried when you didn't come down for lunch and asked me to check on you. I needed to talk to you anyway, so I thought this was a good time to chat."

Clutching the tray, Emma followed, unsure of where this conversation was going. It had been obvious the previous day that Monica had clear intentions of matchmaking her with Juan. Though she found him attractive, she wasn't too keen on people trying to push her into a relationship.

Especially someone's mother.

She hoped that the conversation would steer in a different direction.

"What do you need to talk to me about?" Emma asked cautiously.

Rosie took one of the chairs at the table, forcing Emma to take the other. Reaching across the table, she plucked the cover off the tray revealing the warm, delicious food.

"Since I run the kitchen, I interact with everyone in the Fort. I'm here to discuss your upcoming kitchen duty assignments."

"Kitchen duty, huh?" Emma cut into a tamale with the plastic fork tucked into a groove on the side of the tray. Fragrant steam rose from it, making her even hungrier. "So the women are still in the kitchen."

One of her major fights with Stan when they were together was how he'd expected her to do all the cooking and cleaning.

She hoped the Fort was a bit more progressive in its running.

"We *all* do it, including the men. Even when they argue and throw fits." Rosie grinned, a triumphant look on her face. "Kitchen duty is required of everyone over the age of fifteen who is physically able. I like to find out what people's culinary strengths are before I assign their duties. I ran the school cafeteria back in the day, so I have a lot of experience with running a kitchen that feeds this many people. Trust me. It's like running my own small army."

"That seems fair. I learned the basics of cooking from my grandmother. I can do just about whatever you need as long as you give me a recipe. I can also make a killer peach cobbler from memory."

"That's good! Ed's old peach orchard is providing us with lots of fruit. I'll make a note of that. Just so you know, Yolanda has put you on kitchen duty tomorrow. You've got today off to give you time to rest and settle in."

It made sense that she'd have to work for her room and board, so she had no complaints especially because they'd been kind enough to let her have a day to rest.

"I appreciate the consideration."

"You made a good impression yesterday at the wall. Katarina told me that you're a good shot, something we definitely need around here."

The woman was definitely friendly and her smile genuine, but her dark eyes were scrutinizing everything about Emma. She could feel it in her gut that the woman was sizing her up and evaluating her character.

"My grandfather taught me to hunt when I was a kid."

"You mentioned your grandmother teaching you to cook. Did your grandparents help raise you?"

"Actually, they raised me," Emma answered, forking a piece of tamale into her mouth.

Rosie waited patiently for her to finish chewing. Emma pondered not answering the unspoken question, but thought better of it. It was best to satisfy the curiosity of her new companions to avoid wild speculation.

"My mother ran away from home when she was a teenager. She hated everything about the town, our family, our religion. She wanted to find herself. She ended up in a commune on the West Coast where she met my father. They connected on a 'deep spiritual level,' got pregnant, and decided they didn't connect with *me* on a deep spiritual level. They dumped me off with my grandparents and left for a different commune somewhere in Costa Rica. I occasionally got postcards and birthday gifts from them until the zombie apocalypse."

The smile on Rosie's face had faded during Emma's story. "I'm sorry. I didn't mean to pry."

"Yeah, you did." Emma cut into her remaining tamales with vigor with the side of her fork. "Everyone wants to know who I am. I mean, that's normal, right? Especially now. Who am I? Who are my people? So, I'll tell you. I got my freckles from my redneck Irish family, my killer cheekbones from a German grandfather, and a natural tan from my Lipan Apache heritage. I'm twenty-five, I was a single mother, my ex was a charming jerk who cheated on me, I was going to school to make a better life for myself and my son, and I was poor as shit. None of that mattered once the zombies came and killed my son."

"And then you killed an entire *town* of zombies."

"A *small* town."

"But a town," Rosie said gently. "That's impressive. It says you're a resourceful young woman. Or that maybe you had help."

Emma was convinced she was under interrogation by the woman. Was she doing it on behalf of the Fort leaders or for herself? That was unclear, but Emma didn't like it one bit.

"My grandfather helped me until he died of a heart attack a few months after it all started. Stan died with my son on the first day. I've been alone. I didn't run with any banditos or anything like that."

Rosie chuckled. "I think you're misunderstanding me."

"You're not trying to find out if I'm some criminal element?"

"No. No. Nothing like that."

"Oh." When Rosie didn't expound, Emma considered the

possible conclusions the woman could be drawing. "So you think I'm military?"

"You don't have that kind of bearing, so no."

"Then why all the questions?"

"I watch out for my family."

"So you're here about Juan?"

Lifting her eyebrows, Rosie placed her elbows on the table and leaned toward Emma. "Why would I be here about him?"

Emma wagged her fork at Rosie. "Maybe because your niece was giving off some serious matchmaker vibes yesterday."

Rosie snorted. "Monica is always trying to set people up. It's her thing."

Pointedly taking another bite, Emma waited for Rosie to continue.

"I have to wonder why didn't you show up earlier to ask us for help."

Emma blotted her lips with a napkin and took a swig of diet soda. The beans had a spicy bite to them. "Two reasons. Number one: I wanted to put my son to rest. He disappeared on the first day and I eventually accepted that I wasn't going to find him alive."

"I'm so sorry," Rosie said, meaning it. "I can't imagine what that was like for you."

"I didn't want him to be one of *them*."

Bobbing her head, Rosie said, "I would feel the same way. *But* you could have come here and asked for help, you know."

"That brings me to reason number two. I didn't know the Fort was here."

That surprised Rosie. "Oh, I see. So how did you find out about us?"

"Jenni." Emma enjoyed Rosie's shocked look.

"Jenni is dead."

"I'm not lying. She told me to come here."

"Did she find you on one of her missions? Tell you we were here?"

Emma shook her head. "No. She told me just a few nights ago."

"That can't be. She's dead."

"But not gone, right? Not completely."

Fingers fidgeting on the surface of the table, Rosie gave her short nod and discreetly crossed herself. "Tell me how she told you about us."

"I dreamed about her the night after I put Billy to rest. I didn't know who she was, of course, but she showed up when I was passed out drunk after failing to work up the nerve to kill myself. She told me to come here."

"So how did you know it was Jenni?"

"Juan's son showed me her picture in the memorial garden after I arrived. I recognized her."

Muttering in Spanish, Rosie sat back sharply in her chair. "Troy told me Jenni told him in a dream that a nice lady was coming here and then you arrived."

Taking a moment to collect her thoughts, Emma found it hard to believe that the woman in her dream had actually existed and told her to come to the Fort. Yet, it was the truth. "That dream about Jenni saved me. I didn't want to live anymore. I lost everything in the apocalypse. I came here because..." Emma floundered, unsure of how to express emotions she couldn't clearly define.

"Because you didn't want to be alone?"

Emma's grip on her fork was so tight her fingers were aching. "It's hard to put into words. I guess maybe I just wanted to feel hope. Even if the dream was bullshit and the Fort didn't exist, trying to find it was a more positive, hopeful thing than putting a bullet in my head."

Rosie sighed, her fingers fiddling with the gathered hem of her apron. "I came here to talk to you because my grandson, Troy, likes you a lot. He won't stop talking about you. I just wanted to make sure you're the type of person he should be attaching himself to. Listening to you speak, it helps me understand who you are and what you've been through."

Emma fought the urge to chuckle. Here she'd been convinced Rosie was interrogating her for the powers that be when she was only a concerned grandmother. "I understand."

"If he bothers you, just let me know. I told him to let you get used to living here before he starts to pester you."

"He's sweet."

"So do you, Emma," Rosie replied, her expression warm and kind.

"I'm just a mom who lost her kid who hopes to help other people not lose theirs."

As Emma spoke the words aloud, they became her mission and purpose for living. There had to be more than just mere survival in this dead world and she'd found it. It was natural that her thoughts would drift to someone she already knew was in dire circumstances.

"The mother with the child from yesterday..."

"Yes?" Rosie tilted her head, curious.

"Is she still outside the wall?"

"Sadly, yes. Juan says Travis talked to her over the walkie-talkie he gave her, but she is refusing to leave her poor dead son behind. Juan says she's convinced we're holding out on her."

"Has anyone gone over to talk to her face to face?"

With a sad sigh, Rosie shook her head. "She's moved locations. We don't know where she is now. We can't make her come into the Fort. Everyone has to make their own choices in this world. As cruel as that may sound."

"It doesn't sound cruel. People should be allowed to make their own decisions, even if those choices don't make sense to us." Emma remembered her own despair and the ghost in her dreams, urging her to find a new life. "Maybe she just needs to speak to someone face to face. Someone who understands."

"You?"

"I'm not sure yet. Maybe."

"If I can help," said Rosie, "let me know."

"I definitely will."

An idea was starting to brew in Emma's head, but she wasn't sure it would work. There was only one way to find out.

It was time to get dressed and leave the comfort of her new room.

CHAPTER 9

The Newcomer

The roar of bulldozers pulled Emma's attention out the window of her room. The activity outside the Fort was in full swing. The construction vehicles were in a final cleanup of the area in front of the hotel, removing any signs of the zombie horde. Two big trucks rumbled down the street, packed with the corpses of zombies. She watched until they disappeared down another side road. The battle against the horde must have been epic in scale. Observing the approach of the horde must have been frightening. The good news was the Fort was still standing, and inside its walls was hope for the future.

Which brought her to her mission...

Freshly showered and in her new clothing, Emma stepped away from the view to finish getting ready. She tightened a leather belt around her hips then hooked the buckskin holster she'd inherited from her grandfather onto it. She'd leave her rifle in the hotel room for now, but slipped her pistol into the holster. Tucking two loaded backup magazines into her back pocket, she glanced at the clock. It was a few hours until dinner when most of the population of the Fort would descend on the dining room, but she'd rather not wait until then to track down the person she needed to speak to.

Monica had given Emma the cowboy hat she'd been wearing yesterday. It was woven straw with a longhorn concho bolo around the crown. "You'll need this since you'll be out and about during the day," she'd said.

Emma tucked it onto her head and was satisfied with the fit. Glancing into the mirror over the dresser, she marveled at how different she looked in her new clothing and hat. With her chestnut waves secured in long braids, she looked like someone different. Someone new. That thought appealed to her.

Snatching her denim jacket off the bed, she headed out on her mission.

Unlike the preceding night, the lobby was much quieter when the elevator doors opened. The afternoon sunlight poured in through windows that opened to a view of the high wall that spanned the front of the hotel. The golden rays gave the area a dreamy feel. A few of the elderly residents were reading, crocheting, or doing puzzles. The younger people were missing from the mix, probably out on duty. The imposing check-in counter didn't have anyone behind it. Flowers in a vase, a few prayer candles, and hand-written notes and cards created a memorial to the deceased city secretary and her son.

Emma found her way out through the back of the hotel, nodding to the few other people she passed by in the hallways. Everyone she saw was a stranger, so she kept walking. It was a little unnerving to be around so many people after so much time alone and it was hard to work up the nerve to do more than nod in greeting.

Outside, there were a few people gathered at a folding table laden with large orange water coolers, red plastic cups, and a basket full of protein bars. Without a ton of people milling around, the hard-packed red earth looked barren. The memorial garden was empty, the flowers the brightest color on the block. There were stakes roping off a section near the portable office, a sign announcing it was a future vegetable garden. Yet, overall, the area felt empty.

The back door to City Hall slammed open just as Emma reached the bottom step. Lenore appeared in the doorway, closely followed by a skinny black guy in an Atlanta Braves cap. In the rear was the redheaded man named Arnold. Emma swiftly stepped to one side, letting the heavyset woman pass.

"You couldn't have picked up the pace and gotten here like a month ago?" Lenore groused.

"I don't get why you're angry," the newcomer snapped, pausing on the steps.

"You could've gotten here faster! And then Ken wouldn't be

dead!"

"Is she making sense to you? Because she is not making sense to me," the skinny guy said to Arnold.

"Lewis, she's upset because her best friend, who was gay, died alongside his unrequited love," Arnold explained. "She thinks if you'd gotten here earlier he wouldn't have died because you're gay and he wouldn't have been chasing that other guy."

"Who said I was gay?" Lewis protested.

Lenore swerved around on her heel to pierce him with a disbelieving look. "Really? *Really*?"

"Fine! I'm gay. But just because you put two gays in the same space don't mean they're going to fuck," Lewis shot back.

The unwavering incredulous gaze of the irate woman bore down on Lewis.

"Okay, *maybe* they will, but that don't mean he'd be alive. You can't put this on me! I just got here!"

"I can put it on you because if you'd been here earlier he wouldn't have been pining for that mountain man!"

Arnold raised a finger. "Which is my point, babe."

"Lenore," she corrected. "I ain't your babe."

"Fine! *Lenore*, Ken was into buff dudes. Lewis ain't that."

Lewis was clearly offended. "Excuse you!"

"You're as skinny as a blade of grass," Lenore snorted.

"She means no offense," Arnold interjected. "But you're definitely not Ken's type."

Lenore glowered, but didn't deny what Arnold was saying.

Feeling distinctly uncomfortable, Emma waited for a break in the conversation to speak to Lewis. He'd arrived with the mother and child. Maybe he'd be able to give her insight into how to reach the distraught woman and bring her into the Fort.

Raising his hands, Lewis's attention swiveled back and forth between Lenore and Arnold. "I'm just trying to make friends here. I'm new here. I saw a sister and-"

Lenore grunted. "I ain't your sister."

Lewis drew himself up and met Lenore's angry gaze with an equally indignant one. "*Really*?"

"Babe, give him a break."

With a furious sigh, Lenore's shoulders sagged. "I get what you're sayin', okay? Both of you. I'm pissed off at the universe right now because Ken wouldn't have been so lonely if you'd gotten here weeks ago. He was so lonely." Tears welled in her eyes and she stalked off.

"It'll be cool, man. I promise." Arnold clapped Lewis on the shoulder. "She's just having a rough time of it. I'll put in a good word for you. It's all good." The tall redhead scampered after Lenore.

Pivoting about, Lewis caught sight of Emma lingering nearby. "Is everyone around here crazy?"

"I just got here myself, so I can't speak to that," Emma answered.

Lewis shot her a suspicious look. "But I saw *you* on the wall shooting the zombies yesterday."

"I got put to work right away." Emma shrugged one shoulder. "I guess they wanted to test me."

"Will they do that to me?" Lewis didn't look too happy at that thought.

"I killed an entire town of zombies, so I think they wanted me to prove myself." She might as well get the topic of her legendary status out of the way.

"A *whole* town? You're so tiny! What did you do? Drop a bomb?"

"It took over a year."

"*Oh*! So slow-like. That makes sense."

Emma nodded.

He extended his hand, an open and friendly look on his face. "I'm Lewis."

"Emma."

They shook hands, exchanging smiles.

Crossing his arms over his chest, Lewis eyed her cowboy hat for a second. "You're from Texas, huh?"

"Yeah. A few hours from here. You're from Atlanta, right?"

"How'd you know?"

Emma pointed to the cap.

"Oh, yeah." Lewis laughed, embarrassed. "I'm sleep-deprived and a little shook up right now."

"Totally understandable. Especially after yesterday."

"That was some shit, wasn't it? I can't believe that happened. Just when we thought we were safe, Rickie got chopped to pieces by that trap. Shit. I can't shake that image out of my head."

Emma grimaced. "It's stuck in mine too. I had awful nightmares."

"The worst. Plus, I think I might still be in trouble for crashing that sweet Mustang. That lady who runs the garage keeps giving me the stink eye."

"It was...a choice to take the car," Emma said, trying not to straight up tell him it had been a dumb move.

"I know. I panicked. I just wanted to save my people. This is why I like taking orders, not giving them. I panic."

"We all do at times. It's normal."

Lewis shrugged beneath his spotless white t-shirt. It must be new. "I do it all the time. It's like my default setting."

"Do you mind me askin' how you and your people got here?"

His eyes sparked with eagerness, giving the impression he was anxious to speak about his misfortunes. "Nah, it's cool. I'm fine with sharing. I can tell you it was some crazy ass journey. We started out in a big caravan of cars, but it got bad on the road. Zombies, crazy people, wildfires, tornadoes...we saw some bad shit out there."

"It sounds bad."

Leaning his elbows against the railing, Lewis gave her a somber nod. With the flair of a storyteller, he said, "We started out with a hundred. Lots of people gave up when things got rough. They wanted to just find a place to hunker down and wait it out. It was tempting, but hope kept us going. The idea of a cure! It drove us forward through all the bad shit. When we reached Texas, we thought the worst was behind us. We were trying to get here as fast as we could, especially once we got past I-35. That was some serious shit, I tell you. Cars everywhere. Zombies everywhere. We thought once we got past it, we could just haul ass here. Then everything went wrong. Car broke down, ammo ran out, and we barely avoided a fuck-ton of zombies by hiding in a warehouse. Once the zombies cleared the area, we humped it the last few days on foot. Then we get here and the street starts exploding and there's traps and..." Lewis shook his head in disbelief. "I can't believe some of us made it here alive after what went down. When we started out from Atlanta, we thought it would take a few days to get here. Not months."

"So it is true you were looking for a cure."

Sagging with sorrow, Lewis nodded. "Yeah. For my cousin."

"The little boy with the mask?"

Lewis visibly shuddered, his gaze dropping to the ground. "That's him. Julian got bit by another kid. We were holed up in a high school and these people showed up. A big family. They didn't tell us that the daughter got bit earlier in the day. Julian was trying to cheer her up by showing her his teddy bear when she turned. She grabbed his arm and bit down. He was wearing long sleeves, so she kept at it like a rabid dog, trying to get to his meat. It was fucked up. Can you believe her family didn't tell us she was bit?"

"Yeah, I believe it. Sometimes people go into denial when bad shit happens."

Dark eyes glimmering with tears, Lewis pressed his lips together, composing himself. "Seen it with my auntie when Julian got the bite. It was a small one. We weren't even sure it broke the skin all the way, but I knew we couldn't chance it. So I told him we were going to play ball, put the mask on him, and duct-taped it on his head. I told him it was because it was too big for him. Had to make it secure. We were playing and then he said he was dizzy. He laid down on the ground and...and..."

Emma reached out to touch the young man's arm when he choked on the words. "You don't have to tell me if it hurts too much. I understand."

"My auntie wouldn't let anyone put him down!" The words tore out of Lewis mouth, angry and desperate. Emma got the feeling that he *needed* to share his story. "We locked him in a janitor's closet. Ain't *that* crazy?"

What if Billy had been with her when he'd been bitten? What would she have done? She didn't have an answer. "No, no. Not really. It's hard to know what you'll do when you're faced with something that awful."

"People got so mad at her, but she held her ground. Now she's out there right now. With Julian. Still hoping for a cure that ain't here."

"I want to help her. That's why I came looking for you. Maybe you can tell me something that would help me convince her to let go of Julian and come inside the walls."

"Oh, no! There ain't no convincing my Aunt Macy. I'm telling you right now. I'm stubborn, but she's way worse. She came here because there is supposed to be a cure and now everyone is saying there's not. There's not even a lab! We were told there's a lab here! It was so much bullshit!"

"Who told you?"

"A voice on the ham radio. A dude telling everyone there was a cure in Ashley Oaks, Texas at a fort run by the government."

"You told the leaders here about that, right?"

"Oh, yeah. The moment we got inside they were asking us a bunch of questions. I kept hoping they would tell us they did have a cure and we had to pass some tests, but that wasn't the case."

"I can't imagine why someone told you to come here. If any place would have a cure, it's the CDC. You were in Atlanta, right?"

"We're from outside of Atlanta. Seventy miles east. It's not like anyone could just go up to the CDC building and demand a cure. Atlanta was nuked anyway, so it wasn't an option."

Widening her eyes, Emma found herself speechless.

"You didn't know? They dropped a bomb on Atlanta and Houston on the same day."

"No, I had *no* idea. We only had local stations on our television and the coverage went dead within two days."

"It was about a week after things got really bad that they

started taking out the big cities. New York City was first. Then Washington D.C. and Los Angeles. The idea was to kill the outbreaks in the big cities and save the rest of the country. Didn't work. The bombs didn't stop it from spreading."

"But it could've killed millions of zombies, which is better for us survivors."

"Maybe." Narrowing his dark eyes, Lewis leaned toward her. "Why are you interested in Aunt Macy?"

Emma didn't see the point in not being truthful. Her pain would always be a part of her. "I was a mom too."

"*Was?* Oh, wow. Shit. Sorry."

"I was the one giving her cover yesterday and when I saw your cousin in that condition, it broke my heart."

"You know what's sad? We told ourselves that because he had such a small bite, they could cure him. He wasn't ripped up like other zombies, you know? My aunt clung to that the whole way here. But it was for nothing. I don't think there's a damn thing you could say to her to convince her to give up hope. I tried yesterday. I begged her to come inside. That dude, Juan, he tried the same. I even tried to pull Julian out of her arms. She wouldn't let me. I love her, but she's gone crazy with grief."

"I can't say I blame her."

"Look, Emma, you seem like a nice lady." Pressing a hand against his chest, Lewis said, "It touches my heart that you care about my aunt. It's been months since he died and she's still got hope because some asshole on the ham radio said there's a cure here. I just don't know how you can change that. I love her, but I'm not going to go out there and die with her. And she's gonna die. I hate it, but that's the truth."

"I understand why you feel like that, but I had given up on life when someone saved me. I can't give up on your aunt."

The vision of the dark haired woman in the red sweater reappeared in her mind. Jenni sitting in the shadows, urging Emma to live.

"So whatcha gonna do to save her?" Lewis asked, genuinely curious.

A ghost had saved her, so maybe a ghost was the answer.

Emma moved her gaze from Lewis, scanning the area for the white-haired medium. "I'm going to speak to a friend and see if he can help."

"How'd he change anything?"

"He's a man with inside information."

Lewis gave her a befuddled look which was promptly interrupted by the back door to City Hall opening. Yolanda poked her head out and was relieved to see Lewis.

"There you are, Lewis! I need to talk to you about fixing my computer. No one else around here is that good with them, but you did a fine job with Travis's last night."

"Sure, Ms. Yolanda. Be right there. I'll catch you later, Emma. I appreciate you being concerned about my aunt. If you can get her to come inside, that would be awesome."

"I'll do my best," Emma promised.

Lewis gave her a brief nod and rushed back inside City Hall.

With fresh determination, Emma started her search for Rune.

CHAPTER 10

The Inside Man

It took a few tries to find someone who knew where the white-haired medium was. The first people Emma approached were very friendly though they didn't have an answer for her. That alleviated her shyness, making it easier to ask others for help. It was a good sign that she was gradually adapting to being around other people.

Finally, someone directed her to the garage where Rune was working on his bike. Eagerly, she took the wooden steps over the inner wall into the main entrance to the Fort. It was quieter today since the construction vehicles were stored elsewhere in the Fort and must exit another way. Out of the garage came the sound of tools being used and the hum of large industrial sized fans blowing warm air into the stuffy interior.

Voices from close by drew Emma to a spot on the far end of the building toward the last bay.

"…and tell him he's an asshole for killing himself. I'm a pilot! This isn't my gig!" a woman said testily.

"Patrick ain't around," Rune drawled. "I ain't seen him since he took a header out his hotel window."

Emma found the two people next to an impressive Harley Davidson. Rune was on his knees, attentively cleaning a part of the engine. A tall, thin woman with short, dark hair that curled around her ears and forehead grunted in response and placed her hands on her hips.

"It's bad enough that I'm grounded, Rune, but now I have to run the damn garage because he was chicken shit."

"You'll be back in the air soon enough, Greta. This ain't going to last forever."

"It feels that way."

Rune caught sight of Emma and waved her over. "Hey,

Emma! Have you met Greta yet? She's a kickass helicopter pilot and now runs the garage."

Greta spun about, hand extending. She had a long, angular face with keen eyes that swiftly looked her over, as though evaluating her. "The fearless zombie killer. A pleasure."

"For God's sake, Rune. Have you told everyone?" Emma complained, but clasped the woman's hand warmly. "I'm just Emma."

"Rune actually didn't tell me. Calhoun did. He's excited about your arrival. He thinks you're some sort of alien hybrid that will wipe out all the zombies for the Amazonian Queen."

"Huh?"

"Calhoun thinks Nerit is an Amazonian Queen," Rune explained.

Dropping her hand, Greta shot a grin at Rune. "Would you be surprised if she was?"

"Not one damn bit."

"She is impressive," Emma said. "Kinda scary too."

"Rumor is she was Mossad. I'd believe that."

Rune nodded. "I'd put money on that one."

"Got any inside information on that?"

Rune sat back on his heels. "That's the thing. She ain't got no one haunting her since Ralph moved on. Maybe even the ghosts are too afraid to try to haunt her."

There was a loud clatter nearby and furious cussing.

"I better go check on Carlos," Greta huffed. "He's trying to fix the Mustang that kid wrecked. Good thing I rebuilt one with my dad back in the day. I know exactly what to do. Catch you later, Emma."

Brushing his hands off on his jeans, Rune scrutinized Emma's face. "Hmmm," he said, "you look like a woman with a purpose."

"I need your help."

Rune leaned back against a work bench. "I had a feelin.'"

Emma emulated his stance, resting her back against a pillar, instantly regretting it. It was grimy and left a swath of dirty grease on her clothes.

"Tell me what you need, Emma."

So she told him. Rune listened to Emma, his brow puckered. He grunted a few times, nodding in understanding.

When she finished, he exhaled long and hard. "I'll go with ya to talk to this Macy, but I'm warnin' you now, I will not lie to her. If we get over there and I can't help, you're gonna have to accept that. The dead don't always haunt the livin', though it is a helluva lot more common now. And sometimes, even when they're hauntin', they don't talk."

"I don't want you to lie," Emma assured him. "Even if her kid has moved on, knowing that might help her."

"I think you're being a bit too optimistic there."

"Maybe."

"What did it take to make you let go of the hope you had about your son?"

Emma scrunched up her face at the horrible memory of the moment she gave up. "I went into Stan's house. The windows were shattered. There was blood everywhere. I thought I'd find Stan and Billy dead, but it was Stan's new wife torn to pieces. Her eyes were pinned to one spot in the room. It was the changing table. I found her baby inside the hamper, barely alive."

"Shit, Emma. I'm sorry."

"He died within minutes of me arriving. When I killed what was left of her, she was staring at where her baby had been. Was she staring because she wanted to eat him? Or because she gave her life to save him? There was no way to know." Emma shrugged. "Stan and Billy weren't in the house. If Stan had been there, he would have done everything to save his family. It was then hope started to die inside me, bit by bit, every day, until I put Billy to rest. It was a process. A slow, agonizing process."

"I betcha it's the same for her, don't ya think? What will make her give up that last bit of hope?"

Staring at him straight in the eye, Emma said, "You."

"There's no guarantee of that," Rune replied. "I won't lie. If her son's ghost ain't hangin' around, I'm not pulling some fake ass John Edward's shit."

"I'm not asking that of you. I promise."

Rune watched her, blue eyes pensive, mouth tight with apprehension. "Once I open myself up to the other side, I might get bombarded. Every ghost hanging around might swarm me, demanding I help them find peace. If that happens, I'll have to head out for a while. Give them time to settle down."

"For real?" Emma stared at him in disbelief. "You'd have to leave the Fort?"

"I've done it before. Things settled down a little when the horde came through. Ghosts got their peace and moved on, but that only cleared the way for weaker ones to start manifesting. So far, I've been able to ignore them, but doing this..." Rune lifted his hands in surrender.

Heart sinking, Emma sighed. "I apologize for asking. I didn't know."

"Well, it's not like I told ya. I got the gift. I'm supposed to use it, right? Besides, I thought you were going to ask me if you're haunted by your dead family. That's what most people ask me."

"I see the face of my grandfather and my ancestors every time I look in the mirror and see my reflection. I know they are with me, in my blood and flesh. I never doubt that. I also never doubted that once I put down the monster that took my son's body that his soul would be at peace. I don't need you to confirm it to me."

"Lipan Apache, eh?"

Emma raised her eyebrows. "What?"

"The Native blood running in your veins. Lipan Apache."

"And a good dose of Texas redneck," Emma answered, unsettled.

If Rune noticed her discomfort, he was ignoring it.

Bending at the waist, he leaned toward her, blue eyes piercing and disconcerting. "Your *soul* is Lipan Apache."

"That's what my grandfather always told me."

Her gaze swept over her surroundings, almost expecting to see her grandfather standing nearby with an all-knowing grin on his face.

"But your grandmother hated it. She blamed him for your mother running off. Thought him sneaking her off to the reservation for what she called heathen rituals is what corrupted her and made her leave."

"You're getting personal," Emma said, biting off the words.

"This is what I do. This is what you want me to do to that woman out there. It does sting a bit, huh?"

Closing her eyes, Emma took a moment to compose herself. "Who's talking to you?"

"All of them."

"My ancestors," she whispered.

A shiver ran visibly through his body. "Well, they're definitely not ghosts that are stuck here. They're something different, connected to the very cosmos. Voices whispering out of the stars."

"Sometimes I hear them when I'm afraid."

"I know you want to save this woman, but you're asking a lot of me. I need you to be sure that this is the right move. We could go out there only to discover she doesn't want to hear the truth. Or if she accepts the truth, it could be the end of her."

Rocking back on her heels, Emma lifted her eyes to the stars. She couldn't save Billy or the woman's son, but she could try to save the mother. Jenni had saved her when she'd been so close to eating a bullet.

"I need to do this. I will go find her and try to convince her with or without you. I know I am asking a lot of you. If it is too much, I will accept you saying no without complaint. I didn't realize just how much I was asking of you."

"Jenni was a loud one, but she's not here anymore. Last thing she did was pop into one of my dreams to tell me to help Emma. 'Who the fuck is Emma?' I said when I woke up. And then you arrived. So I'll help ya."

"Why do you think she brought me here?" Emma dared to ask the question she hadn't even wanted to ask.

"Well, Jenni liked to save people to make up for not saving her kids. That burden weighed heavily on her. She gave her life to save another woman's children. A way of balancing the scales. If I were to guess, I'd say Jenni saved you so you could continue her work. Just like you want to do with Macy."

With a sharp inhalation, Emma accepted his words as truth. It sounded right somehow.

"You two would've been friends, I think. Though Jenni would have driven you fuckin' crazy. It was hard to tell what was goin' on in her mind one second to the next. Honestly, the only person who could actually handle her was Katie. They had a bond born out of loss and the struggle to survive. But you would have gotten along with her once Jenni figured out you weren't a threat."

"To her and Juan?" Emma arched an eyebrow.

"Nah, to her and Katie. Katie was her family. Mom, sister, best friend, everything."

"Why are you telling me this?"

"Because if you're going to pick up the mantle Jenni left for you, you should know a bit about her and who she cared about. I have a feeling Jenni probably also summoned you here to watch over Katie."

"Does she need watching over?"

"Nope. But Jenni would've kept on worrying about her. Besides, once Katie is back from maternity leave, you'll be dealing with her a lot. Travis is mayor, but Katie is the power behind the throne. Trust me on that."

"Is she like Nerit?"

"Scary? Nah. Katie is cool as a cucumber, that one. She doesn't get riled easily."

Despite Rune's reassurance, Emma was intimidated by the thought of meeting Katie. Jenni had definitely sent her to the Fort, but Emma wasn't sure she was comfortable with picking up any mantle. At the very least, she shared a mission to help others with Jenni.

"So when do we go find Macy?" Rune asked.

"You're going to find Macy?"

Emma whirled about to face Juan. He was flushed from the heat and wiping the back of his neck with a kerchief. Beyond the garage, a teenager was guiding a horse toward the stable. Rune altered his position so he could stare past Emma and Juan as though looking for something unseen.

"I want to try to get her to come inside the walls," Emma explained.

"There's no sign of her out there. I took a look around," Juan replied. "I'm worried about her. She's really messed up over there not being a cure."

"I just got a lead on where she might be," Rune said in a nonchalant manner.

"Oh?" Emma and Juan said at the same time.

"Someone just showed up who wants a final word with her. It looks like we're all on the same mission," Rune explained, one long finger pointing to an empty spot near the garage doors.

"Her son?" Emma whispered.

"Nope. Her husband."

CHAPTER 11

Hiding Places

The big red truck slowly rolled down the red-brick streets of Ashley Oaks. Juan drove while Rune sat shotgun. Seated on the bench in the back of the cab, Emma craned her head this way and that to study the facades of the buildings, peer down alleyways, and scrutinize the wild tangle of foliage in empty lots. Rune joining her mission increased the odds of a positive outcome, or at least that was what she was hoping. Unfortunately, they hadn't spotted any signs of Macy yet.

It had taken a half hour to get their little excursion approved and a vehicle assigned to their mission. It was peculiar to Emma just how organized the Fort was despite the apocalypse, but it made sense for such a huge operation.

"See your ghost?" Juan asked.

He'd asked the question multiple times since departing the Fort.

"Nope. He just told me to head northwest," Rune replied. "Then he vanished."

"You gotta ask for details, man. I keep telling you that."

"And I keep telling *you* that the dead aren't like us. They got their own priorities."

Juan swore under his breath in Spanish.

"You can't blame them, Juan," Emma said. "They don't have to worry about the shit we do. They've already had the worst possible thing happen to them. They're dead."

"Emma's right. They're setting things right, getting revenge, or figuring out that they're dead," Rune agreed.

Juan made a scornful noise. "How could you not know you're dead?"

"Denial is a powerful thing, man," Rune said. "How many people died those first days because they couldn't believe

Night of the Living Dead was suddenly a real thing?"

"You mean the *Dawn of the Dead* remake. That's when the zombies got fast," Juan said with nerdish authority. "Which I *still* think is bullshit. Zombies should be *slow*."

Rune grunted. "Fine. Whatever. My point remains the same."

Peering out the windows, Emma said, "I wish they started off slow. Maybe it wouldn't have gotten this bad."

Juan turned the pickup down another road. "Whoever made them broke the zombie rules. I'd like a harsh word with them, but they probably got eaten when the zombies broke out of the lab."

"You think they were made?"

"Yeah, Em, I do. Someone watched too many Romero films and thought it was a great idea because they're *pendejo*."

"Rune, got any inside info on how we got zombies?"

"Nope, can't say that I do. And it don't matter no how. Where they came from doesn't change that they're here."

The medium had a point.

The conversation lapsed for a while as they all watched for any sign of Macy.

The town had once been beautiful. Parts of it still were, but time had destroyed some of the quaint beauty of the Texas boomtown. The old railroad station told a story Emma knew was a common and sad part of the history of the region. Towns had popped up alongside the railroad, bursting with new commerce and migration to the area. Once new lines were laid down, bypassing old stops, a lot of towns had faced a hard economic downturn. Ashley Oaks appeared to be one of those towns. The pickup rolled past what had once been a dance hall. It was crumbling, the interior filled with a bramble of trees and wild grass.

"Wait! I just saw him. Doorway of that building over yonder." Rune pointed toward an old three-story brick apartment building. The windows were covered in newspaper and a few others were broken and boarded over. The windows on the higher floors were intact.

Juan pulled up to a buckled and broken sidewalk, wild grass

and weeds poking up between the crisscrossing cracks. Peering up at the building, he tapped his fingers against the steering wheel.

"You sure, man? This place looks hardcore abandoned."

"I'm sure."

"The dirt in front of the entrance is disturbed. You can see where the door swung outward." Emma leaned forward and pointed to the deep grooves in the accumulation of dirt and leaves. "Someone is in there."

Juan killed the engine and reached for the shotgun tucked between his seat and the console. "Okay. Then we go in and Rune does his magic."

"Ain't magic."

"Whatever. You talk to the fuckin' dead, man. Sounds like magic to me."

There was anger in Juan's tone, and Emma wondered why. There had been some strain between Rune and Juan since they'd climbed into the truck. Rune gave Juan a long, hard look, his hand resting on the door latch. He appeared confused too, but shrugged off the tension and exited. Emma squeezed out behind him, scrutinizing their surroundings. There hadn't been any sign of zombies in this part of town, but that didn't mean they weren't lurking about. The sound of the pickup might have caught their attention, so it was best to stay on alert. Emma slid her pistol out of its holster and trailed behind Rune as he skirted around the front of the pickup with a Glock in his hand.

Juan slapped the keys onto the roof of the truck and joined them. "In case I get eaten, you guys can get away" he said, answering Emma's inquiring look.

"Oh."

The front steps were red brick and solid despite one corner being chipped. The front door was thick metal with a leaded glass inset.

Tapping the spray painted mark on it, he said, "It should be clear of z's in there. We already did a sweep of the building."

Juan tugged on the door to find it locked. "Of course, it

wouldn't be easy."

Rune returned to the sidewalk, searching for another way inside. "Better hurry up before the zombies show up."

Emma jogged past him toward the corner of the building. "There's a side door. I saw it when we pulled up."

The wooden fence surrounding the side yard had long ago fallen over and was trapped beneath the heavy mesh of weeds and wild grass. A stone fountain was in pieces and the wrought iron benches set around it were orange with rust. Barely visible beneath the browned foliage, a flagstone path wound alongside the building to a wooden door warped with time and rain.

"Careful, Em," Juan warned, joining her.

"I know. Crawling zombies."

"Nah. I was thinking rattlesnakes."

With those words, Juan brushed past her and cautiously started along the pathway. Emma followed, with Rune taking up the rear. The breeze stirred the thick overgrowth, making it undulate. It was easy to imagine a zombie scuttling along beneath it toward them. As a precaution, she kept her pistol trained on the ground, watching for any signs of the undead.

A jack rabbit erupted from a hiding spot nearby, darting through the shrubs and into the alley. Though all three of them started, no one panicked and shot at the frightened creature. Emma's confidence in her two companions solidified. She liked that they could keep their wits about them even when under the threat of a possible zombie attack.

Juan reached the rickety wooden steps leading up to the door. With a firm hand, he shook the structure. It fell apart in his grip with a loud clatter. The noise sent grackles into an angry tirade in the nearby trees. A rapid search of the staircase remains revealed one solid piece of wood which he used to pry open the door. It swung outward on creaky rusted hinges. There was a loud crack when the top hinge sprang free of the doorframe and the door buckled over, striking the side of the building. The grackles furiously protested the racket, hoping from branch to branch to squawk.

"She definitely knows we're coming," Rune muttered.

Bristling, Juan shot Rune a sharp look. "You couldn't have done it any quieter?"

"You need to take it down a notch. Now is not the time."

"When will it be time, Rune?"

"I told you, I can't control them."

"I don't know what this is about, but we just made a shit-ton of noise. We need to get moving," Emma cut in, giving both men a disapproving glower. "Macy is what's important right now."

Juan responded with a curt nod.

"I agree. Let's see what we got here." Rune edged forward to peer into the open doorway that was about five feet off the ground. "Good news. He's waiting for us in the hallway. We're on the right track."

"I'll take lead." Hoisting himself up into the doorway, Juan disappeared for a few seconds. "These are the only two entrances," he said when he returned. "I can see her footprints in the dust heading upstairs. No sign of anyone else following, so we should be good. Let me help you up, Em."

Emma holstered her pistol and extended her hands. His calloused ones closed around hers and he easily lifted her off the ground. His t-shirt clung to his muscled chest and shoulders, drawing her admiration. Catching herself, she looked away. Juan set her down on the filthy and warped linoleum floor, his hand briefly squeezing hers. It was such a rapid gesture, when he let go she wasn't sure if it had actually happened. Ignoring the sudden flush of her face, she drew her weapon and stared down the long, gloomy hallway to a window covered in yellowed newspaper. The doors on the bottom floor were spray painted with the distinctive markings of the Fort. At the far end, barely visible in the dim lighting, was another hallway and the bottom steps of the staircase.

Rune hauled himself up to join them and wiped his hands off, then redrew his Glock. "He's pointing up the stairs. I'll take lead since he's guiding me."

Juan waved her forward after the biker. "After you, Em."

The floor was solid beneath her feet despite the popping noise of the linoleum cracking apart beneath their footsteps. Hard wood peeked out from beneath the ugly yellow fake tile. The building was old, reeking of mildew. She wondered if the Fort would ever expand far enough to absorb it. It would need renovation, but it appeared the bones of the structure were solid. The stairs were old, worn, and solid wood. They creaked enough to let anyone upstairs know that visitors were on their way up.

A few steps ahead of her, Rune answered an unseen person a few times, nodded his head, pointed in one direction, then grunted in agreement.

"What's up?" Juan asked.

"He's getting chattier the closer we get to his wife," Rune replied. "She's on the third floor and knows we're coming. Also, she ain't happy."

The second floor was worse than the first. A busted window had let in the elements. Mold covered one wall that was damp from a recent rain and rotting debris covered the floor. They hugged the far wall, making sure to bypass any parts of the surface that might be too fragile to walk on. The staircase to the third floor was narrower and Macy and her son's footprints were plain in the thick film that covered the steps.

The air was humid, stale, and speckled with the dust stirred by their passage. Emma sneezed a few times, then tucked her face into the collar of her shirt. The hallway at the top of the stairs was brightly lit from the sunlight flooding through a big hole torn in the roof. A dead tree branch lay on the floor near it. It was easy to surmise what had happened.

Rune gestured to a door down the hall. "Corner room on the left."

The closer they drew to their destination, the tighter the knot of anxiety grew in Emma's chest. It wasn't rooted in fear of the undead, but in the possibility of failure. She had lived the last year and three months of her life in a tiny, hot, and sometimes squalid Airstream. For most of it she'd been alone with the ghosts of her past and fears of the future. The thought of Macy living in such a decrepit building while clinging to hope made her chest heavy. It hit too close to home.

Rune reached the door, once a bright red now faded to maroon, and knocked.

A woman's tired voice answered, "Come in."

Rune gently pressed the door open, taking a moment to scrutinize the situation beyond the threshold. With a nod to the others, he stepped inside. Emma scuttled in behind Rune and holstered her weapon. She didn't want to appear to be a threat. Rune also put away his Glock. Juan had his shotgun, but aimed at the floorboards.

Emma finally got a good look at the other woman. Macy had large, dark eyes with thick eyelashes and her slender face was framed with thick curls that formed a halo around her head. Tall and leanly muscled, she was wearing different clothes from the previous day: jeans, a black tank, and an unbuttoned chambray shirt with the sleeves rolled up. She was perched on a rickety old chair next to a card table covered in empty water bottles, cellophane wrappers, and a can of air freshener. A backpack filled with canned and boxed food rested against the wall alongside two jugs of water. Emma knew the woman hadn't traveled with those items, so the Fort must have provided the supplies, along with a sleeping bag stretched out in one corner.

In the opposite one, Julian, in his mask, was pacing restlessly at the end of a leash his mother had tied to the radiator. Growling low in his chest, the little boy pulled at the end of the thick leather strap, his small hands clawing in their direction. Beneath a layer of air freshener, the room smelled of rotting meat.

"I thought you said you'd let me decide my own fate," Macy said, directing an angry glare at Juan.

"Yes, it's your decision to join us or not."

"But you're here," Macy said, her annoyance evident.

Emma stepped forward. "We want to help."

"And you are?" Marcy didn't move from her chair, but tapped her fingers lightly against the surface of the table.

"I'm Emma. This is Rune."

"So Emma, Rune, and Juan, you tracked me down after I blew out of that other building in the middle of the night so I wouldn't be bothered by you folks. So unless you're here to offer me the cure, I gotta say I'm not feeling too hospitable."

The two men gave Emma expectant looks. It had been her choice to come, so it was only right that she should take the lead. She cleared her throat.

"Macy, I want to help you. I know you're in a lot of pain and-"

The woman let out a sound of derision. "You think?"

"I *know*. I lost my son too."

"I didn't lose my son. He is right there. Waiting for a cure."

"We told you, Macy-"

"I know what you *told* me, Juan." Macy shot him a furious look. "I heard you loud and clear."

Silence fell over the room, only disrupted by the growls of the zombie child.

"We're not here to do you harm," Rune said, breaking through the uncomfortable quiet.

"There is nothing you can offer me other than a cure."

"We gave you food and-"

"Take it back then," Macy cut in, glaring at Juan. "I'll find my own supplies."

This was not going the way Emma had thought it would.

"That's not what I'm saying," Juan said, raising his hands in surrender.

"Then what *is* it you're saying?"

"We're here to help, ma'am," Rune said in a gentle voice.

The situation was getting away from them swiftly.

Julian snarled in the corner, straining on the leash, which made it difficult to think straight. The radiator let out a metallic groan as it pulled away from the wall. Julian flung himself at Emma, the zombie child's fingers gripping her arm in a painful vise.

CHAPTER 12

Time to Move On

The tiny fingers of the zombie child were surprisingly strong as they dug into the tough fabric of Emma's denim jacket. Growling, Julian slammed the face guard of the mask he was wearing against her arm. Behind the slim metal bars, his teeth snapped together as he strained to bite her and the smell of rot that emanated from his blackened mouth was overpowering. Gagging, Emma attempted to jerk her arm away from the child's bruising grip, but couldn't break free.

With a cry of dismay, Macy dashed across the room and grabbed her son about the waist. The child's hold tightened on Emma's sleeve as his mother attempted to yank him off. Grunting, the dead boy thrashed in Macy's arms, fighting to reach his prey. He slammed the face mask into Emma's arm over and over again, frantic to bite her.

"Julian, stop it! You know better!"

Juan joined the struggle. He attempted to pry the dead child's fingers off of Emma's arm, but Macy shoved him away and shot him a furious look.

"Don't! He's delicate!"

"I can't hurt him," Juan protested. "He's dead!"

"He's rotting. You might pull off a finger, or even his arm," Rune soberly remarked.

Macy glowered at Rune, but didn't refute his assertion.

Though dead for months, his dark skin discolored, his fingernails blackened, and his once dark eyes pale and lifeless, the boy didn't look as decomposed as other zombies. He was gradually decaying. The virus slowed the natural process of decomposition in the zombies. Emma had observed that herself while clearing out her town. Julian looked deceptively alive from a distance, but up close it was evident he was a zombie.

At last, Macy managed to pull her son off of Emma and dragged him to the corner. "Julian, I told you not to do that! You can't bite people!"

Eerily calm, Macy re-tied the leash to a more solid part of the radiator. She ignored Julian as he clawed at her, his fingers hooking into her afro and jerking her head toward him. Once his leash was secure, she focused on the zombie child and patiently removed his hands from her curls.

"No, Julian. Be a good boy," she chastised him in a patient, loving tone.

Emma exchanged disbelieving looks with Juan and Rune, who were clearly unnerved by Macy's interaction with Julian. The mother was acting like her dead child was just being naughty instead of a monster attempting to tear into Emma's flesh. Her denial of his condition was startling and unsettling.

When Emma had seen Billy's zombified corpse, her only thought had been to release him from his terrible existence. The difference between the two mothers was that hope of a cure had given Macy time to grow accustomed to her son's condition. She was blinded by hope and love to the truth. For the first time, Emma realized they might not be able to convince Macy to join the others at the Fort. Their task was definitely more daunting and complex than Emma had thought, and she realized there was a good chance they would leave without Macy.

Rune crossed his arms over his chest, his eyes downcast and his expression grim. A sigh escaped his lips and he nervously tugged at his mustache. Since he was privy to a world Emma couldn't see, she wondered what was so unsettling. She moved closer to him and nudged him with her elbow.

"Do you see something?"

Rune nodded once.

Juan ventured over to Macy's side to make doubly sure the leash was tied securely to the radiator and probably to make sure it would hold. While he worked, the distraught mother lectured her growling zombified son while holding his arms firmly to his sides to keep him from lunging at her.

"What do you see?" Emma asked.

Rune let out a ragged breath. "The boy's spirit *is* tied to his body. I didn't see it at first. He was hiding in the shadows by the radiator, but he's there."

A sudden head rush left Emma dizzy. She steadied herself with one hand on Rune's shoulder. He caught her elbow and gave her a moment to compose herself.

"Emma, your boy moved on. He ain't here."

Swallowing hard, Emma gave him a short nod. "Thank you for telling me that."

"Julian, though, is confused and afraid. He's tethered to this reality."

"Because she won't let him go?"

Rune inclined his head. "Yeah."

Macy shot them a curious look over her shoulder. "Why would I let him go? I'm his mother. He's safe with me."

Realizing they'd been overheard, Emma turned to face Macy while Rune sheepishly looked away. Juan paused in his task, his expression guarded.

"We didn't mean to let go of his zombified body," Emma responded in a careful tone.

Giving Emma an incredulous look over her shoulder, Macy scowled. "You're not making sense."

Emma took a deep breath before proceeding. "Macy, your son isn't at peace because you're not letting him move on."

Releasing her son's shoulders, Macy stood and swiveled about to face Emma. "How dare you!"

Julian instantly lunged at Juan, who straightaway pinned the snarling kid to the wall with one hand. Agitated, Macy jerked her son away from Juan and dragged the thrashing zombie to a nearby door. Opening it to reveal a decrepit bathroom beyond the doorway, Macy pushed her son inside.

"You're having a time out, Julian."

The leash caught on the doorjamb, stretching it taut. Macy held her son's body at arm's length and shut the door, pulling her hand free just as it clicked shut. The zombie immediately banged on the wood with his small fists.

"Calm down, Julian, and I'll let you out in a few minutes."

"This is so bad," Rune muttered to Emma. "He's so scared."

Macy faced them, her chin lifted in defiance. "Don't tell me how to parent. He's not scared. He's…he's…" She struggled to find the right words that wouldn't upset her precariously balanced conviction on her son's condition.

"He's scared," Rune repeated, his tone heated and edged with frustration.

Juan scooted over from the radiator with a shiver. "Kinda cold there, Rune."

Rune responded with a sober nod. "It would be."

Realizing he wasn't looking at the bathroom door, but the darkened area near the radiator, Macy gave the spot an uneasy look. "Why are you looking there?"

"That's where he's hiding," Rune replied.

Macy lifted her eyebrows. "No he's not. He's in the bathroom."

Stepping toward the mother, Emma swallowed the lump in her throat threatening to choke her. It was not the time to let the memories of her own loss get the best of her. "We're here to help you and Julian, but you have to accept that your son is not in that corpse locked in the bathroom. He's-"

"Don't you start lecturing me about him being in heaven! I've heard that enough from Lewis."

"He's not in heaven. He's over there. In that corner. Afraid."

Rune's bluntness made Emma flinch.

Looking peeved, Macy blurted out, "That's nonsense!"

Emma moved in front of Rune, taking charge of the increasingly emotional situation. "Macy, Rune is a medium. That's why he came with Juan and me. To help you realize that your son isn't in that decaying corpse. His spirit is tethered to you because you haven't let him move on."

"Bullshit! Mediums are scams."

"No, ma'am. I'm the real deal."

"Prove it."

Squaring his shoulders, Rune glanced to one side and waited a few seconds before he replied. "Clive says you're stubborn, but you have to listen to the truth."

Macy scowled. "Lewis could have told you my husband's name. Besides, he's not dead. He's with his mother and brothers."

With a weary sigh, Rune shook his head. "I hate to be the bearer of bad news, but he met his end two weeks ago along with the rest of his family. They got overrun in the middle of the night."

Macy rushed at Rune, coming so close to him her nose nearly touched his. Wagging her finger accusingly, she shouted, "How dare you lie to me! Lewis told you we split up over Julian, didn't he? How dare you try to manipulate me!"

Rune calmly took a step back from the upset woman. "I haven't spoken to Lewis."

Emma inched closer to Macy, drawing her attention. "I did talk to your nephew, but not about your husband. I didn't even know his name."

"Same," Juan said. "I didn't get any background about your personal past when I talked to Lewis."

"No, no! You're all lying. How else can *he* know Clive's name?"

"He's a medium," Juan insisted. "The dead talk to him. Clive is here with us right now talking to him."

"No, no!" Macy backed away from Rune, shaking her head wildly. "Clive and his brothers would've kept their family safe. They were all former military."

Rune swallowed hard, his blue eyes red and watery. Emma thought he looked a little pale in the dim afternoon light coming through the windows. His interaction with the other side appeared to take a lot out of him. "Yes, ma'am, they were doin' a fine job until a horde from Chicago swept through their town. It was massive. There was no way they were going to survive. When the fence came down and the front door was breached, Clive and his brothers held their ground while the family members took their lives upstairs. The mothers made the children lay down with their stuffed toys and shot them in the back of their heads. They had no choice, Macy, but to give their kids peace. This is the same choice you face."

Macy staggered backwards, collapsing against the far wall next to the shuddering bathroom door. "No. You're making it up. Someone told you about Clive. You're trying to trick me so I'll go to your damn fort!"

Rune took a deep breath, steadying his nerves. When he exhaled, his breath was a frosty mist. "Clive says he should've stayed with you, but he couldn't bear to see you coddlin' your son's dead body like it was actually him. Now that he's on the other side, he regrets that choice. He knows now that he should've stayed with you."

"You're lying. You're making this all up! Lewis told you enough for you to concoct this lie!"

"We've got no reason to lie," Juan said defensively. "We're trying to help."

"Tell her something that Lewis couldn't know," Emma urged the empty air in front of Rune, hoping Clive could hear her.

Tilting his head to one side, Rune bobbed his head while apparently listening to the ghost of Macy's dead husband.

Juan edged around Rune to stand at Emma's side. She was surprised when he took her hand, but quickly realized it was for his benefit, not hers. He was trembling. Gently, she squeezed his fingers.

When Rune spoke, his icy breath plumed from his lips into the warm, putrid air. The air freshener couldn't push back the scents of rot and decay. "Clive says that when Julian was born you had real bad postpartum depression. It hit you like a freight train, but you hid it well. In fact, he didn't realize you were strugglin' at all. You always seemed to have everything handled. You were an office manager and a damn good one. You always had everything under control at work and at home. You gave the impression you had motherhood licked. That is, until one night he found you holdin' Julian and sittin' in the back of the closet in the nursery crying. The baby wouldn't sleep, wouldn't stop cryin', and you were failin' your baby. You were overwhelmed. You felt like a failure. Clive kneeled beside you and assured you that you weren't a failure, that you were doin' your best. He promised to help more and took you to the doctor the next day. He never told anybody that you had to take medication to fight against the crushin' depression. It was important for you to look strong in the eyes of your family since they were always so hard on you. He understood that and wanted to protect you. Now his greatest regret is that he didn't protect you when you needed him to again."

"Oh, my God!" Macy gasped. "Clive would never tell Lewis that. Lewis is the family gossip. Everyone would be in my business in no time. My mother would've given me so much grief for taking medication. She thought I should be able to pray through all difficulties in life."

"I don't pull that John Edward's bullshit. I'm the real thing." Rune pulled over the chair that Macy had been sitting in earlier and sank into it. He was visibly shaking.

Blinking her eyes rapidly, Macy swept her gaze over the room. "So Clive is here? Now?"

Rune extended his pointer finger and indicated a spot near the radiator. "Right there. With Julian."

Her bottom lip trembling, Macy stared at where Rune indicated. "With Julian?" Her eyes drifted to the shuddering door, where the growling zombie struggled to get out.

"He's not in that corpse, Macy," Juan said gently. "Your son is not that *thing* in there. You have to let him be at peace."

Macy hugged herself, dragging a shuddering breath into her lungs. Emma could tell she was struggling to accept the truth. "I brought him all this way to *save* him. People died to get me here. Rickie died so that Julian could be cured."

"You did your best by him. Clive and Julian both know that," Emma assured her.

Rune wiped his brow with a trembling hand. "You'd be doing him a kindness letting him go, ma'am."

Macy shook her head adamantly. "No. You don't understand. I kept him clean. I made sure his wound was wrapped. I didn't let him bite or eat anyone. I've kept him from *becoming* one of those things out there. If I can just find someone with the cure, they can bring him back!"

"He's decaying, Macy," Emma said motioning to the air freshener. "It's happening real slowly, but it is happening. No one can come back from that."

Tears trailed down Macy's cheeks and she wiped them away with the back of her hand. "No. The man on the radio said that if the body didn't have lethal wounds the cure would work."

"But there isn't a cure," Juan reminded her softly. "It was a lie."

"Why would someone lie? Why would that do that to me and the others?" Macy flung up her hands and paced in front of the door. "No, no. Somewhere around here there has to be a lab and-"

Shakily, Rune stood and reached out to stop Macy in midstride. "Macy, Clive says you need to let go of Julian. Let him take your son into the light and give him peace. Julian is chained to you. He hasn't moved on because he's confused. The corpse bewilders the boy because he knows it ain't him, but you talk to it like it *is* him. Julian is afraid because he doesn't understand. He is struggling because he feels guilty about dyin' and not being able to climb back into his body. He's tried, Macy, so many times. For you."

"Oh, God," Macy whispered. "Oh, God, what have I done?"

Rune released her arm and she turned away, hands over her face.

"We've all lost people we love," Juan said gently. "All of us have gone through the hell of loss. At some point, we all have to let go. No matter how hard it is."

Nodding, Macy lowered her hands. "I know. I just thought…"

"My daughter and grandson died the first day. I found out because they came to warn me about the end of the world." Rune set his hands on his belt buckle and lowered his gaze. "It was hard to see them like that. Ghosts often carry the wounds of their deaths on their spirit bodies until they cross over. Julian is a handsome boy. He didn't suffer the death my daughter and grandson did. That was a blessing. Take it and hold it close to your heart. You did your best and now you have to do what is right."

Eyes flicking toward the bathroom door, Macy didn't immediately reply. Seconds ticked by, loaded with many possibilities. Juan released Emma's hand, patted her shoulder, and stepped to one side while swinging his rifle into position. Cautiously, he approached the windows. Emma wondered if he'd heard something and was about to follow to investigate, when Macy broke the silence.

"Maybe I should leave him here. Just in case."

"If you leave him here, ma'am, you will keep your son's spirit trapped. Julian will stay here. Do you want that?"

Emma expected Macy to say she was fine with that proposition, but was pleasantly surprised when the mother shook her head. Tears glistening on her cheeks, Marcy stepped closer to the radiator. She stared hard into the shadows.

"Are they both there?"

"Yes, ma'am."

"Clive will take him to heaven, right? If…if…" Macy glanced toward the quaking door.

"He will take him into the light."

Emma was about to edge toward Juan, when Macy trained her gaze on her.

"What would you do, Emma?"

"My son died and came back. It took me over a year to find him, but when I did I put a bullet through his head and buried him." It was difficult to keep a steady voice, but somehow she managed it.

"How?" Macy shot her a disbelieving look. "How could you do that?"

"To give him, and me, final peace. I couldn't stand the idea of him wandering around like that. Chewed up, dead, trying to kill other folks…I did what I had to do."

"I need some time to decide," Macy declared, sniffling.

"You don't have time," Juan said from the window. "We've got company of the dead kind and it's those damn zombie-rules-breaking fast ones."

CHAPTER 13

The Haunted and Hunted

Emma joined Juan at the window and squinted through the dirty, smeared glass. A half-dozen runners dashed back and forth in front of the building, heads jerking about.

"They're hunting," Juan said.

"Did they hear the truck when we arrived?"

"Maybe, but they're tracking a noise right now. Watch their heads. Doesn't it look like they're trying to locate a sound?"

"Our voices perhaps?" Macy offered.

"Possibly." Juan glanced at her, his jaw tightening with resolve. "You don't have time to drag out your decision. Either you come with us or stay here. We can't wait to see if more show up. We gotta move or we'll have more of those assholes here than we can handle."

Macy's lips parted in surprise, obviously not expecting an ultimatum.

Juan bristled at her expression. "We risked our lives coming here to try to save yours. If you choose to ignore what Rune said and stay here with your dead kid, I'm not going to stop you. I didn't lie to you yesterday. We won't force you. You have a choice to join us. The same way we have the choice *not* to risk our lives for you and your zombie kid."

Emma fully expected Macy to rip into Juan. The anger filling the woman's eyes was understandable. Juan had ground the brutal truth into every word he spoke. Macy clutched her hands at her sides and set her lips into a tight line. She looked away from the windows and Juan to stare at the empty corner.

After a few tense seconds of contemplation, she turned to Rune. "What is my anniversary date?"

Rune listened to a voice only he could hear, nodded, and replied, "March twelfth."

Blinking back tears, Macy pulled a shuddering breath into her lungs, exhaling explosively. "Okay. You're the real deal. I don't want my son to suffer because of my...issues. What do I do?"

Rune glanced at the quaking door. "Julian's corpse needs to be put down so his spirit can move on." His hand moved to Glock. "I can do it for you."

"No. I'm not going to have a white man killing my boy. *I'll do it.*"

Rune pulled his firearm and held it out to her.

"No," Macy said, shaking her head. "I have my own way."

"It's better not to use a gun anyway," Juan spoke up. "The runners are pacing around. They don't know we're in here yet. Let's keep it that way."

"We'll have to kill them when we head to the truck if they're still hanging around," Emma pointed out.

"If we're spotted, Juan, it's going to be messy one way or the other."

"I'm trying to think of a plan, Rune. Just help her do what she needs to do to get her kid through those pearly gates."

"Once his corpse is put down, the tether will break."

Macy leaned over and pulled a knife from a sheath strapped to her ankle. The blade was sharp and glinted in the pale afternoon light. Holding the tan hilt firmly in one hand, Macy sighed wearily. "This was Clive's bayonet when he was in the Marines. It only feels right to do it this way."

"I'm sorry," Emma said. "I wish there was another way."

The crack of the rifle from just a few days ago echoed in her memories. Billy's small body collapsing would forever haunt her, but she knew it had been the right thing to do. Hopefully, Macy understood that the act she was about to perform was one of love and deliverance.

Macy fastened her gaze on Rune, fingers twitching around the hilt of the fighting knife. "If I...kill the zombie, it will set both of them free, right? Clive will take Julian to heaven?"

"Yes, ma'am. Your husband is here to do two things: apologize to you and take Julian into the light."

With a defeated look, Macy said, "Okay then. I need you to leave the room. I have to do this alone."

Juan and Emma exchanged wary looks, but Rune was already walking to the door. While Juan took one more moment to study the activity in the street below, Emma walked over to Macy's side.

"I know this is the hardest thing you've ever had to do, but it's the right thing to do for yourself and your son."

Macy gave her the saddest smile. "What do I live for once he's gone?"

It was a question Emma had grappled with for some time. She had found her answer at the Fort. "Yourself. I know it's hard. Trust me, I do. But every life left on this planet is important. We all have a role to play."

Macy studied Emma's face, perhaps gauging her sincerity. "Do you really believe that?"

Emma nodded. "Now more than ever."

Juan tore himself away from the window and hurried across the room to Emma's side. The urgency in his stride spoke volumes. "Okay, Macy, make this fast. The runners are moving away from us and heading down the road. Once we exit the building, we'll be in their sights."

"Maybe you should just let them wander away," Macy tersely replied. "It will give me more time."

Juan's green eyes were alight with his frustration and a surprising amount of anger. "We're losing sunlight and there ain't no assurances that they won't double back and bring more friends. We got a chance to get out of here and we have to take it. You gotta do what you gotta do."

Macy stared down at the blade clutched in her hand. "Fine, but I want to do this alone."

"You got two minutes."

Juan exited the room through the open doorway, clearly expecting Emma to follow. Instead, she rested her hand on Macy's wrist.

"Love means sometimes letting go," she whispered.

Her expression unreadable, Macy lifted her head. "I'm

learning that. Thank you."

Emma's despair over her own loss threatened to resurface and choke her. Leaving the room, she quietly shut the door behind her. A terrible thought filled her mind and she forced herself not to barge back inside.

Juan asked Rune the question that Emma was wondering herself.

"Think she'll do herself in?"

"If so, it's her choice." Rune tilted his head to gaze up through the broken roof at the late afternoon sky. It was growing gradually darker, stars poking through the dimming sunlight. "We can't save everyone."

"Yeah, I noticed," Juan snapped, his irritation with Rune obvious.

The medium bristled. "I don't know what happened to Ed's group. I *told* you that."

"Your ghosts are pretty worthless at times, "Juan groused.

Rune glared at Juan. He looked a little pale, but was steadier on his feet. "They came through when it counted most. Jenni warned us about the horde."

"*She's* the exception because she was *always* loca."

"She made an effort to save all of us. That was *her* choice. I can't control the ghosts. I can't make them show up and tell me what's up. I ain't no fraud. I won't lie."

"Yeah, I know. Not like that John Edwards shit."

"I'm legit. The spirits come to me. I'm their conduit. I can't make them do jack shit. I get that you're upset over Belinda, but now is not the time. We got other shit to deal with."

With a curt dip of his chin, Juan brushed past Rune to watch the stairs. Rune remained near the door, his hand on the wall, eyes closed. Emma wasn't sure what he was doing, so she lingered further down the hallway to give him space.

Two minutes ticked away, but Macy didn't make an appearance.

Emma silently prayed that the woman wasn't taking the easy way out. She knew how alluring that option was when everything seemed lost.

The wind picked up, whistling through the broken ceiling, but another sound caught her attention. Straining to pluck the sound out of the ambient noise, Emma drew her weapon. Juan glanced her way, his expression questioning. He pointed to his ear and she nodded. Among the creaking and groaning of the building, she detected feral moans.

Juan tiptoed over to a shattered window that overlooked the garden below. Craning his head, he looked downward.

Rune's head snapped up. "It's done."

Emma whipped about, her heart leaping with fear. Before she could ask him what he meant, Macy opened the door and staggered out into the hall. She shut the door behind her, blocking out the view of her son lying stationary on the floor. The dagger in Macy's hand was dripping with black blood and reeked, but she didn't appear to notice. Sobbing, she struggled to control her grief.

"You did good. I felt them move on," Rune said kindly.

Her dark eyes filling with relief, she gave him a faint smile. "I'm glad. Now I'm ready to leave."

Juan motioned for Emma to draw closer as he joined Rune and Macy. "I think there are zombies downstairs outside the rear entrance. I can hear them below us. The noise they're making is locked to one spot, so I don't think they're inside yet."

Rune lifted an eyebrow. "Maybe they're trapped outside the back door. Without stairs, they ain't gonna be able to climb up. They're dumbshits."

Emma agreed with Rune, but was worried. "Maybe the noise they're making is what is pulling the runners to the area."

Macy somberly wiped off the bayonet on her pants. "They do flock together, don't they?"

"So we move fast, head downstairs, go out the front door, and run for the truck. I'm driving. Rune, you got shotgun. Macy and Emma, you need to climb into the back on the passenger side. Make it quick, understand?"

Juan's directions were acknowledged by nods all around. He took point, striding down the hallway with his shotgun at the ready. Emma followed with Macy at her shoulder. Rune followed in the rear.

With the afternoon sun descending, the murky atmosphere inside the building was deepening. Emma followed close behind Juan down the rickety stairs. They reached the second floor and cautiously traversed the rotted area. The floor groaned beneath their feet and the moans that Emma had detected earlier grew louder. She slid the safety off on her pistol.

Their descent down the next staircase seemed so much noisier, every step eliciting a loud creak, but maybe it was because she was worried about the runners hearing them. The growls and moans of the dead increased in volume and reverberated through the building. The zombies gathered at the rear entrance definitely knew they were close by.

When Emma neared the bottom floor, she glanced over the railing at the open doorway down the hall. Three of the slower, dumber zombies were clawing at the floor and doorframe, clueless as to how to climb inside the building. Their swollen, blackened faces beneath their gnarled hair were cracked and oozing. They were fresher than most of the zombies Emma had seen recently, which was worrying.

At the sight of the humans, the zombies grew even louder, banging on the floor as they desperately tried to clamber inside. The doorway was too far off the ground for them to easily crawl into the building and the slow zombies were terrible climbers. Juan reached the ground floor and motioned for the others to hurry, pointing toward the front door down the entry hall. Emma's foot had barely touched down on the cracked linoleum when pounding footsteps pulled her focus back to the open doorway.

A runner vaulted over the slower zombies, landed on their shoulders, and launched himself into the building. Emma raised her pistol to fire at him, but a shot behind her beat her to the punch. The bullet tore through the zombie's forehead, a plume of brains and blood splattering the walls and floor.

"Clive taught me to shoot," Macy said, hurrying past Emma.

Knowing that more runners were on the way, the women ran toward the front door, their footsteps reverberating through the old structure.

The shotgun fired and Juan shouted, "Hurry!"

Rune barreled down the hallway with Juan at his heels. "Got more coming!"

Breathing heavily, Macy pushed a heavy magazine rack away from the door that she must have placed there earlier as a barricade. Once it was out of the way, she started to twirl the locks on four deadbolts.

"Cover the porch, Emma," Juan barked.

She stepped to one side so that when Macy opened the door she'd have a clear view of the front steps. Juan and Rune faced the back of the building, waiting. Loud thumps announced the arrival of more runners in the rear hallway. Just as the first one rounded the corner, Macy pulled the front door open.

The shotgun fired behind them, followed by the sound of a body crashing to the floor. The front stoop was clear and Emma slid out, finger sliding onto the trigger. She checked both sides of the porch and the street.

"Clear."

"Get to the truck!" Juan ordered.

More gunshots followed, the shotgun and Glock roaring over the growls of the runners and the clatter of the shell casings striking the floor. Emma trusted the men to cover their retreat to the big red truck, but Macy hesitated to view the battle.

"Should we help them?"

Trying to keep an eye on the road, Emma took a quick look. The runners were closing in on Juan and Rune, leaping over their dead comrades to try to get to the men. They were so determined in reaching their prey, the runners crashed while attempting to push each other out of the way. Rune covered Juan as he reloaded while both men backtracked to the doorway.

"They've got it," Emma said to Macy. "Let's go!"

Racing to the truck, Emma pivoted about, making sure that none of the runners were coming around the side of the building. A few stray slow ones shuffled along the road, but they weren't an immediate threat.

Behind her, the gunfire continued.

"Emma, you're driving! Hurry!" Juan shouted.

"They just keep coming!" Macy gasped behind her. "There's more down the road. Slow ones!"

"Cover me, Macy!"

Emma reached the pickup, jumped onto the side step, and rose to her toes to snatch the keys off the roof with her free hand. She didn't want to let go of her pistol, so she fumbled a little until she hit the button on the car key fob. It didn't beep, but the locks popped. Yanking the driver's side door open, she cast a wary look over the road, measuring the distance between the pickup truck and the slower zombies. They were closing in surprisingly fast and would soon be a threat. Macy scurried around the front of the truck to the passenger side.

At the same time, Rune and Juan reached the porch while shooting at several persistent runners in pursuit of the men. The fast zombies were erratic in their movements making them difficult targets.

"Can they make it?" Macy asked, climbing into the truck.

It was always better to think positively even in dire situations. "Yeah. They can."

A turn of the key brought the engine to life. Foot on the brake, Emma switched gears while Macy slid onto the rear bench. Juan and Rune hurried along the sidewalk toward the truck, weapons at the ready.

Two runners lunged out of the entrance and into the fading daylight. Without dead bodies obstructing their path, the runners headed straight toward the men. Rune had a clearer shot and took both out in quick succession.

The men scrambled to get to the vehicle.

Emma kept an eye out for more runners, nervously checking the mirrors.

Pivoting around, Juan got off a few shots at the shambling zombies closing in on their location. Rune pulled the passenger door open and Juan climbed into the back with Macy. Settling into the seat, Rune slammed his door shut.

"Let's get out of here, Em," Juan said, gripping the back of Emma's seat and leaning forward.

From around the street corner, a small pack of runners appeared and aimed toward the front of the truck. They were fresh, their wounds leaking blood, leaving a trail of gore in their wake.

"Shit! That's the Vargas kid! One of Ed's people!" Juan exclaimed, slamming his fist against the console.

"Are those the missing people?" Emma's heart was beating so hard, she could hear her pulse in her ears.

"Some of them. Shit! Shit!" Distraught, Juan sank back on the rear bench.

"We need to go! Those bastards will punch through a window to get to us!" Macy exclaimed.

Emma started to drive forward, but Rune unexpectedly shouted, "No! Stop!"

Rune stretched out one hand toward an empty spot in the street. "Quiet!"

"We should go. Now!" Macy urged. "More are coming behind us!"

Emma glanced into the rearview mirror and saw that the other woman was right.

Rune slammed his hand on the dashboard. "I said be quiet! I gotta concentrate!"

Macy started to retort, but Juan covered her mouth. A second later, he yelped when she bit him.

His gaze fastened not on the runners, but something beyond them, Rune frowned, his wrinkles deepening around his eyes. He slumped back in the seat. "Okay, go."

Seconds before the runners reached the truck, Emma switched gears, reversed, smacked two slow zombies out of the way with the rear bumper, and did a sharp U-turn. She drove fast in the opposite direction, casting worried glances at the runners in her rearview mirror. Following Juan's terse directions, Emma eventually lost them in the maze of the downtown area. After a few minutes, they headed toward the

Fort.

It wasn't until the tension of their escape dissipated that Juan leaned forward again. "Who did you see, Rune?" He sounded afraid to hear the answer.

"Ed."

"Shit! What did he say?"

"Nothing."

Juan's expression in the rearview mirror was not a happy one. "Nothing?"

"Who is Ed?" Macy asked.

"A friend who left the Fort," Juan said.

Macy's second question was directed at Rune. "And he's dead and not talking?"

"Nope. But he did relay a message."

Emma slowed as they neared the Fort's outer gate.

"So what was it?" Juan demanded.

"He pointed."

"Pointed at what?" Macy asked.

"That's what we need to find out," Rune answered.

"Maybe he was pointing to other survivors," Juan muttered. "Maybe Belinda is alive."

"Those runners were a good chunk of Ed's group. We'll be lucky if there are survivors."

Sounding close to tears, Juan whispered, "Fuck this apocalypse."

The gate creaked open and Emma drove forward.

CHAPTER 14

Sunset Woes

Emma parked the car where she was instructed by Juan and hopped out of the driver's seat. Handing the keys over to a mechanic, relief washed over her. She was back behind the high walls and she'd never felt so safe. Her heart rate was gradually returning to normal as the tightness in her chest diminished. It was scarier being out with a group than it had been out killing zombies alone. She'd only been accountable for her life then, and the increased responsibility added stress to dealing with the zombies. But, she had to admit, she liked the feeling that came with bringing someone into the safety of the Fort walls.

Macy cautiously stepped down onto the blacktop, taking in the bustle of the Fort. She looked about with awe in her dark eyes. Now that the terrible deed was done, Macy stood straighter and the worry that had shadowed her face was gone. While Emma suspected the woman would never admit that she was relieved to not be struggling to contain her zombified son, she looked like a great burden had been lifted from her.

"I didn't expect this, Emma."

"They've got some operation, huh?"

"It's impressive," Macy admitted.

Juan jumped down from the truck and landed with a thump beside Emma. To her surprise, he briefly clapped his hand on her shoulder. "You did good out there," he said with a broad smile. "Great driving."

Emma's cheeks heated up. She was never good at accepting compliments, but she was glad that things had worked out, especially because it had been her idea to approach Macy. "No problem. Just doing my job."

"It was nice not to be running for my life or dealing with

those traps," Macy added. "So thanks."

"We have to take care of each other," Emma said, reddening further. It was incredibly awkward feeling heroic.

"Speaking of taking care of each other," Juan peered past Emma and Macy. "Where's Rune?"

"He walked off in that direction," Macy said, pointing toward the far end of the garage.

Bette and two guards arrived in front of them.

"It's that time again," Bette said. "Time to get fondled."

Juan held out his arms while Bette examined him for bites. Macy looked taken aback for a moment, then realized what was happening.

"Does my cousin know what you're up to?" Juan teased as Bette swept her hands down his legs.

"That joke is getting so old." Bette rolled responded, rolling her eyes. "You're clear."

Emma went next to give Macy a few more seconds to accept the coming pat down. Bette was thorough and fast.

"Has anyone managed to get past you with a bite?" Macy asked when it was her turn.

"No. One guy tried, but he failed."

Macy frowned. "Why would he try to fool you?"

"He had an unhealthy dose of denial. You're clear."

Rune stood alone away from the bustle of the Fort activity with his head down and shoulders hunched. Bette and her guards approached, but he didn't appear to notice.

"Rune, we need to get your info to Nerit," Juan called out, following the others.

Emma started after him, uncertain of where to go next, and Macy trailed behind her.

Rubbing his forehead, the medium acknowledged Juan's comment with a nod but didn't move from the spot where he was rooted. He looked a little disoriented while Bette patted him down.

"You're clear, Rune," she said.

The medium gave her a quizzical look for a second.

"You okay?" Bette asked.

"Yes, ma'am."

Although Bette didn't look convinced, she moved on to check the people coming through the gate.

"Rune, we need to talk to Nerit," Juan said again.

"I heard you the first damn time." Sounding cranky, Rune dramatically swept his hand in front of him. "Along with the rest of them."

Emma grasped what he was implying. "The other ghosts found you, didn't they?"

Rune blinked his eyes rapidly, as though trying to avoid looking at something, then turned to face the three people staring at him worriedly. "Let's make this fast. I can't stay."

Juan bristled. He'd been on edge with Rune all day and his expression hardened. "What do you mean? We need you to show us where Ed was pointing!"

"I *will* show you, but I can't stay here!"

"Dudes, chill," Macy chided both of them, holding out her hands in a soothing manner.

"I'm trying, ma'am, but it's hard when I'm being bombarded by a pack of ghosts with separate agendas."

Giving Rune a bewildered look, Macy took a step back from him. "Who are these ghosts? You said that my son-"

"It's not anyone you know. It's not anyone *I* know. It's a bunch of lost spirits trying to resolve their issues so they can move on and they're damn *loud*."

"Rune, you can take care of them later. Right now you have to help us find out what Ed wanted," Juan insisted.

"Juan, I like you, but you need to back off," Rune responded, a clear warning in his tone. "You don't know what this is like. I can only help so much before I'm teetering on the edge of losin' my damn mind."

Exhaling with frustration, Juan set his hands on his hips and stared at the other man. "Okay, I know I'm being an asshole, but if any of Ed's people are out there we gotta save them."

"We both know this is about Belinda, but I can't tell you if she's alive or dead," Rune said. "Ed didn't speak a word about anyone or anything. All he did was point."

"*If* she's alive, I have to try to save her."

"Hey, Juan!" a woman's voice called out.

Katarina strolled toward them, her rifle slung across her shoulders. The homely woman's red hair was French braided tightly against her head and slung over one shoulder. Emma couldn't help but wonder who Katarina had been in her former life. She exuded quiet strength and pure grit, but didn't necessarily come across as someone who'd been in law enforcement or the military. Seeing Macy, she paused and spoke into her walkie-talkie while Juan jogged over to join her.

Emma cautiously approached Rune, recognizing his distress was because of her request to help Macy. His keen blue eyes flicked toward her.

"I'm sorry," Macy said, feeling awkward and guilty. "This is because of me."

"I made the choice to help. Not just because you asked, but because Clive also asked."

"I do appreciate what you did. When I...when I..." Macy struggled to retain her composure. "I felt something when I did what I had to do. It was like the world sighed with relief. Julian is at peace because of you. I thank you for that."

"I did what needed to be done. Which is why I need to head out soon."

"It's dangerous out there," Emma said.

While listening to Rune and Macy, Emma kept an eye on Juan and Katarina. They were in a deep discussion and Katarina lifted her walkie-talkie to her mouth a few times.

Rune rubbed his temples, wincing as though in pain. "I'll go fuckin' crazy if I stay here. One dude in particular will not shut up."

Clearly concerned, Macy leaned toward Rune. "I don't want you to run off because of me. Can I do something?"

"There ain't nothin' you can do. Once the ghosts know what I am, they bombard me. It's like having a room full of people just yellin' at ya nonstop. I have to leave the area to get any damn peace."

The guilt Emma was experiencing blotted out her earlier joy

at their rescue of Macy. "Can you come back?"

Rune nodded. "Eventually."

When Yolanda and Lewis appeared, Emma wasn't surprised. The Fort people were efficient. Katarina had probably called in Macy's arrival. Lewis ran to his aunt, his arms outstretched, and Macy caught his skinny body and held him tight.

"Auntie!"

"Hey, baby."

"I didn't think you'd come!"

Macy kissed his cheek. "I didn't think so either, but I'm here."

Tears in his eyes, Lewis hugged Macy again. Though he was taller than his aunt, he looked child-like in her grasp. Emma recognized how much Lewis had needed his aunt while she'd been focused on her dead son. Maybe Macy recognized it too, because she held him tighter, tears glimmering on her cheeks.

Yolanda stopped a few feet away, beaming at the reunion.

It did feel good to see a family brought back together after suffering so much.

Rune, meanwhile, slunk off, clutching his head in both hands. Emma started after him, but a voice distracted her.

"Happy family reunions are rare nowadays."

Pivoting about, Emma saw Nerit standing close to her. She hadn't even heard her approach, which was a little unsettling.

"I wanted to help Macy," Emma admitted. "It was wrong to leave her out there."

"You're a capable fighter and have a good heart. It's a good combination." Nerit's chin length hair was tucked behind her ears, and despite the sunset, her dark sunglasses were over her eyes. Dressed in jeans and an olive green shirt, she looked as physically fit as any of the younger people in the Fort.

Emma checked on Macy to see she was firmly under the care of her nephew and the city secretary of the Fort. "Miss Yolanda can set you up with a room and stuff, Auntie," Lewis was saying. When the three walked toward the stairway that would take them into the main area of the Fort, Emma sighed with relief.

"She was a tough one to crack," Nerit noted.

"We couldn't have done it without Rune, although it came at a cost for him."

Nerit studied Rune, taking in his pained expression. "I see."

"He says the ghosts are bombarding him."

"That has to be a pain in the ass."

"I don't know if it's my place to say, but he saw Ed out there."

Nerit's head swiveled toward her, and Emma wished she could see her eyes. Had Emma stepped out of bounds? It was impossible to tell.

"Not alive I take it."

Emma shook her head.

"Well, shit." Nerit set her hands on her hips and returned to observing the medium. "Did Ed say anything to him?"

"No, but Rune said he pointed to something."

"That doesn't sound ominous."

"Rune says he has to leave because of the ghosts."

"We can't make people stay, Emma. Don't worry too much about him. Rune can handle himself. He's left before and returned. That being said, let's find out what he learned from Ed."

Pleased to be included, Emma walked with Nerit to where Rune stood. Katarina and Juan joined them.

Katarina glanced at Nerit. "Juan says Rune has news."

"That's what we're about to talk to him about," Nerit replied.

Rune watched them approach with a bleary look in his eyes.

Nerit stopped in front of him and sighed dramatically. "So, Ed's gone."

Rune nodded. "Yes, ma'am. I saw him when we got charged with runners."

"Some of them were Ed's people, including the Vargas kid," Juan added.

"Mateo? Damn. He was a good kid." Katarina shook her head sadly.

"Emma said he pointed at something. Any idea what it was, Rune?"

"Not sure, Nerit." Rune indicated the hill that loomed over the west side of town. "That's where he pointed, but no explanation. I assume it's the hill, or something on it."

Juan turned to look, his brow creasing with confusion. "That doesn't make sense."

"There's nothing up on that hill. Just the cellphone tower," Nerit said.

Katarina shook her head. "Actually, you're wrong. It used to be a picnic location. People would go up there on the Fourth of July and stay until evening to see the fireworks over City Hall."

"Any structures?" Nerit asked.

"The only building up there is a restroom. It used to scare the shit out of me, literally, when I went to the toilet, since you're basically perched over a deep hole. It's also where high school students used to go to make out until the old sheriff started patrolling up there."

"Someone could have taken the old road up there looking for refuge when the horde came through!" Juan said excitedly. "If Belinda and any of the others are alive, we've got to save them. And if she's not alive, I have to do right by her."

Nerit stared toward the hill, pushing her sunglasses back on her head. Lifting her sniper rifle, she peered through the scope for a minute. "I'll take a squad out."

"I'll get a vehicle ready." Juan started to dash off.

"In the morning," Nerit added.

Swiveling about, Juan gaped at her. "We can't wait!"

"Yes, we can. The sun is going down and we need to plan and not run off half-cocked. Katarina, I'll need a map of the area. Draw it if you need to."

"You got it, Nerit."

Juan bent toward Nerit to get her attention. She met his desperate look with a calm one. "Nerit, if Ed was pointing up there, it's important. You know that."

"Which is why we're going in the morning."

"But what if people are up there right now? What if they're trapped?"

"Juan, I understand your concerns, but I'm not risking people at night. We've got heavy cloud cover and no moonlight. Additionally, we don't know the road conditions. We haven't bothered with that hill since it was deemed irrelevant to the protection of the Fort. We'll find out what's up there. In the morning." Her definitive tone said the argument was over.

Sputtering with frustration, Juan shook his finger at her. "I'll talk to Kevin and Travis."

"Go ahead. They'll back me up," Nerit responded with a cold as ice smile.

"We're all concerned," Katarina said to Juan. "You're not the only one. Nerit is right and you know it."

With a frustrated grunt, Juan reluctantly gave in. "Fine, but I want to go with you."

"I'll consider it."

"Nerit, you can't make me sit it out!"

"Yes I can if you can't prove to me that you can calm your ass down."

"I'm calm!"

"Prove it."

Juan wilted under Nerit's stern glare. With a weary sigh, he lowered his head, pressing his palm to his brow. "Okay. I will."

"Katarina, you're coming with me. Who else do you want on the team?"

Emma raised her hand. "I want to go with you. I can handle myself. I'd like to help, since this is my new home."

Nerit gently pushed her hand down with her warm, rough one. "You're in, Emma. How about you, Rune? You sticking around for a rescue?"

"I can't. I won't be any good to you. They're getting louder and distracting me."

"Okay. That's fine. Just take care of yourself out there."

"Will do, Nerit."

"Get an early breakfast and meet me in the garage at 6:30 in the morning. We leave at sunrise. I'll recruit the rest of our team tonight and let Travis and Kevin know what's up."

With that, Nerit walked off with Katarina falling in behind her.

Emma turned to check on Rune, but he was already heading into the main area of the Fort. Alone with Juan, she swiveled about to face him, although he darted off.

   Alone, she lifted her head to gaze at the sun setting over the hills. Today had been a good day. Hopefully tomorrow would be as well. In a world filled with zombies, a good outcome was never a sure thing, but she was ready to make damn sure she did her best to tilt the odds in their favor.

CHAPTER 15

Asshole Ghosts

Emma waited for Rune, leaning against the wall near his bike in the old newspaper building. On the other side of the bay, a mechanic worked on one of the vehicles. Tejano music with a polka beat blasted away from an ancient boom box in the corner. The activity in the main entry area had dissipated with the setting of the sun, leaving the area tranquil and rather comforting. The night had brought a cool breeze that swept through the dimly lit garage and dispelled the humidity and heat of the day.

Stomach grumbling, Emma wondered if maybe Rune wouldn't leave until daybreak. She was hungry, but didn't dare go to dinner for fear of missing the medium. He'd been so desperate to get away when they'd arrived back at the Fort, she was convinced he'd leave as soon as he could pack. Tapping her foot to the Selena song playing, she resolved to keep waiting.

It was comforting being alone again. The mechanic wasn't even visible. She was glad the mission to bring Macy into the Fort had been successful, but somehow the aftermath was bittersweet. She couldn't quite put her finger on what was niggling at her and was the source of a surprising restlessness.

When Rune appeared, he was carrying his leather motorcycle saddlebags over his shoulder and clutching his rifle in one hand. A Harley Davidson bandana was wrapped around his forehead. Clad in a leather jacket, gloves, and jeans, he looked every inch a biker. Emma didn't get the vibe off of him that he was new to life on a Harley traveling across Texas on the back roads. He'd probably been a biker for a long time.

"Hey, Emma," he said with a somber nod when he spotted her.

"Hey, Rune."

He cast a wary look at her. "What can I do for ya?"

"I'm just here to say goodbye."

That answer brought a relieved grin to his face. "That's mighty appreciated."

The sound of swishing liquid came from his jacket when he leaned over to strap his bags to the bike. The top of a bottle of Jack Daniels poked out of one pocket.

"Does that help?" she asked, pointing to the liquor, genuinely curious.

"Somewhat. It's got the noise level down since I'm feelin' a bit numb, but that one asshole ghost is determined to wear me down. City folk. Even dead they think they can boss my redneck ass around."

"Is it safe? Drinking and riding?"

"Don't *you* get on my ass. You already remind me way too much of Lainey and she always got onto me about my drinkin' and ridin'."

Emma lifted an eyebrow. "Who's that?"

"My loud-mouthed daughter." Rune quirked a crooked smile at the memory of his child. "Bossy little cuss right from the start. Always tryin' to mother me. She kept forgetting who was the parent."

"Was she like you?"

"Oh, yeah. A total rebel. Did what she always wanted no matter what me or the old lady told her." Despite the liquor on his breath, Rune deftly secured his bags with nimble fingers. "You got that same steel and fire. I can see it in ya."

Emma folded her arms across her chest and leaned against a pillar while watching him prepare to leave. "I never thought I did before all of this."

"You just had some asshole holdin' ya back."

"In my defense, Stan was a *charming* asshole."

He'd also been a manipulative asshole who made sure she got pregnant so she'd stay in her hometown with him and not attend college. In Emma's heart, she'd known from the moment the pregnancy test was positive that he'd won. He'd known her personal beliefs would keep her from having an abortion.

"Still an asshole. Men like that are shit. Stay away from men like that."

Whether he meant to or not, Rune sounded like a dad, something she'd never had. It made her chest a little tight.

"You got some inside information on me, Rune?"

He shot her a wry look. "Nah. I've just lived long enough to know that a woman like you is only held back by asshole men."

"Are there a lot of asshole men here in the Fort?"

"A few. Some would say I'm one."

"You? You're nice."

"Shut your mouth! Don't go spreadin' rumors like that," he chided her.

Emma giggled. "Fine, but I'm sure other people have figured out that you're a softy at heart."

Grumbling, Rune secured his rifle to the bike. "Only when I *like* people. I do like you. As I said, you remind me a lot of my daughter, which is why I'm gonna give you some advice. If you'll allow it."

"I'll allow it."

Staring her straight in the eye, Rune said, "Give him time."

Tilting her chin, Emma gave him a quizzical look. "What?"

"You heard me. Don't play innocent."

Emma knew he was talking about Juan and was a bit rankled. Yes, she experienced an undeniable pull toward the tall, handsome man, but that didn't mean anything more than she'd gone a very long time without sex. It made her uncomfortable that a few people made it obvious that they suspected there was more than sexual attraction brewing between them. After all, they'd just met, and Emma didn't believe in fate.

"Even if I had designs on him, he's got all his attention on his unrequited love. If she's alive."

"Even if she is, Emma, time is on your side."

It bothered her that his words gave her a tiny bit of hope. So she shut it down with a heaping dose of denial and snark.

"Are you sure? Because the world ended, remember? Time doesn't seem to be on anyone's side. The longer you live, the better the chance that something will go wrong and you'll end up dead."

"Now you're just shit talking to avoid listening to my advice."

Bristling, she shot him a defiant look. "I listened."

Sitting on his bike, Rune flipped his long white braid onto his back and regarded her somberly. "There are two different kinds of ghosts. The ghosts of those who have died and refuse to move on are the most famous. But the harder ones to get rid of are the ghosts that live in your head. Memories of what was, what coulda been, what was hoped for. A lot of people here are haunted by both types. Lord knows I am."

Attempting to not think too hard about his comment, Emma shrugged. "Maybe that's all we have left after the reality of the old world is stripped away."

"Ghosts?"

"Yeah. The kind that lives in our head. I'm trying to let go of mine, but at night, when I'm falling asleep, I like to pretend that none of this happened. That I'm in my old bed and my son is sleeping in his room down the hall."

"But that's all bullshit and you know it."

"That's a mean thing to say."

"But it's true. What's real is that you're here, right? Finding a new life? Reality isn't your memories. You know I'm not shoveling bullshit at you."

Emma reluctantly nodded.

"Jenni brought you here for a lot of different reasons. I feel it. I know it. But despite whatever designs she had on you, you've still got your free will. You can hop on the back of my bike right now and ride out into that big, dark world and find your own path. You understand that, right?"

It was eerie how perceptive he could be. A part of her had considered leaving with him. It had been the briefest flash of a thought, but it had been there. Not because she didn't like the Fort or its people, but because she didn't want to feel there wasn't a choice other than to stay. Emma didn't believe in fate, but the ghostly intervention in her life made her newfound role feel inevitable. Jenni had diverted her life just as Stan had.

Jenni had saved her life, but she'd also handed her legacy over to Emma. That was not only daunting, it made Emma feel like she was caught in a snare. Now it was clear why she was so restless. A piece of her feared she was trapped by forces beyond her control.

"I'm not here to take over someone else's life. I'm not here to be Jenni 2.0."

Bushy silver eyebrows lowering over his eyes, Rune gave her a hard look. "Has anyone told you to do that?"

"No. Actually, people have told me the opposite. That they don't expect it. Yet..."

"You think maybe Jenni foisted her destiny onto ya, huh?"

"I guess."

"Did you consider that maybe she sent you here because we *needed* you? You're an asset to everyone here."

"Yet, you're leaving because of what I asked you to do."

"It's my curse, hon. It's got nothin' to do with you."

While Emma wasn't too sure of that, she held her tongue. She asked another question that had been on her mind. "Do the ghosts keep you safe? Out there? Warn you?"

"Sometimes. Oftentimes. It suits them to keep me alive."

"That makes me feel a little better."

"If I run into a bunch of zombies, though, I may not make it out alive."

"You're okay with that?"

Rune shrugged. "I know death ain't the end. That makes it easier. But I do feel I perform a valuable service in the land of the living. I do plan to come back. I just need to shake a certain asshole ghost *THAT WON'T SHUT THE FUCK UP!*"

"Where is he?" Emma asked curiously.

Rune pointed to a spot in front of the Harley.

Emma swiped at what felt like a pillar of cold air with her fist a few times. "Go away! You're not wanted here! Go away!"

Chuckling, Rune said, "You're so much like Lainey."

"Did that work?"

"Actually, a little bit. Now he's damn insulted and just glaring at you."

"Good."

"So...you gonna hop on and go on an adventure with this old man?"

"As exciting as that sounds, I do want to stay here," Emma said, and meant it.

"You've done good here." Rune pulled the Jack Daniels from his pocket and took a long swig. He offered her some and she gratefully took the bottle.

The whiskey burned all the way down. "I hope so."

"Worried about tomorrow?"

"No. Maybe. I guess. I'm just wondering what we'll find." After one last mouthful, she handed the bottle back.

"Whatever is up there was important enough for Ed to point it out." Rune took another swig, then tucked the bottle away. "If it's any consolation, I know you can handle yourself. You'll do fine."

"It's getting used to the team thing. I don't call the shots now."

"Nerit won't steer you wrong. Trust her. And with that bit of advice, I'm gonna get."

Surprising him, Emma hugged Rune. He clung to her for a second, sniffled, then pulled back. His blue eyes were rimmed with red.

"You sure do remind me of Lainey."

Emma found it a little hard to speak. "I accept your compliment. She was lucky to have you as a dad."

"Take care, Emma. I'll see you when I see you."

She hadn't had a father and her grandfather was long gone. She hadn't known Rune that long at all, but he was already starting to feel like family. It grieved her that he was leaving. When the bike roared to life, she stepped back and tucked her hands into the pockets of her denim jacket. Watching Rune ride to the gate, she sighed heavily and kicked at the cold spot.

"Stupid asshole ghost," she muttered.

Emma waited until the gate opened for Rune and waved when he turned back one last time. Then the medium was gone and she was alone.

CHAPTER 16

Dawn of the Possible Dead

Dawn crept over the horizon, pushing away the darkness to fill the world with pale gray light. Mist floated over the ground where Emma waited near the old newspaper building. Up early, she'd been one of the first people to arrive at breakfast in the hotel dining room. When she hadn't seen any of the other people who were supposed to be on the team, she'd departed for the garage clutching her breakfast tacos and coffee hoping she wasn't late. The only people in the garage were the mechanics checking out a heavily modified short bus. Realizing she was the first one of the volunteer team to arrive, she found a stool to perch on near the door that opened to the interior of the newspaper building and ate in silence.

After her talk with Rune, Emma had been up for hours carefully sorting out her feelings about the Fort, her new life, the successful rescue of Macy, and her attraction to Juan. She found peace with her chosen role at the Fort, but she was uncomfortable about Juan. He hadn't done anything to upset her. She liked him quite a bit and wanted to get to know him better. Yet at the same time, it was as if there was an invisible cord connecting her to him. When she'd first arrived, he'd acted like he felt it too. There had been an unspoken familiarity in their initial interaction. It had been both comforting and unsettling.

Now it was just unsettling.

Finishing her breakfast tacos, she tossed the foil into a nearby trash bin and sipped her hot coffee from a disposable cup. She didn't want to think too much about it, but the reason her instant camaraderie with Juan was so troubling was because it felt so natural. Emma didn't believe in fate. She believed that the future was shaped by her choices. The choice to have her son had set her on a path that was difficult and often soul-crushing. Billy had brought joy to her life, but she'd also slid deeper into poverty while trying to support him. Though Stan strutted around like he'd won, she'd done her best to limit his influence over her life. That included kicking him out of her bed and taking charge. Sending Stan on his way had been an important milestone in her life and a valuable lesson learned. She had to keep that in mind. She needed to remain focused on finding her niche in the Fort and not on the hot Latino.

As though on cue, Juan exited the garage office door clutching a steaming cup of coffee. He was bleary-eyed, but handsome in jeans, a blue t-shirt, and a leather jacket. He smelled good, like soap and shampoo. Beneath the brim of his cowboy hat, his freshly washed curls clung to his brow and neck.

"Hey, Em," he said, leaning against the worktable next to her.

"Morning."

"The rest of the team ain't here yet, I take it."

"Just you and me."

"Early riser, or couldn't sleep?"

Not wanting to give anything away about her state of mind, she opted to change the subject. "Nerit decided to let you join us, huh?"

"Actually, no." Juan gave her a charming smile. "But she can't make me stay here."

Emma lifted a skeptical eyebrow. "You sure about that?"

"Maybe she could, but I gotta see what's on that hill. I couldn't sleep all night. I kept tossing and turning. If Belinda and the others are up there, I gotta have a part in saving them."

His words were yet another reminder why Emma shouldn't even entertain any delightful ideas about Juan. "Belinda means a lot to you, doesn't she?"

"We've known each other since we were in diapers. She's my childhood sweetheart. I gotta save her if I can. I promised to always be there for her and I intend to be. I always looked out for her when we were growing up. I can't stop now."

Though his words made sense, they took unpleasant bites out

of her resolve not to be drawn to him. It was damn attractive that he was determined to save someone he cared about.

"I'm sure she'd appreciate that, Juan. If she's on that hill, I know we'll save her."

The sun finally made its appearance known, pushing up over the horizon. The fiery glow turned the morning sky a bright orange and pink above the hills. It was officially sunrise.

Right on time, Katarina strolled into the garage. Dressed similarly to Juan, she had her hair braided tight to her head. It was the best way to keep long hair out of the reach of zombies. Emma's own hair was in braids under her cowboy hat.

"You on the team?" Katarina asked Juan, skipping over pleasantries.

"Not officially, but yeah," he answered.

Katarina narrowed her eyes. "You able to keep it together?"

Juan looked insulted. "Keep it together? I'm a bad ass."

"Hmm." Katarina didn't look convinced and focused on Emma. "You ready for this?"

"Yep. Venturing out into the zombie-infested world is pretty routine for me. I'm used to putting zombies down, but I'm up for a rescue."

"If they're alive," Katarina said pointedly.

"They're alive. They have to be," Juan said, sounding a tad too desperate.

"We don't know what Ed was pointing at. It might not be survivors. Maybe he was warning us about something else."

Definitely not liking this opinion, Juan folded his arms over his chest and scowled. "Ed would want to take care of his people, which is a good reason to be a ghost."

Approaching footsteps pulled Emma's focus back to the outside. Nerit was walking briskly toward the garage with Arnold right behind her.

"Ed was also a part of the Fort. He might want to make sure we're safe," Katarina replied.

Emma was slightly confused with her logic. "But he didn't want to be here. Ed and his people left."

"Which is why this mission is completely voluntary," Nerit

announced, also skipping over the usual conversation starters. "When I talked to Travis last night, he said I could check out what Ed was pointing at and take a few people with me, but only if they wanted to tag along. Also, this excursion is on the down low. Though Travis respects Rune's abilities, he's not too keen on a mission ordered by a dead man. He doesn't want it getting out that we're chasing ghosts. Despite what some of us experienced in the last few weeks, a lot of the Fort population don't believe in ghosts."

"Lots of people saw what went down with Curtis," Juan grumbled. "Who cares what everyone else thinks?"

"Comments like that are why Travis is mayor and you're not," Nerit said with a broad smile, poking Juan in the ribs. "So, to be clear, is everyone here a volunteer?"

There were short nods all around.

"Good. Arnold is our driver." Nerit gestured toward the lined-up modes of transportation. "Juan, which vehicle is ready to go? I assume you arranged for one."

"We're taking the short bus over there. Junior's already got it gassed up and ready," Juan answered.

"Good. As soon as Monica arrives, we're ready to go." Turning to Emma, Nerit said, "We do five people crews when we go out. We found out that works best. Since you are pretty adept at taking out zombies, I'm confident you'll do well in our fifth slot."

"I can handle it," Emma assured her.

"I'll say. You took out a town of zombies," Juan said with a grin.

"So that's true? It's not bullshit?" Arnold looked impressed. "Damn. I thought it was just rumors."

"It did take me over a year."

"But still... a whole town. That's Lenore level of badassery."

Nerit cleared her throat, keeping Arnold's worship of Lenore to a minimum. She looked relieved when Monica jogged up.

"I'm here! Sorry! Got stuck in line for breakfast." Monica waved a breakfast taco wrapped in aluminum.

"Let's proceed now that we're all here," Nerit said. "Katarina, thoughts on how to approach this so-called make-out point?"

Katarina took out a hand drawn map and laid it out on the worktable. "There's only one road that leads to it and the entrance is on the side of the hill approaching the town. We should head out of the Fort, turn east, take the road that circles the outside of town, and approach from the west so we don't pull any straggler zombies into town."

Nerit nodded with approval. "Agreed."

"Since we've got only one way up on a narrow road lined by trees, we're not going to have any visibility until we're at the top where there's the clearing. Usually, you can fit around ten cars on the gravel parking area. People would also park between trees. We might not have much room to maneuver if that's where Ed's people are, so we need an expert driver."

"That's me. I can drive anything on wheels. I can parallel park a transport vehicle," Arnold said with confidence. "I'm better at driving than a Hollywood stuntman."

Juan dug into his jeans and pulled out a green lucky rabbit foot keychain with keys dangling on it. Tossing it to the other man, he said, "You might have to prove it."

"What else is in the clearing, Katarina?"

"I've only been up there a few times, but I recall the restrooms are in a concrete structure with a corrugated metal roof. There was some plan a while back to make it a tourist spot. Some folks wanted to put a big metal cross up there, kinda like the one in Fredericksburg, but the idea got shot down. Since people were already going up there to picnic, the town built the restrooms and had plans to expand the road and pave it. When we ended up with a new city council the whole thing got shut down. So we got dense foliage, a narrow and winding road, a restroom, gravel parking area, and a few old picnic tables."

With a somber look, Nerit said, "So plenty of places for the zombies to be lurking."

"It's not like they hide," Monica said around a mouthful of taco.

"No, but if Ed's people did take refuge up there, some may have run into the trees or restroom to hide and died from their bites," Nerit reminded her.

"You've got a good point," Monica admitted.

Nerit started toward the bus and everyone followed. "We may have to improvise once we've reached the top of the hill since we're uncertain of the situation and what we're exactly looking for."

Shifting from foot to foot and rubbing his chin, Juan gave her an incredulous look. "It's survivors. We all know it."

"It's a possibility," Nerit replied, completely unruffled by his glare.

Arnold unlocked the bus door and shoved it open. "How many people left with Ed?"

"Twenty-three," Nerit answered. "Martin spotted Eddie. Juan identified six others."

"And we could have stragglers from the horde who followed them up there," Juan said.

Monica waved her taco around for emphasis. "Why would Ed's people come back? They were a pretty salty lot when they took off."

"My guess is they ran into something dangerous on the road that made them reconsider and turn back," Nerit replied.

"Another herd?" Juan wondered.

"Banditos," Monica grunted.

"Or maybe they had a change of heart. It's rough out there," Emma said. "They were used to being safe behind high walls. I don't think it would take too long for them to reconsider. I wouldn't want to be out there again."

"Whatever the reason they turned back, we need to be careful. Let's move out." Nerit followed Arnold up the steps into the bus with Monica right behind her.

"Ready?" Juan asked in such a way that Emma understood he was giving her a way out if she was reconsidering volunteering.

Squaring her shoulders, she wrapped her fingers around the strap connected to her rifle. "Ready."

CHAPTER 17

All Signs Point to Bad

The small bus shifted gears and roared up the winding narrow road leading out of town. The few zombies that had given pursuit after the rescue team had driven out of the paddock quickly fell behind.

Emma watched the scraggly creatures flounder in the dust tossed up by the wheels until the bus turned a corner. The undead were old and slow, definitely not the newer zombies that were a threat to the people who lived inside the Fort.

With a sigh, she settled into her seat near the back of the warm bus. The air conditioning barely put a dent in the heat that had accumulated inside the vehicle during its time being stored in the garage. She ran her palm over the back of her neck, sweeping the beads of sweat away. The only signs of life on the outskirts of town were birds hopping about in the trees and a squirrel running along the edge of a porch.

Spray paint markings decorated the exteriors of all the buildings. There was uniformity to the marks, evidence they'd been made by people from the Fort. She'd also tagged buildings as she had meticulously cleared her town. It was another spot of familiarity in this new world, and she found it comforting.

The last block consisted of mostly empty lots filled with abandoned cars, machinery, and derelict buildings overwhelmed with foliage. Soon the whole world would look like that, she supposed.

Except for the Fort.

Hopefully.

The town remained in view through the lattice of tree branches while the school bus circumvented the main roads. It was prettier away from the recent war zone. Flowers bloomed along the shoulders of the road and the sky was a brilliant blue overhead. Staring out at the hilly countryside brushed by the morning light, Emma discreetly wiped an unexpected tear away. It was hard to wrap her mind around just how much her world had changed so swiftly. While walking through the Fort, she was often tempted to pinch herself just to make sure that she wasn't dreaming this new life.

After spending so much time alone, she was finding it difficult to adjust being around other people. The scents wafting off their bodies were strong and she'd often discreetly rubbed her nose to stifle the odor. It wasn't just the natural body odor that was assailing her, but the reek of cigarette smoke, aftershave, and coffee.

What Emma found particularly embarrassing was that she jumped every time she heard a voice after a long pause in conversations. It was too easy to fall back into a silent world, but she was learning to appreciate the hum of people talking around her.

At the front of the bus, Juan wrapped up a discussion he was having with Nerit and sauntered down the aisle toward her. He'd rolled up his jacket sleeves, revealing more brown muscled skin. Emma tried not to notice his attractiveness, but it was hard. Sliding into the seat in front of her, Juan slumped against the window and took off his cowboy hat to run a trembling hand through his damp curls.

"Everything okay?" Emma dared to ask.

"Yeah. It's good. Sorta."

"That's not encouraging."

"It's nothing bad about the mission. I just have this feeling I forgot to do something before we left."

"You have your pistol, rifle, and machete. Your team. A plan." Emma ticked the list off on her fingers.

Juan nodded at each bullet point and then smacked his forehead with his palm. "Shit! I forgot to let the kids know I was heading out. They were sleeping, but I should've woken them up to say goodbye."

Emma winced, understanding parental guilty panic well.

"Probably, but maybe it would upset them to know what you're doing."

"Maybe. I was so worried about Belinda that I completely spaced it. Gawddammit."

It was evident that Belinda was extremely important to Juan. The mere mention of her left him looking stricken. Of course, he was worried about his old friend who could be stranded on the hill, or worse—dead. Emma was starting to wonder if there was more to the equation than Juan having unrequited feelings for Belinda.

"I can't believe I did that, Em. *Shit!* I'm learning how to be a dad, you know? I love those kids, don't get me wrong, but sometimes I get hyper-focused and forget how to parent."

"Juan, we all fuck up as parents. Billy once cried and refused to talk to me for three hours because I forgot to kiss him goodbye before going to the grocery store. I felt like a criminal. Parents get distracted, Juan. You have to forgive yourself."

"I know you're right, but Jason is going to be pissed."

"The oldest kid, right?"

"Yeah. We're pretty tight now. He hated me for a while, but we got past that. He's a teenager so he knows it all and loves to lecture me about how I'm fuckin' up." Juan grinned with affection. "He's such a great kid."

Emma barely knew Juan, yet she cared about his situation and feelings. Of course, she was attracted to him, since she was a sucker for men with bodies chiseled by hard work, deeply tanned skin, and curly hair. But there was also kindness in his green eyes, a vulnerability, which called out to her. Again, she pushed back at the connection she sensed between them. Emma kept telling herself that after being alone for so long she was just craving companionship in all its forms.

"He might be mad for a little bit, but he'll get over it. I'm sure he knows you love him."

Juan folded his arms over his chest. "Jason was mad when I didn't tell him about going out to find Macy. It's mostly because the second I'm late, Margie, my oldest girl, thinks I'm dead and gets the younger ones riled up. It doesn't help that Jason worries because his mom..." Closing his eyes, Juan gave himself a few seconds to compose himself. "Jenni died on a scavenger mission to get medical supplies to save my life."

"So then you don't disappoint him by dying."

Maybe her straightforwardness startled him, but Juan gave her a surprised look.

"We do what we have to, save who we can, and go back in one piece," Emma continued. "Just like we did yesterday."

"Em, you're pragmatic as fuck. I can see now how you wiped out your entire town."

Emma wasn't sure it was a compliment.

"Juan, I can't allow myself to consider dying. It'll freak me out, gum up the gears in my head, and slow my reflexes. I just concentrate on the job. I do what I need to do. I stay focused. I just don't consider death an option."

Emma was lying a little. Her last night in the trailer, death *had* been on her mind. She'd planned an exit, but when she dreamed about the woman with the long, dark hair and black eyes who told her about the Fort, she'd decided to give life one more shot. Now she was determined to hold onto her new life and see where it took her. Which evidently was on dangerous missions to find out what a ghost had been pointing at. Life was weird.

Staring at her, Juan searched her expression. What for, she wasn't sure, but he appeared to find what he was looking for and nodded. "I hear ya and will do, fearless zombie killer."

Rolling her eyes, Emma laughed. "I'm not going to live that title down, am I?"

"Nope."

The bus downshifted.

Emma glanced out the window to see a steep and narrow road turning off from the one they were traveling on. It sliced through a thick bramble of undergrowth and closely clustered juniper trees.

"This is it," Juan said breathlessly, sliding to his feet and leaning his forearm against the window to observe their ascent. The fear and anticipation in his eyes only reinforced how much

Belinda meant to him. Despite what Rune said, Emma knew she had to keep Juan squarely in friend territory. His clenched fist resting against the window was shaking, and not from the bumps in the road.

"Look at all the dead fuckers!" Monica exclaimed from where she was perched at the back of the bus. "Whoa!"

Limbs, entrails, and other meaty parts of zombie bodies were strewn along the sides of the road. There were tire treads clearly visible on a partially-smashed head.

Juan was fighting to keep his breathing even, but his excitement was evident. "Someone took 'em out with their vehicle."

Monica stared at the destroyed corpses as the bus passed by. "Those bodies are mush, run over by something really heavy. Ed's people took Durangos. It must be them."

At the front of the bus, Nerit stood holding onto a pole to keep upright, also scrutinizing the area. "It's starting to look like we might be on a rescue mission."

"Or maybe Ed just wants us to know where they died," Arnold offered. "So we can bury them."

"There's someone alive on that hill and we all know it!" Juan clearly wasn't going to listen to any other theories on why Ed had directed them to the hill.

"We're about to find out the truth," Nerit replied. "But it's looking like a promising possibility."

As Arnold turned the short bus onto the narrower roadway, Emma noticed that a huge swath of foliage was trampled flat not too far from the intersection.

"That's where the herd came through," Juan said, pointing.

"Ed and the others must have nearly run into them," Monica decided. "That's why they took the turn."

"To a dead end," Juan grumbled.

"If you're desperate, you do stupid shit," Emma said. "If I saw that zombie horde coming at me, I'd shit myself."

Monica gave Emma a grim look. "Trust me, I almost did when Bette and I played Pied Piper to try to redirect the horde."

"Okay, that's a story I want to hear," Emma said.

"Over drinks tonight," Monica promised.

Emma studied the area as the bus rolled through, contemplating the possible path of a pursuing herd. "No downed trees and scrub here."

"Maybe they weren't followed up the road. They could be safe up there," Juan said hopefully.

Emma hated to be the voice of reason. "Then why haven't they come to the Fort?"

"Maybe their vehicle broke down, or ran out of gas. Maybe they weren't sure about coming back to the Fort after they decided to leave in the first place."

"All possibilities, but we shouldn't get our hopes up too high," Nerit said reasonably.

"We don't give up hope until we know for sure what happened," Monica said.

"Amen, cuz."

Emma turned away from Juan's hopeful face and looked out the window at the passing scenery. A zombie impaled on a broken tree branch flailed weakly as the bus climbed past it. It had probably been knocked off the road by a fleeing vehicle. No matter how hopeful the cousins were about saving their friends, one thing was certain.

Zombies were definitely up on the hill.

The question was just how many were there.

CHAPTER 18

Keep Calm

"Emma!" Nerit called out, waving her toward the front of the bus.

Grabbing her rifle, Emma immediately joined her. "How can I help?"

"You spent a lot of time scouting through dangerous areas, right?"

"Yeah, I did."

"What's your assessment of the situation?"

"The main horde didn't follow Ed's people up to the picnic area. They might have been able to turn off the road without being spotted by the zombies. There'd be more damage to the terrain if they had been seen and followed," Emma explained. "That being said, I am certain that there will be zombies up there to deal with because of that zombie impaled on a tree back there."

Nerit looked impressed with her evaluation. "We never did clear this area of town. There wasn't anything worth salvaging out this way. There could have been zombies up here all that time."

"There's also the possibility of zombies climbing up from a different direction we can't see from the road."

Nerit nodded. "I agree."

"That's *not* a comforting thought," Arnold muttered under his breath.

Emma struggled to keep on her feet. The road was cracked from disuse. Grass and other plants pushed up from underneath the broken asphalt. A few more corpses, old and rotted, littered the road. They were clearly not Ed's people, but dispatched zombies. The bus ambled around a curve, revealing a clear view of the hotel and the Fort around it. It was a pretty sight, the green hills framing the hotel with its windows glimmering with morning sunlight.

"Hold up," Nerit ordered.

Arnold immediately obeyed, the engine idling as Juan and Monica joined the group at the front of the bus. Nerit opened the side door and dropped out next to a body lying at the edge of the asphalt. It was face-down with the back of its balding head blown out. Nerit kicked the corpse over, revealing the dead man's face. A bullet hole punctured the wrinkled forehead and a bite was visible on the sagging skin of his neck.

"Ed," Monica whispered.

Juan punched the ceiling with a fist and swore in Spanish.

The noise startled Emma and she shot him a disapproving look. He acted far more on edge than yesterday.

"This doesn't mean they're all dead," he said defensively to Emma, misreading her expression.

"Someone had to have shot him," she agreed.

"Right, Em. Right." Juan nodded vigorously, clearly grasping onto a tiny shred of hope.

Climbing back onto the bus, Nerit clucked her tongue with annoyance. "Dammit, Ed. You shouldn't have left, you stupid old fool."

Arnold shut the doors. "That confirms that Rune saw his ghost, doesn't it? So we're on the right track."

"Yes, we are." Nerit frowned, her hands settling onto her narrow hips.

"Bullet to the head," Monica noted. "Was he a zombie?"

Nerit glanced at Ed through the glass panels in the door. "He doesn't look like he turned. The bullet wound isn't self-inflicted since there aren't any weapons on him."

"Then it was a mercy kill," Arnold said. Nerit studied their surroundings with a critical eye. "Which means we have at least one survivor. Ed probably stuck with the group to help them get to safety, but he must have been close enough to turning before they reached their destination that he was put down."

"Or he lied about getting bit, huh?" Arnold rolled his eyes.

"People who do that are shit."

"Ed wouldn't have done that. He was an asshole, but he was a *noble* asshole," Monica said.

"Who abandoned us," Arnold shot back. "When we needed him most."

"Monica is right," Nerit interjected. "Ed would've have told his people he had a bite. He was probably close to turning and a liability. Someone gave him an out. Someone who might still be alive."

Juan vehemently nodded. "So Belinda and the others might be up there waiting for rescue. Can we go now?"

"Not yet. I don't like the way this feels," Nerit admitted. "Too many unknowns."

Juan gripped the section of the pole above Emma's hand. "If Belinda and the others are up there, we have to help them!"

Emma could feel the heat radiating off his body and his breath brushing over the top of her head. The uncomfortable response of her body was a reminder of just how long it had been since she'd been with a man. She focused all her attention on Nerit, who gave Juan a withering stare.

"We're not turning back, Juan," Nerit said. "But you need to consider the worst, while hoping for the best."

"I can't accept the worst. I have to save Belinda."

Monica sighed, frustrated with her cousin. "Juan, we don't know who is alive up there. Belinda might not have made it this far."

"Until I see her body, there's a chance to save her."

Emma winced, his words reminding her of the deep denial she'd experienced the first few days after the apocalypse started. She hadn't considered the possibility that Billy was dead until it was evident he couldn't feasibly be alive.

The thick juniper trees swayed in the wind, creaking loudly. The shadows beneath the leafy canopy didn't give birth to zombies. The bus had been stationary for a few minutes without being attacked.

"Zombies aren't coming for us," she noted.

Nerit nodded. "A good sign that the area isn't as infested as we feared."

Juan breathed out in relief. "Maybe this will be easier than we thought."

Nerit clucked her tongue at him. "No, no. Never say that. Never jinx the mission."

Monica punched his arm. "*Pendejo.*"

"I may be a noob, but even I know that," Emma drawled.

"Sorry. I'm fuckin' going nuts here. I just want to get up there and find out what or who Ed was pointing at."

"We all do, cuz," Monica said, clapping him on the shoulder.

Realizing everyone was staring at him with concerned looks, Juan relaxed his shoulders and averted his eyes in an apparent attempt to look calmer. "I'm ready when y'all are."

"Arnold, drive on," Nerit said.

The short bus rumbled up the road and past a sign that said "Lookout Point."

Nerit gestured to Emma to get her attention. "When we disembark, stay close to me. You're my partner, watch my back. Monica and Juan will veer right. We're going left. Arnold will provide cover from the bus."

"I'm also your comic relief and getaway driver," Arnold said jovially.

Nerit's lips set into a grim line. "This isn't a bank robbery."

"If some of Ed's people are alive, we're stealing humans from zombies. That counts, right?"

Nerit speared him with a sharp look, but Arnold grinned. It was a forced expression, his eyes not matching his broad smile. They all had coping mechanisms to endure the apocalypse.

Another sharp turn and they were on a narrower road lined with tall grasses. Mexican Hat wildflowers dotted the terrain. The yellow petals clustered at the base of their spikey center were ruffled by the summer breeze. It would have been a pretty sight except for the scene just beyond the flowers.

A Dodge Durango, riddled with bullets, slathered in zombie guts, and sporting a rear flat tire, had crashed into the concrete building housing the restrooms. Chucks of cement were strewn across the roof and hood. Most of the windows were broken and blood stained the glass. There didn't appear to be anyone inside. Even more worrisome, a number of the undead milled around the vehicle. Most were weathered by time and the elements, but a few among them looked freshly dead.

"Stop," Nerit ordered

Arnold brought the bus to a hard stop.

"What do we do? Leave? Back up? There's no one alive in that Durango for sure," Arnold whispered.

"We can't just leave without checking it out!" Juan protested.

"Keep your head on straight, Juan."

He wilted under Nerit's stern look. "Yes, ma'am. It's just that after everyone we lost, if I can't rescue-"

"This isn't about your need to be a savior. This is about rescuing any possible survivors up there. I need you to focus. Monica is your partner on this mission and I won't have you putting her life at risk because you're-"

"I get it, Nerit!"

"Do you?"

"Yeah." Juan met her gaze defiantly. "I'm good. I won't let my cousin down."

"Good, because if you did, and I turned zombie, I'd eat you." Monica nudged him with her elbow. "I got your back, so have mine."

"I'm fine. Really." Juan folded his arms across his chest and directed his gaze away from Nerit to watch the zombies milling outside the Durango. Lips pressed tightly together, he was clearly waiting for Nerit to continue.

Emma didn't know Juan well, so it was hard to tell if he really was okay. Watching him flex his hands and roll his shoulders, she had quite a bit of sympathy for him. She knew what it was like to want to be a savior. Hopefully, he wouldn't have to become executioner to his turned loved one.

Nerit waited a minute, allowing the tension to die down, before turning to Monica. "What's *your* assessment?"

"There are about fifty zombies," Monica said, her fingers fiddling with her holster strap. "If someone was alive in that Durango, they'd be swarming it."

"But they *are* gathered around the building," Emma pointed out.

"Which is suspicious," Nerit said with a nod.

Staring at the scene, something caught Emma's eye. She climbed onto a seat and peered through the metal grating welded to the window frame. She lifted her hand to shade her eyes so she could study the scene. So far, they hadn't been spotted. The wind was carrying both sound and scent in the opposite direction of the dead. Also, the bus was far enough away from the zombies to not be noticed. Squinting, Emma stared at the building and crashed Durango. There wasn't a sign of life anywhere. She started to look away when something caught her eye again, but she wasn't sure what it was exactly.

"See something?" Monica was at her elbow, straining to look.

"Movement, I think. Or maybe it's the trees behind the building, but..." Emma glimpsed it again. "There!"

A hand, straining upward, was visible on top of the roof of the restrooms for just a second before disappearing again.

"We have a survivor," Emma announced. "On the roof of the building."

Nerit raised her sniper rifle, peered through the sight, and waited. A minute later, she lowered it and nodded. "You're right."

"Can you tell who it is?" Juan asked, his lips trembling.

"No," Nerit replied.

Somehow, Emma knew she was lying to keep Juan calm.

"But we're going to save them one way or the other," Nerit promised. "Here's the plan..."

CHAPTER 19

Are Traitors Worth It?

Emma shoved the hatch to the roof upward. It swung open with a creak. Bright sunlight flooded through the opening and a hot breeze swirled over her upturned face. Feet braced on the backs of the seat benches, she maintained her grip on the rope attached to the handle and gently lowered the door onto the roof. Once it was lying flat, she gripped the edges of the hatch and hoisted herself up. The fingerless leather gloves she wore protected her palms, but her fingertips burned against the hot metal roof. She raised her body only high enough to gaze over the top of the bus. Muscles straining, she memorized where the handholds were placed, along with the safety harness attached to a ring bolted to the roof.

Strong hands suddenly gripped her hips, holding her up and giving her arms some relief. Since she'd told Juan she could handle the assignment without any help, Emma was annoyed. She wanted to prove herself to the people of the Fort. Tales of her zombie killing exploits were rapidly spreading, and she wanted to live up to expectations. It was important to show everyone, especially Nerit, that she could work with a team to rescue others.

"I'm climbing up now," she informed those waiting below.

Hoisting herself onto the hot surface, she quickly grabbed the nearest strap, slid across the roof, got to her knees, and lifted the binoculars Nerit had handed her earlier. Focusing on the figures trapped on top of the restrooms, Emma ignored the undead scrabbling at the small structure. She never paid any attention to zombies unless they were her target. It was too disturbing to see their desiccated faces and wonder what sort of person they had been when alive.

The magnified view told a very sad story. A woman and two

men were trapped on top of the building. They were laying flush against the roof, keeping away from the edges. Badly sunburned by the harsh sunlight, the trio used their clothing to protect their reddened skin from the heat radiating off the corrugated metal roof. Emma panned over the surrounding area in an attempt to spot anything that could prevent the bus from moving into a rescue position other than the crashed Durango lodged in one corner. The picnic tables were close enough to the restrooms to make a quick getaway difficult. Arnold wouldn't have an easy time turning around.

Skidding backward, Emma edged her way through the hatch until she could drop down into the aisle below. The rest of the crew was waiting for her expectantly. Juan looked the most aggravated, gnawing at his disfigured thumb. His green eyes settled on her, undoubtedly nervous for her report on his friends.

"Nerit, it looks like we got two guys and one gal up on that roof."

"Only three?" Arnold gasped. "Out of all the people that left, there's only three?"

"That's all I saw. They don't look like they're in good condition. They may have been up there for a few days. The one young blond guy looks pretty burnt up."

Nerit frowned, the lines in her face deepening with concern. "That sounds like Kurt, Ed's younger son."

Juan's body was literally vibrating with his barely contained anxiety. "What about the girl? What did she look like?"

"Maybe my age. Long, dark hair."

"Belinda for sure," Monica said with relief.

"Thank God," Juan whispered.

Nerit gave Juan a piercing look. "So we're saving Belinda *and* Kurt for certain. Tell me what the second man looks like."

"A middle-aged guy, receding hairline, brown hair, maybe a little bit pudgy in the middle, and fair enough that he looks like a tomato right now," Emma answered Nerit with a wince.

Juan glanced at Nerit. "Sounds like that new city guy that went with them. I can't remember his name though."

"Ted," Arnold said. "Ted Buck from Fort Worth. He was a lawyer or something like that."

Nerit brushed her chin-length hair behind one ear while peering out the window toward their destination. "I was hoping all of our regulars had survived. It may be a little bit more difficult dealing with somebody who wasn't fully integrated into the Fort. I guess in the end it doesn't matter who he is as long as he follows instructions. Did you spot any obstacles preventing us from pulling up to the building?"

"Other than the Durango and a bunch of zombies, there's some picnic tables close enough to make it hard to turn around. They're hidden by the zombies crowding the area."

"Duly noted," Arnold said.

"If we can get close enough on the right side, Nerit, I'm certain we can get the survivors onto the top of the bus. My only concern is that they look pretty weak, so I don't think they'll be able to do it on their own," Emma went on.

This news did not go over well with those around her. The people from the Fort couldn't have believed this would be easy. There were a lot of zombies between the bus and the survivors.

"That makes things harder," Monica muttered. "I hate roof rescues."

"I mean, we could always go back and get more people to help us. Right, Nerit?"

"Calling for reinforcements is not an option, Emma."

Monica made an irritated sound from where she was perched on the back of a nearby bench. "Nerit, there's a whole lot of them and not many of us. We could use some backup. Roof rescues suck. Jenni was good at them, but she's not here."

"The road is too narrow. There's not enough room for maneuvering as it is, and we're not putting any more people at risk. We came up here to see why Ed was pointing to this hill. Now we know the herd came through and Ed's group didn't make it to safety." Nerit made a point of looking everyone directly in the eye one by one. "We have to handle this ourselves, so I need to know everyone is on board with this rescue. If not, we can leave right now. Travis gave me full discretion on this mission, but I want to hear your thoughts before I decide whether we proceed or not."

Juan took a sharp step toward Nerit. "You can't be serious? Those are our people out there! Of course we have to rescue them! We don't have another choice! No way we can turn back now!"

Nerit shook her head. "No, they're *not* our people anymore, Juan. They abandoned us. Remember? They left because they didn't trust us to stick to the plan to defend the Fort against the herd. Now the Fort is still standing and most of the people who left with Ed are dead. So technically, they're not our people, Juan, even if they were once our friends."

"How the fuck can you say that?" Juan exclaimed.

Monica let out a noise of disbelief. "Nerit, you're fucking with us, right? These people stood with us through tough times."

"But not when it counted, right?" Arnold met Monica's furious gaze steadily. "When we needed them to stand against the herd and defend the Fort's walls, they vamoosed. They found a bullshit reason to leave because they were afraid to stand with their friends. I liked Ed, but he did us dirty."

"Arnold, I'm not saying they're perfect. Yeah, they turned chicken shit, but we can't turn our backs on them." Monica slid off the bench and leaned toward Arnold. "Look me in the eye and tell me you haven't done stupid shit since the zombies started chomping people."

"We all do stupid shit, Monica. But I can say I *never* abandoned my friends. We don't owe them a damn thing, so we better consider our odds of surviving if we try to rescue them." Arnold gestured toward the zombies. "This is gonna be a tough one."

"That's *Belinda* out there! My childhood friend! And you're telling me to let her die!" Juan shouted.

"Juan, keep your voice down, or we're going to have more problems than we have right now," Nerit said in a commanding tone that shut down all protests from the upset man.

The silence that followed was uncomfortable. From the grim

expressions surrounding Emma, it was clear that everyone was on edge. The tension in the small bus was only growing as each second ticked by.

It was difficult for Emma to find her voice in the face of such high emotions, but her life was on the line too. "Look, I know I'm new here, but every life is valuable. I tried, but couldn't save *anyone* in my town. I kept hoping I would find people alive, but everyone was dead by the time I found them. So the fact that I'm standing here among the living is blowing my mind. You don't know what it's like to not see another living face for over a year. If humanity is going to have a rat's ass chance of survival, we have to save everyone we can. I don't know the people out there, but I'm willing to put my life on the line for them."

It was evident from the look of approval on Nerit's face that Emma had said exactly what she wanted to hear. Emma had the impression she had passed some sort of test.

"She's right," Monica declared, glaring at Arnold. "They may have bailed on us, but I'm not ready to bail on them."

"Besides, don't you have mad driving skills, Arnold?" Monica lifted an eyebrow.

"Fine. But if they run away again, I ain't stopping them."

"Then we're all agreed. We save them." Nerit patted Juan on the shoulder and he visibly relaxed. Bending over the driver, she said, "Arnold, let the Fort know our status."

While Arnold relayed the information, Juan leaned against the windows, straining to see the people on the roof.

"You're good people, Em," Juan whispered.

"Thanks, Juan."

His approval did mean something to her. He was the first person she had met when she'd arrived on the outskirts of the Fort and she felt an affinity to him for the losses he'd experienced.

Nerit straightened after the conversation over the radio ended. "The Fort is standing by for further updates. Now we need to plan our rescue. Arnold, I need you to park the bus as close to that building as possible, but away from the Durango. How close can you get us without risking the bus?"

"The picnic tables are right there," Emma said, gesturing.

Arnold leaned forward, resting his arms on the steering wheel, and peered out the windshield, a frown on his face. Giving the area a long, scrutinizing look, he remained silent for nearly a minute.

"Nerit, I can get us close," Arnold started with clear trepidation in his manner, "but the second we're near that building, we're going to be swarmed. This bus has been souped-up to deal with zombies, but it has limitations. There's no telling how many of those fuckers are in the trees. We get enough of them hemming us in and we're not going anywhere."

"So we move fast," Nerit replied. "Emma, you volunteered to be up on top, but if you're having second thoughts let me know now."

"I can do it. I'm stronger than I look and have plenty of experience scaling buildings, trees, vehicles, you name it. I basically had to learn parkour to survive this last year."

Nerit grinned. "All right. Arnold, you pull up to the building with Emma already on top and the rest of us in position to pick off the zombies when they attempt to swarm us. We thin out the numbers while Emma gets our survivors on board. As soon as they're secure, we leave."

Arnold scrunched his face. "Nerit, I might not be able to turn around, so I'll have to back out of here. Which means I could potentially drive off the hillside."

"I trust you *not* to do that," Nerit said, patting his shoulder.

"You can do this, Arnold. I have seen you do some crazy ass driving," Monica said.

"Arnold, you're the best driver the Fort has. We all know this," Juan added. "You said you can parallel park a tank."

Arnold frowned. "I did *not* say a tank."

"I'm sure Nerit wouldn't ask you to do something she didn't think you could do," Emma added encouragingly.

"I truly appreciate y'all trying to build up my confidence, and it's working. Let's do this!"

Emma moved up the aisle to where the hatch was located. Craning her head, she stared at the blue sky through the opening. As she had done a hundred times before, she pictured exactly what she needed to do in the next few minutes. It was like playing a short film in her mind over and over again until she memorized every action. It was this ritual that had kept her alive throughout the last sixteen months.

"Are you sure you got this?" Juan asked.

"I know what to do."

"Are you sure?"

"I've been doing this type of thing since the zombie apocalypse started. I'm sure I'll be fine."

Juan appeared doubtful, but he nodded. "Maybe I should take your place."

Nerit stepped toward Juan and gestured toward a nearby window. It had a heavy metal grating over it with an opening that would allow a weapon to be aimed through it. "I need you there taking out every goddamn zombie you can." She hooked a thumb at the roof. "I need someone lightweight and fast up there."

"Nerit, Emma says some of them are in bad condition. I can be of help to save them," Juan protested.

The older woman took him by the hand and lifted her chin to stare into his green eyes. "You're too emotional. Too connected to what's happening. I need you to take out all your anger and fear on the zombies."

Juan exhaled in obvious frustration, ready to protest.

"Juan, I may look skinny, but I'm pretty spry. I know what I'm capable of. I can get your friends back on this bus safely as long as you're giving me cover."

There was no way in hell Emma wanted him on the roof with her. Juan was obviously carrying way too much emotional baggage where Belinda was concerned. Nerit knew him much better than Emma did, and it was evident she also believed he was too caught up in his need to be a hero to risk him taking point.

"Em, just promise me that you'll bring her back to me. I can't lose someone else."

"I promise, Juan, I will do my best."

Nerit yanked on Juan's shirt to get his attention. "I need to know you're good with this plan."

"I'm good. I'll do my part."

Swiveling about on her heel, Nerit walked back to Arnold's side. "All right, Arnold. Time to save our friends."

CHAPTER 20

People are Assholes

As soon as the bus shifted gears and rumbled toward the outdoor restrooms, Emma started to have grave second thoughts about the plan. She'd promised Juan she could handle the rescue and she didn't want to let him down.

The short bus rambled along the gravel drive at a steady pace toward the parking area and the restrooms. Once in the line of sight of the undead, the bus would be swarmed and the situation would become even more perilous and unpredictable. She wished that Arnold would speed up so they could get this over with as soon as possible, but slow and steady was the best way to go about it. With so many zombies in the area, it would be easy to make a miscalculation when traveling at a higher speed, which would put the team in a bad spot.

Gripping the back of the seat in front of her she planted her feet wide to prevent being jostled about. Staring straight ahead through the windshield, she witnessed the moment the zombies heard the bus. In unison their heads swiveled toward the approaching vehicle and their voices rose in one stomach-churning wail. It was the sound that haunted her nightmares every time she closed her eyes to sleep.

Since the first day when the zombies became a part of the world and started the slow disintegration of civilization, Emma's brain had done a splendid job of creating coping mechanisms. The sound of their wails became white noise while their mottled, dissected bodies blurred into gray figures. They would remain that way until she had to concentrate on individual ones to kill.

Around her, the faces of the rest of the team were grim and resolved. She was adapting to working with an organized group and trusting them was difficult. Her grandfather had taught her to hunt when she was ten. Their history enabled them to work seamlessly together after the first day of the rising when the zombies had stopped being myth and became reality. They understood each other's frame of mind and actions when facing the undead. Emma didn't know those seated around her. Juan had competently had her back yesterday when they'd rescued Macy, but he was frazzled, too invested in Belinda's survival. Nerit was the only one on the bus she was certain could handle any threat for she had the bearing of an ancient warrior. That was the only reason that Emma had any sort of confidence in their rescue plan. If Nerit believed the team could pull off the rescue, Emma would trust her judgment.

The bus bounced over some dips in the uneven terrain, jostling the passengers. Zombies attempting to headlong charge its front bumper were swatted away by the deer guard, their broken bodies careening into the brush. Arnold was true to his boast and deftly maneuvered through the thicker clumps of zombies while evading the hidden picnic tables to pull alongside the building on the opposite side from the crashed Durango.

As planned, Emma rapidly scrambled up through the open hatch, her gloved hands reaching for the nearest handholds. She hauled herself onto the roof, the metal scorching her fingers, and quickly secured herself with the harness. It took a few seconds to get accustomed to the belay device that would control the mountain climbing rope attached to the bus. It made her a little nervous to be so dependent on the equipment. It would instantly tighten if she fell, hopefully keeping her out of the grasp of the dead.

The zombies swarmed the bus and the all too familiar sound of hands beating against the metal filled the air. The first gunshot cracking through the air startled Emma. For a long time, no one other than her had fired a gun in her vicinity. It was yet another thing she needed to get used to.

She rapidly scrutinized the situation that confronted her, and recognized that this rescue was going to be a little bit more difficult than anticipated. Arnold could not pull up flush to the building, leaving a three-foot gap between the sloping edge of the top of the bus and the corrugated metal roof of the building. The space between the bus and the building filled up with the dead. Emma briefly glanced down and shivered at the sight of the murky eyes gazing up at her. Blotting out their presence, she planted her feet on the section where the bus roof started to curve and tested her line. It was taut and secure, ready to hold her weight.

Dehydrated, gravely burned by the sun, and weak, the three survivors gingerly crawled toward her. The woman, Belinda, was helped along by Kurt, the younger blond man. The dark-haired middle-aged man, whose name was Ted, Emma recalled, reached the edge of the building first. His face and neck were red and blistered from his days in the sun and sweat glistened on the tip of his hooked nose. Shaking violently, he climbed to his feet, stepped to the edge and looked down.

"Ted, my name is Emma. I'm here to save you, but you gotta listen to me. First, you need to not look down. You need to concentrate on making it safely to where I am standing. Don't get distracted."

The man was unsteady on his feet, and clearly terrified. "No, absolutely not! You can't expect us to jump in our condition! You need to pull up closer to the building!"

"That's not an option. We can't get that close."

The continuous gunfire made it a little difficult to hear, but it was the incessant cries of the undead that was most distracting. Ted's gaze remained riveted to the decayed faces squeezed into the gap below.

Ted shook his head. "You can't expect us to jump! We can't do that!"

Their situation had been more precarious than Emma had realized. The roof had not been constructed to hold so much weight and it protested loudly, the metal and wood creaking beneath him.

Kurt and Belinda edged forward, each step they took tentative. It was evident that Belinda was in the worst shape.

Blisters had popped on her shoulders and forehead, oozing pus and blood. Though she had a darker olive complexion, the sun had done its damage. The blond haired man identified as Kurt was beet red. All three were probably severely dehydrated. Emma considered calling out for Juan, but thought better of it. He was too emotionally attached to the situation.

"How do we get across?" Belinda asked over the cries of the dead.

Emma had wanted them to jump across the three-foot expanse, but now understood that was not a possibility without help. With a sigh, she accepted she was going to have to put herself at risk to save them. Giving herself enough slack, she planted one foot firmly on the roof of the bus and kicked out to set the other on the roof. She was muscular and physically fit, yet she could still feel the strain in her thigh muscles. The rubber soles on her boots helped her maintain a steady stance while the harness around her waist gave her the semblance of being secure. If she slipped, the belay device would lock and keep her from falling too far.

"Hurry, we need to get outta here before more come," Emma urged. "I'll help you across."

"Belinda goes first," Kurt said.

"I'm closer," Ted interjected.

Seizing Emma's hand, Ted prepared to jump. His soft, doughy physique was a worry. He honestly did not look capable of making the leap.

"Ted, it might be easier if you do what I am doing. Straddle the gap then shift your weight so you can reach the handhold over there." Emma pointed to the metal grip near the edge of the roof. It was wrapped with leather to provide a better hold and protect against the heated metal surface.

Ted tossed a look at Emma that said he was not someone who liked to be told what to do. Clearly agitated, his fingers dug into her hand as he prepared to jump. Emma took a deep breath, hoping that the harness could hold both their weight if he fell.

"Ted, just do what the lady is telling you to do. Stop making things difficult," Kurt said, instantly making the situation even tenser.

If the middle-aged man didn't like Emma telling him what to do, he sure as hell did not like the younger man giving him orders.

"It's only three feet," Ted retorted with a snarl on his thin lips.

With those words, he made a desperate leap across the gap. He wasn't in the best shape to begin with, but if he hadn't been so weak from dehydration, the heat, and lack of food, he might have had a shot at cleanly making the jump. His feet landed on the curved edge of the roof and he started to slip. Instead of releasing Emma's hand and reaching for the handhold, he jerked her toward him, causing her to lose her footing on the building. Thinking fast, she threw all her weight toward the bus as she fell. The harness tightened around her torso, squeezing the air out of her lungs. Her gloved hands gripped the line as her body slammed into the curved edge of the roof of the bus, her legs dangling over the side. The impact stunned her and left her gasping with pain. Her knees and feet throbbed from where they impacted with the grate over the window. Expecting to feel the hands of the undead on her at any second, she kicked her feet violently while attempting to hoist herself upward.

There was a loud thump and then someone gripped her wrists. Raising her head, she saw Kurt pulling her onto the roof. It took some effort on both their parts to get her safely onto the bus. He was weak from days of exposure and she was gasping to force oxygen back into her lungs.

"Stupid asshole almost got both you killed," Kurt grunted.

"Did they get him?"

It was the only reason Emma could think of as to why the zombies hadn't grabbed hold of her when her legs had been dangling over the edge.

Kurt shook his head. "No, but he has their attention. I'll get the idiot."

Emma glanced over her shoulder and saw that Ted had managed to grab one of the handholds and hook his knee over another. His other leg dangled dangerously close to the grasping hands of the zombies teeming below. Getting to her feet, Emma edged forward on the shuddering bus to help Kurt drag Ted to safety.

Throughout the entire ordeal, the gunshots never stopped as the team did its job thinning out the zombies in the gap between the building and the bus. Emma swept her gaze over the area long enough to see numerous corpses dotting the ground. More zombies staggered out from the trees. They were in bad shape, most likely stragglers from the herd. Nonetheless, zombies in large numbers were a serious threat. The team was running out of time and needed to leave soon.

Digging her fingertips a little harder than necessary into Ted's soft arm, she helped Kurt pull him fully onto the roof. Ted crawled to the hatch and disappeared inside without even a word of thanks.

"Asshole," Kurt grumbled.

"Scared asshole. Now to get Belinda."

"If you give me the harness, I'll get her," Kurt said.

"You sure?"

"I'm taller and have longer legs. I'll straddle the gap and lift her across to you."

"Sounds good."

Emma started to unbuckle the harness, but was distracted when Juan climbed through the hatch. He glanced at her and Kurt briefly before rushing forward, preparing to leap across to the building.

"No! Don't! It's not safe!" Kurt cried out.

It was too late. Juan jumped, sailed easily over the gap, and landed with a resounding thud on top of the roof next to where Belinda was cowering. There was a loud cracking sound and then the roof crumpled beneath them.

CHAPTER 21

People are Stupid

The roof of the building partially crumpled, creating a dangerous makeshift slide that disappeared into the darkened depths of one of the restrooms. With a scream, Belinda disappeared from view into the bathroom below. Somehow Juan managed to hook his fingers around the lip of the corrugated metal panel as it pitched down at a slant.

The thunderous noise of the roof collapse immediately caught the attention of the zombies. Redirecting their focus from the people on top of the bus, they surged through the entrances into the two separate bathrooms.

Emma froze, unable to fathom the stupidity of her fellow Texan. The tall man was trying to reach into the building, which was a good sign that Belinda was among the living. Next to her, though barely able to stand on his feet, Kurt started forward.

Emma caught his arm. "You're too weak to help them. I'll do it."

The young man started to protest, but was distracted by the appearance of Monica climbing out of the hatch.

"Kurt, get below and help thin out the zombies. Emma and I will help my damn fool cousin and Belinda," Monica said.

"We got this, Kurt. You already did your best to help her. Now it's our turn."

Kurt reluctantly retreated through the hatch while Monica leaned over and hooked a new harness to the roof of the bus. Pulling it on, she gritted her teeth, the fury in her eyes obvious. She was a powerful-looking woman with muscular arms and legs beneath her clothing. There was a good chance that between the two of them they could rescue both people as long as the zombies hadn't reached Belinda yet. Only a minute or two had passed, but that was all it took in the zombie apocalypse to lose a life.

"We need to get Juan back over onto the bus and then get Belinda. You know, if she is alive." Monica glanced toward her cousin, who was yelling down into the bathroom and completely ignoring them. "Sorry again about my ridiculously stupid cousin."

"I understand desperation. I would've done anything to save my loved ones."

"*My* loved one is an idiot." Monica worked feverishly to finish securing her harness while shooting worried looks in Juan's direction.

"Let's save your cousin's ass and chew it out later."

With a grim expression, Monica finished her task. "That sounds like a plan to me."

The other woman probably didn't fully understand how lucky she was to have the chance to save someone she loved. Emma envied her.

The walls of the structure were about a foot thick and provided a ledge to stand on. Monica made the leap across to the building with astonishing surefooted finesse. Maintaining her balance, she extended her hand toward Emma.

"I've been working on the construction crews, so this is a cakewalk. Just don't look down and you'll be fine."

After making sure she had enough slack in her line, Emma took Monica's hand and stepped across the gap. It took all her willpower not to look at the swarm of zombies fighting to enter the restroom. When she was sure of her footing, she pushed off from the bus. It took her a second to catch her balance. In that time, her heart almost came to a complete stop.

Monica placed a stabilizing hand on her arm. "Gotcha. You're good. You've got this."

Emma cautiously dropped into a kneeling stance to study their predicament.

The corrugated metal roof had been bolted to supports. There had been three panels lying side-by-side and in the collapse two panels had wrenched apart. This was the only reason Belinda was still alive. She'd dropped into a stall, while one of the panels had fallen outside of it and was wedged against the stall door. The stainless steel walls of the stall shuddered under the violent assault of the zombies crowding into the bathroom.

Juan held onto the inclined roof panel with one hand while reaching with the other toward Belinda. She was standing on the toilet stretching to catch his hand, but her small frame was far too short to close the gap. Exhausted from her ordeal, she swayed on the toilet seat. The door to the second stall was open and it was filled with the dead. The dividing wall was starting to dent under the desperate beating of decaying hands.

Juan wasn't in a great position either. The panel holding his weight rested against the top of the neighboring stall and was bent at an angle, so that his legs were suspended over the undead crowd. He was in just as precarious position as the woman he was trying to save. How he had expected to rescue Belinda made no sense to Emma. He was clearly on the verge of losing his grip and falling. There wasn't a plausible way he could reach Belinda and hoist her up.

"Juan, we'll get her! You need to pull yourself up onto the roof! You're just dangling dinner over the zombies and making the situation worse! Get up here!" Monica barked out with an authority that Emma appreciated.

"I need to save Belinda!"

"You're being a fucking moron, Juan de la Torre! Get your ass up here before you get both of you eaten!"

The writhing bodies beneath Juan's feet were growing more agitated by the sound of human voices. Time was swiftly running out for everyone, including the rescuers. They had to move fast. Emma tested the remaining intact roof panel. The metal was scorching hot beneath her gloved hand. It groaned as she leaned some pressure on it, but remained in place.

"Those rusted bolts are holding," Monica pointed out. "But I don't think it will support too much weight."

Emma tested her safety line again. She had just enough slack to implement her quickly forming plan. "I'll have to risk it. Crawling onto it will get me close to where she is so I can lower myself down to get her. Once I have her, you and Juan can hoist us up."

"Did you hear her, Juan? Get up here and help!"

Perhaps some sense penetrated his thick skull and it had registered in Juan's mind that he was in just as much danger as Belinda. Or maybe it was the prospect of being part of Belinda's rescue. Either way, Juan made an effort to catch the edge of the roof with his other hand. The twisted panel holding him up made it difficult, so his cousin moved to assist him. Monica straddled the top of the wall so she could brace herself as she leaned over to help.

Fear etched onto his expression, Juan desperately reached for his cousin's hand. Kicking his legs in an attempt to propel himself upward, he only managed to stir up the zombies beneath him. That worked to Belinda's benefit by temporarily distracting the undead from their attacks on the stall she was trapped within. Emma had planned to wait until Juan was safely on the wall and then climb down, but she decided to take advantage of the zombies focusing on him.

The top of the stainless steel stall partition was only a few feet below her perch. In normal circumstances, it wouldn't be difficult to lower herself and climb down into the stall with Belinda, but currently the space around it was completely crammed full of the rotting, foul-smelling creatures.

Belinda sank against the wall and slowly slid down until she was crouched on the toilet lid. Head craned, she watched Emma, her gaze pleading for rescue. Emma cautiously rolled onto her stomach and lowered her legs over the edge of the roof, her feet searching for purchase on the top of the stall divider. Inching slowly downward, Emma clutched a peak in the corrugated metal. The last thing she wanted to do was lose her grip and fall. It was a relief when her heels hooked over the top of the partition. With a grin, she lowered the rest of her body into the building, squatting down so she was below the roof. Emma's appearance over the heads of the zombies immediately sent them into a new frenzy. Their hands started to hammer against the divider beneath her, rattling her, and only her grip on the roof above kept her from pitching into them.

The situation was far worse than Emma had realized. The constant press of the zombie bodies against the stalls was forcing the partition to gradually slant toward Belinda, and already a few brackets had torn free from the wall. Only the collapsed roof panel, the fact the stalls were floor-length, and sheer luck had kept Belinda out of the reach of the zombies.

"This whole thing is about to come down on us, Belinda. I need you to take my hand right now so they can hoist us up." Emma didn't look behind her to check on Juan's progress. She had to trust that he would make it to safety and that his strength combined with Monica's would be able to pull them up.

At first she thought Belinda was going to ignore her, since she appeared frozen with fear, but slowly, the woman forced herself to stand. Bracing her hands against the solid wall behind her, Belinda climbed onto the seat. Emma's fingers dug into the corrugated metal roof to keep steady while stretching out with one hand toward Belinda. The partition Emma was perched on rocked under the onslaught of the zombies. Belinda was about to grasp her hand when something gripped Emma's ankles. Tossing a startled look over her shoulder, she saw a tall male zombie scrabbling at her boots. Before she could decide what to do, he pulled Emma off balance and she tipped forward. As she fell into the stall, the line tightened sharply around her torso. Again, her breath was nearly knocked out of her, but she was secure. Emma grasped Belinda, jerked her into her arms, and the two women dangled over the toilet as the stainless steel partition started to bend toward them.

"Pull us up!" she shouted, hoping Juan and Monica were ready to rescue them.

Her answer was a sharp yank on the line.

"We got you!" Monica replied.

"Hold on to Belinda!" Juan called down.

In painful, jerky tugs, Juan and Monica pulled the two women up. There wasn't too much distance from where they hung to safety, but every second was terrifying as they dangled helplessly, protected only by the slowly-collapsing stall. When they neared the edge of the remaining section of the roof, Emma dared to plant her boots on the stall divider to hold them steady. A few rotting fingers scrabbled on the soles of her boots. Juan leaned over and gripped Belinda's wrists, dragging her up and out of sight in one swift motion. The roof panel shuddered beneath their combined weight.

The metal partition gave way beneath Emma with a loud groan.

"Shit!"

Emma quickly pulled her knees up to her chest. Holding onto the line, she rapidly swung over the zombie heads toward the wall. She kicked up her legs just before she struck it, but only managed to hook one ankle onto the top. Because there wasn't any slack in the rope, she was unable to maneuver to safety and was stretched tight in a precarious position above the rampaging zombies below.

Behind her, the stainless steel partitions crumpled with a loud metallic moan, wrenching the dividers away from the walls so the brackets tugged free of the cement. The destruction sent a tremor through the entire building. A substantial amount of the zombies were instantly trapped beneath the falling debris. The undead thrashed about, attempting to free themselves, but only managed to become more entangled with the limbs and clothing of their companions.

"Emma, we'll get you! Hold on!" Monica yelled.

A second later the remaining part of the roof caved in on the zombies below. Emma's safety line was snagged on the edge of the corrugated metal and she was wrenched from the wall. She swung over the heads of the downed zombies and slammed into the other wall.

Trapped at the far end of the bathroom opposite the open doorway, she could see the exterior of the bus. The zombies knocked over from the collapsing roof were struggling to get up, giving her a little precious time. It took only a second for her pistol to be in her hand. She immediately aimed at the zombie closest to her. It was male, fresh, and on its knees a few feet from her. With a howl, it lunged toward her. She put a bullet through its brain and straightaway aimed for the next nearest zombie.

"There's no way in hell I'm dying here," she muttered.

Just as she was about to unstrap herself from the harness so she could risk running over the fallen zombies for the exit, she was hoisted upward. A second later, Juan set her on the top of the outer building wall and steadied her with his hands. She noticed they were bloody from where he had gripped the rope while pulling her up. The line remained caught on the fallen roof, so Juan swiftly helped her unbuckle the harness.

Glancing over her shoulder at him, she managed to rasp out, "Thank you."

Juan gave her a brief nod and pointed to the bus where Monica was lowering Belinda through the hatch. "We gotta go."

Emma gratefully took his hand and he pulled her to her feet. He guided her along the narrow pathway back to the bus. She broke her own rule and glanced down once or twice. The tilted heads of the zombies below pivoted as she moved along the wall to safety. They raised their gnarled hands toward her and moaned in unison. A chill swept down her spine. She wouldn't have made it if she'd tried to run for the doorway.

When they reached the gap between the building and the bus, Juan grabbed her under her armpits, swung her over the heads of the zombies below, and tossed her onto the bus. She landed with a hard thump on the roof. It took only a few seconds to climb through the hatch into the safety of the bus. Juan dropped down behind her. Emma noted his eyes instantly sought out Belinda. Rune's words echoed in her mind, but she muted them.

"Arnold, get us out of here," Nerit ordered.

The bus started backward, Arnold skillfully maneuvering through the growing herd of zombies. The older dead splattered against the rearguard, splitting apart like overly ripe melons. The newer, faster dead attempted to grip onto the sides, desperate to reach the living inside.

Emma held onto a seat to hold herself upright. Now that she was out of immediate danger, the adrenaline was leaving her system and making her knees a little wobbly. She didn't want to show any weakness in front of her new companions, so she remained standing.

"Monica, where's Belinda?" Juan asked, panicked.

"She's with Kurt at the back of the bus," Monica replied. "Leave her alone. She's really shaken up and he's the one she turned to."

Juan whirled around to observe Kurt in the back row of the bus with his head bowed over his lap. Belinda wasn't visible, so she had to be lying down. Emma didn't know Juan well enough to read his gaze, but she got the impression he was both relieved and possibly disappointed.

When Juan started down the aisle, Monica grasped his arm.

"Monica, I should-"

"No, you shouldn't."

When the bus reached the road that wound down the hill, zombies flowed out of the woods. There had been many more than they had realized. The faster ones assailed the bus while Arnold futilely attempted a three-point-turn. The bus rocked under the onslaught.

"I knew it! I knew it!" he grunted. "I can't turn around. We're getting boxed in and the tires are gummed up with zombie guts. We're stuck!"

CHAPTER 22

Not Part of the Plan

"We need to get out of here!" Ted exclaimed. Face flattened against a window to peer out, he was visibly shaking.

"We're working on it, bro. Calm down," Juan said.

The space around the bus was filled with the undead, making maneuverability difficult. Emma had faced similar circumstances in the past and knew that driving through such a large throng was not a good idea. A few months into the apocalypse, Emma and her grandfather had tried to drive through a pack of the undead. Shattered bone had punctured a tire and the blood and guts had gunked up the wheels. Her grandfather had barely saved them from the jam by reversing down the road until he could do a sharp U-turn. Even without the zombies, the current area wasn't ideal for doing a U-turn in such a large vehicle.

"We're stuck!" Arnold pounded on the steering wheel. "Nerit, this bus doesn't have that much horsepower. I can't risk a turn with all those zombies. They could be hiding things like boulders or barbeque pits that could take out the axle."

"You said you could drive in reverse. It looks like you'll have to do just that," Nerit answered in such a way it was obvious that she wouldn't allow an argument.

"Shit! Do you know how hard it's going to be going down a winding road backwards with my tires slipping and zombies following and-"

"We don't have a choice, do we?" Nerit motioned to the zombies crowding the area making maneuverability difficult, if not impossible. "And you said you could do it."

"Fuckin' fine! I need people on both sides of the bus guiding me!" Arnold changed gears, every movement agitated. "I can only see so much with these mirrors!"

"We're on it," Juan assured him.

Emma slid onto a seat on the left. "I'll take this side."

Monica took the seat opposite her. "I got the right."

Juan ran down the aisle to the rear. "I've got the back end!"

The bus inched backwards down the narrow strip of asphalt curving sharply around the hill. It had been daunting on the journey up to lookout point, but it was downright terrifying traveling in reverse. The zombies crowded the short bus, beating on it while howling with hunger. The faster, stronger ones shoved aside the weaker of their kind. A towering zombie lunged out of the throng and startled Emma by slamming his massive fists against the grate covering the window she was gazing through.

Breaking her own rule, she reflexively glanced at his face. For a split second, she thought it was Stan, her long dead ex, and her heart leaped in her chest. Then she realized his nose was too big, his face too long, and his murky eyes too bulging. Additionally, she had put Stan to rest on the same day as her son.

The bus slid past the zombie, and he disappeared from view.

Despite her grit, she was shaken. It was foolish for her to believe she could have put the last year behind her so quickly. The ghosts of her past were on her heels no matter how much she tried to ignore them.

Pressing her hands to the glass to steady herself, she blotted out the mutilated faces of the dead screaming at her so she could concentrate on the task at hand. The bus maintained a good three feet from the guardrail and the brush lining the blacktop. Beyond the gnarled mesquite trees, the town dwelled below, appearing deceitfully tranquil.

"You're good on the left," Emma called out.

From the other side of the aisle, Monica chimed in, "Fine on the right."

"So far, so good, boss," Juan said from the rear of the bus.

Ted slid into the seat behind Emma's and stared in horror at the thick bramble of trees lurking a few feet away. "We're going to crash. You need to turn this bus around. This is dangerous!"

"Can't turn around and risk getting hemmed in," Emma replied.

"I'm not talking to you," Ted snarled. "Driver, you need to turn around and-"

The bus ran over something large in the road, jarring them. Emma smacked her forehead against the glass while Ted's face impacted with a meaty thud. It sent sparks shimmering through her eyesight and she blinked them away. The throbbing pain she could ignore, but the instant splitting headache made focusing a little more difficult.

Ted gripped his nose, blood seeping out from beneath his fingers. Stunned, he slumped on the bench. Emma switched seats, leaving Ted to whimper. At least now he wasn't complaining.

A pack of faster zombies raced alongside the bus, leaping at the windows. A few succeeded in grabbing onto the metal grill welded over the windows to hoist themselves up, making it difficult for Emma to see past their squirming bodies.

"It's hard to see with these assholes holding on!"

The engine growled, the gears grinding. Arnold hit the accelerator to pick up speed, probably hoping to escape the snarl of zombies clinging to the sides.

"I got one bugging me too." Arnold sounded annoyed.

A quick look toward the front end revealed that the big zombie who reminded her earlier of Stan had clambered onto the hood near Arnold's position. The zombie was struggling to tear off the windshield's protection. The rattling sound of metal against glass filled the bus. The big zombie was determined to get inside and rip Arnold apart.

"Should I shoot this one?" Emma asked.

"Save your bullets. We might need them if we have to disembark and go on foot," Nerit ominously replied.

"Fuck this guy!"

Arnold veered toward the low-hanging branches to knock off the zombie, a risky move on such a narrow road. The sound of the tree limbs hitting the bus was deafening. The big zombie clung to the grate, growling loudly. Nervously, Emma checked how close they were to the drop off. Although the branches striking the bus made it difficult to see, she spotted the rusted guardrail looming far too close to the tires.

"Arnold, you're getting too close to the edge!"

Swerving back onto the road, Arnold struggled to keep the bus from shimmying. For a few seconds he fought the steering wheel until the bus was firmly back under his control.

"The protective guard is holding. You're safe. Concentrate on driving, Arnold," Nerit instructed.

"This zombie on the hood is doing a damn good job of scaring me shitless," Arnold testily replied.

"Just keep driving."

"He's got the one corner of the grill bent back. You better save me if he breaks through the window!"

"It won't happen."

Emma had seen a fresh zombie shatter a window with its head, but it had taken on so much damage she'd easily dispatched it. Of course, she'd been in a parked car at the time and not driving backwards down a narrow incline. With Nerit at his side, Arnold was in a better position than Emma had been.

"How am I on the left, Emma?" Arnold called out.

Once they hit the curve, there wouldn't be any more trees on the left-hand side. "Trees are thinning out. You're coming up on that big curve."

"Clear on the right. So far," Monica reported.

That was not unexpected since the rock face of the hillside was on Monica's side.

Arnold again attempted to scrape the zombies off the side of the bus by running them through the low hanging branches of the trees lining the road. A few tumbled off into the greenery, but the big one continued his assault on the windshield grill. Zombies clung to the side of the vehicle, their claw-like fingers hooked into the protective mesh. There were a few digits without a body stuck in the metal grill near Emma.

"You might want to slow down!" Juan shouted. "We got

zombies on the road. Looks like stragglers from the horde."

"How many?" Nerit asked.

"Maybe thirty," Juan replied.

"Older?"

"The slow ones, but they're not too rotted," Juan said.

"Can we catch a break?" Arnold groused.

The bus slowed as it neared the intimidating curve with the sharp drop off.

The view below was beautiful, but deadly with its steep incline and tall oak trees. Emma caught a flash of light from below. Concentrating on the spot, she made out the crumpled remains of a vehicle.

"Someone crashed below," she said. "Looks like a Durango."

Struggling with the wheel, Arnold said, "That won't be us."

Kurt spoke up. "It's the other Durango that was with us. It went off the road trying to avoid the zombies."

"We're the only survivors," Ted muttered. "No thanks to Ed. I never should have listened to him."

"My dad was doing what he thought was best," Kurt snapped back. "He gave his life so we had a chance to escape."

"We're not out of here yet. And this redheaded jackass can't drive." Ted gestured toward Arnold.

"You can get out! I'll pull over and throw you out myself!" Arnold again shifted gears, the bus decelerating even more.

"Slowing down is not the best idea right now," Juan said, waving toward the zombies.

"We're on the curve. We don't have a choice," Nerit replied in her steely, no-nonsense way.

The bus backed into the small herd, the impact of their bodies against the exterior sending shudders through the frame. Blood and gore painted the rear windows and door in thick dark ochre. Emma was flung into the seatback in front of her. The impact stung her ribs, but she managed to grip the seat to stabilize herself. The bus shimmied, bouncing over zombie bodies and across the road to sideswipe several trees on the right. Arnold overcompensated, sending the bus in the opposite direction toward the drop off. It careened through the zombies, skidding toward the ledge.

Everyone on the bus shouted at the same time. "Stop!"

When Arnold hit the brakes, the bus slid along on the zombie muck for several more yards. Only Arnold's expert skills kept them on the road. The bus sluggishly drifted along the curve, coming to a hard stop on the road's narrow shoulder, striking the guard rail. The barrier absorbed the energy from the impact, saving them from a plunge over the side.

Emma barely kept on her feet throughout the ordeal and landed with a hard thump on the seat when the bus came to a rocking stop. Pulling herself upright, she warily glanced at the view outside her window. They were scarily close to falling down the hillside. While Arnold fought with the gear shift and the engine grumbled as he attempted to pull away from the edge, the surviving zombies crowded the bus.

"What's wrong?" Ted demanded. "We need to move!"

"Arnold, we got a shit-ton of zombies pushing up on my side," Monica said, completely ignoring Ted's panic.

"I can't get traction." Arnold continued to struggle up front, the engine roaring.

"We've got a tire hanging over the edge," Juan said from the back. "That's why we're not moving."

Nerit remained silent as she scrutinized the situation, moving from one side of the bus to the other. At last she said, "Stop, Arnold. We can't move until we clear the area and sort out how to get this bus moving before the next wave of zombies arrives."

Ted blotted his broken nose with the hem of his shirt. "They're going to push us off the hill! We'll go over the edge. We have to go *now*!"

Monica pointed to the back door. "You want to go on foot? Be my guest."

"Should I call it in?" Arnold asked Nerit.

"Another vehicle won't fit up here safely. They'd also have to back down the road. There's no room to turn around. That being said, let them know our situation."

"You have to call for help!" Ted shouted at Nerit. "We can't stay here!"

Eyes blazing, Monica poked Ted's arm to get his attention. She shushed him as Arnold started to speak with the Fort. "We're working on a plan, Ted."

Staring down the slope of the hill, Emma listened to the arguing voices. When she'd been on her own, her choices had shaped her fate. Now whether she lived or died was dependent on others.

It was unsettling.

Hearing footfalls behind her, she glanced over her shoulder to see Nerit sliding open a window and aiming her sniper rifle through a gap in the metal mesh. She hesitated, closing it back up without firing.

"We're at a bad angle. Kurt, take my pistol and start thinning out the zombies up against the bus. Use the portholes and be careful. The zombies will try to snatch the gun right out of your hand. Juan, Arnold, figure out how to get this bus moving. Emma, follow me. Monica, grab the bag of ammo." Nerit handed her firearm to the badly sunburned man then a few more magazines. "Can you handle this?"

Kurt nodded. "I've got it covered."

"What should I do?" Ted asked.

"Sit there and be quiet." The look on the older woman's face instantly quashed any of his protests. "No more arguments. We kill the zombies, find a way to get this bus moving, and go home."

Without another word, Nerit climbed onto the back of one of the seats and lifted herself onto the roof.

Picking up her rifle, Emma followed.

CHAPTER 23

On The Edge

The hot wind blasted Emma's face, reeking of the dead crowding the bus nestled into the scrub brush and guardrail on the shoulder. Beyond the sharp drop off was the breathtaking view of the greenery of the countryside and the town nestled into the hills. On the other side of the narrow road, the imposing rock face rose up to Lookout Point. They'd only have to worry about zombies approaching on the road. That made the situation a little more manageable.

A gunshot fired from within the bus drowned out the unsettling moans of the zombies beating on the sides of the vehicle.

"We need to cull the numbers. Emma, help Kurt clear the area around the bus," Nerit ordered. "I'll take care the ones coming down the hill."

The sun was higher in the morning sky and blazed down on them, the metal beneath their feet and knees scorching hot. Emma set her rifle aside and shrugged the harness Monica had used earlier over her shoulders. Nerit hoisted her sniper rifle and took up a position close to the front of the shuddering bus. Monica appeared, tossing a bag onto the roof and pulling herself up.

"I'll reload," she said.

Emma scooted closer to the edge of the bus. She deliberately tightened the line and leaned forward to get a good view of the assault on the bus. A handgun was better at this range, so she set the rifle to the side and pulled out her first pistol. Below her, the upturned dead faces with hungry eyes and snapping jaws were the monsters of her waking hours and nightmares. Their blackened skin, snarled hair, and torn clothing obliterated most of their humanity, but there were a few that retained some semblance of who they'd once been. This was the part she didn't enjoy. Observing life-like faces and wondering if there was anything left of a soul trapped in the rotting corpses. One woman was wearing her nurse scrubs. Another was in a school uniform. A smaller zombie, clearly a child, was wearing its school backpack. Shaking her head, Emma tried to keep herself from falling into the trap of feeling compassion for the creatures. She glanced at the nurse, and the zombie woman's head jerked as one of Kurt's bullets blew out her brains.

"You okay?" Monica called out.

"I'm fine. Just getting the lay of the land."

The rocking of the bus forced her to make some adjustments to her stance. She found the rhythm and it helped her aim. Kurt killed the zombies rammed up against the windows, but it was increasingly obvious why he needed Emma's help. The ones pushing up from behind pinned the dead zombies to the side of the bus forming a shield. That meant she should concentrate on the outer edge.

Emma took a mental note of the bullets she'd already fired from the weapon earlier, calculating how many shots she could fire before reloading.

She slid her finger over the trigger.

She pulled.

The pistol fired with a sharp pop.

One bullet, one zombie gone.

"Like shooting fish in a barrel," Monica said.

It was a phrase Emma's grandfather had often used and her heart ached with the loss of him. He used to be her partner when she went on her killing runs, and now he was gone. Just like her son, Stan, and most of the world.

Emma aimed at the next zombie and dispatched it.

Behind her, Nerit fired her sniper rifle at regular intervals, only pausing to reload.

Emma counted each of her shots, handed off the magazine to Monica, and slapped a freshly loaded one into the pistol.

"Can someone kill this muthafucker trying to break the

window?" Arnold yelled from within the bus.

Monica slid across the top of the roof on her tummy, hooked her foot onto a handhold to keep herself secure, and aimed with her Glock at the target. The pistol fired and the sound of something heavy falling down the hillside followed.

"Thank you!"

Over a year's practice made Emma fast and efficient. She killed the zombies one after the other in fast succession, only pausing long enough to reclaim her reloaded magazines. The bodies piled up, throwing off the balance of their undead brethren. A few tumbled to the ground, knocking more down. They clawed at each other, struggling to get up. Emma killed them too. The stink of offal and old blood wafted over her, a stench she would never get used to for as long as the apocalypse lasted. The bus stopped rocking when the last of the zombies fell. A quick look around revealed Kurt had killed all the zombies close to the bus. Nothing moved in the heap of bodies below her.

"All clear on this side," Emma announced.

The road above their location was littered with corpses that Nerit had sniped. The older woman surveyed her handiwork for a moment then said to Emma, "We have some coming down the hill after us, but we have a little time until they're here. I took out the fastest ones."

The back door clanked open and Juan jumped out. "We got a plan! I just need to get something wedged under this tire so it can get some traction. I need help!"

Emma glanced down long enough to see Juan kicking dead zombies out of his way while searching the terrain for an object sturdy enough to lodge under the back tire.

"On my way!" Monica pushed the ammunition bag toward Emma. "Keep us covered," she said, and disappeared through the hatch.

"We need to buy Juan time." Nerit pointed at the zombies shambling around the curve in the road. "I'll pick off the ones coming down the hill. You keep an eye out on the lower road."

"Gotcha," Emma said.

While Nerit stood near the front of the bus, sniper weapon ready, observing the slow, steady march of the undead from Lookout Point, Emma remained near the rear. The walking corpses pursuing them were far enough away to not be a threat. As long as the bus was in view, the zombies would continue to shuffle toward it. The creatures were annoyingly persistent in seeking out the living.

There weren't any zombies on the road below their position. Or so it seemed to her naked eye. With so many trees and high brush, it was hard to declare the area clear. Gunshots didn't always draw out the dead since sound reverberated in the hills, making it difficult for the zombies to locate the source.

Scrutinizing the area, Emma mentally made plans if things went sideways. If on her own in the same situation, she'd already be on the move. She learned early in the zombie apocalypse to ditch vehicles if they broke down. Being trapped in a hot, stranded car was not a fate she'd wish on anyone. The Texas sun would cook a human in no time. She knew that horror from experience. A month after the end of the world, she'd found a station wagon with an entire family dead inside. A flat tire and bloody handprints smeared on the outside of the vehicle had told a terrible story. Trapped, the family had faced a terrible end. She'd seen many things that haunted her, but she'd learned a lesson from staring at the small bodies wrapped in the arms of their parents.

Keep moving.

Don't get trapped.

Glancing over the side of the bus and past the crumpled guardrail, she contemplated the steepness of the hill and the possibility of scaling it. The trees jutting out of the hillside might help slightly with the climb, but the incline grew sharper further down. One wrong move would result in a deadly fall. The harness attached to the roof could be used to lower the injured, but they'd have to move fast to avoid being spotted by the zombies. Otherwise, the undead would hurl themselves down the incline after the living. The chances of escape going that way weren't good, especially with wounded people. Emma killed the idea, not even bothering to bring it up to Nerit.

Walking was another option. Slow zombies could be outpaced if everyone was healthy and capable of maintaining a brisk walking speed or light jog. She doubted the people they'd rescued could do either and discarded that possibility as well.

Which just left the one option. Finding a way to get the bus unstuck. Another glance at Juan revealed he hadn't had success yet and was scouring the area for something to use to wedge under the tire. Monica lingered at his side, weapon drawn and ready.

"Find anything?" Emma called out, impatience getting the best of her.

"Trying. Everything is too small, too rotted, or too big," Juan groused.

"Zombies are coming! We need to go now!" Ted yelled. "Stop wasting time!"

"We're dealing with it! Stop blocking the back door. Get inside!" Monica shouted back.

"We should just leave on foot!"

"I said to get back inside, Ted! Don't block the doorway!"

"We can go now! The coast is clear heading down the road," Ted persisted.

Juan poked around a tree, testing some of the fallen branches. Without looking up, he said, "You wouldn't make it, Ted. You're dehydrated and can barely stand. Shut up and do what my cousin told you."

"But I-"

Emma slammed her foot down on the metal roof.

Ted yelped, obviously startled by the sound.

Juan flashed a grin at Emma and returned to his task. Monica trailed behind her cousin, casting scornful looks at the back of the bus. Ted was probably lingering in the doorway. Emma wondered if he was foolish enough to attempt to run.

Kicking at the brush, Juan muttered in Spanish. The brittle sticks and dead leaves skittered across the blacktop. His frustration was evident as he flung away yet another rotted branch.

Squatting down, Emma scrutinized the area. The asphalt was crumbling along the shoulder, but those pieces were too small. There were spots where deep fissures cut the road into jagged slices further down the road in the shadow cast by the peak of the hill.

"Hey, Juan! What about that area?" Emma pointed to a section beneath a canopy of gnarled juniper trees. "It's badly cracked. Maybe you can pull up a chunk?" "Thanks, Em! I'll check it out!"

Juan jogged toward the location with his cousin. It made Emma uneasy that they had to venture so far away from the bus. Watching the swaying shadows beneath the trees lining the blacktop further down the road, Emma reached for her firearm.

The noise of Nerit's sniper rifle firing caught Emma's attention. The true threat of the moment, the small herd that had followed them down the hill, closed in on the bus and the front line of zombies was in range. With the sun looming behind the herd, it was hard to get a headcount, but it was large enough to push the bus over the edge of the road if they were allowed to get close enough. She wished they could just leave instead of sticking with the bus.

Nerit fired once more.

A zombie collapsed to the ground.

"Emma, I could use some help," Nerit stated.

Plucking the bag of ammunition off the roof, Emma hurried to Nerit's side and concentrated on picking off the front edge of the herd heading their way. Although her shoulder started to ache after the first rounds, Emma only hesitated when she had to reload.

After a few minutes, Nerit said, "I can handle this now. Watch the other side of the road. All this noise might draw more to us."

"You got it."

Emma gathered her stuff and hurried to the rear of the bus. The heated metal was burning through her soles. The sun was higher in the sky, sunlight blazing against her skin. Wiping her face, she wished they could get the hell out of the area and soon. The blistering heat wasn't helping her nerves. Down the road, Monica gave Juan cover while he pried a chunk of the asphalt free with a three foot long branch. It was thick and sturdy, but the end was rapidly splintering apart. Emma was uneasy. Even though the immediate area was clear, Monica and Juan were in a vulnerable position.

Lifting her gaze toward the top of the hill looming over their heads, Emma shivered despite the swelling heat. The treetops swayed, obscuring Lookout Point. How many more zombies were looming up there? Were they all marching toward the bus?

"Got it!" Juan triumphantly hoisted a huge chunk of asphalt off the road. It was the size of a concrete brick and he struggled to carry it back to the bus.

Monica diligently stayed by his side, guarding their return, while Nerit culled the front end of the herd approaching the bus.

With a meaty thump and cloud of dirt spewing into the air, a body landed a few feet from the base of the hill on the shoulder of the road. It had not been there before.

Monica jerked around, searching for the source of the sound. "What the fuck was that?"

Emma cocked her head and studied the top of the hill where moving figures dwelled in the gloom beneath the trees. "I think it fell from up there."

A second later, another body tumbled into view. The uneven rock face and occasional scraggly shrub bounced it around and slowed its fall until it landed with a meaty splat on the road. There was no need to put a bullet through its head since there wasn't one left, only a mash of bone and brain.

Monica gestured to the top of the hill. "Holy shit, they jumped from up there!"

They'd worried about being attacked from the sides, not from above.

"More will follow!" Emma instantly grasped the danger of

the situation and began to unhook the harness.

Zombies traveled in swarms. It only took one moving in one direction to spur others to follow. In their constant quest to seek out the living, the undead were relentless. Devoid of emotion, the need for self-preservation, or the ability to feel pain or fear, they sometimes stumbled into deadly situations which a living person would avoid. The first zombie probably had been drawn to the edge by the gunfire, spotted the bus, and fell.

Another toppled over the edge, spinning through the air. It landed with a loud thump much closer to the bus.

Nerit barked out orders while hurrying toward the hatch. "Juan, hurry up! Emma, get inside!"

Another zombie struck the ground only a foot from the bus. The plunging bodies were a deadly threat to the humans below, not only because of their velocity, but because the road was so narrow some would likely strike the vehicle. Within seconds, Juan and Monica were dodging the dropping bodies. Like lemmings, the zombies leaped from the cliff, desperate to reach the living far below.

"Shit! Shit! Shit!" Juan barely managed to hold onto the chunk of concrete and asphalt in his hands.

The zombies struck the ground with loud, fleshy thwacks. Emma expected them to explode, but to her horror, most barely appeared fazed by their fall and struggled to stand. Only a few were so mangled they fell apart on impact. One zombie clawed at the ground, its intestines falling out in long gray-pink ropes.

"Move, Emma," Nerit said, pushing her toward the hatch.

There was a loud clang, an explosion of glass, and the shriek of bending metal when a zombie struck the roof of the bus, leaving a huge dent in the top of the vehicle. It tumbled off onto the road.

"Oh fuck," Emma gasped.

Nerit dropped through the hatch and Emma scrambled after her, remembering to grab the bag of ammunition at the last moment.

CHAPTER 24

The Escape

Emma dropped through the hatch and landed in the aisle behind Nerit.

"Help Juan and Monica, Emma!" Nerit directed. "Kurt and I will provide cover."

Emma sprinted for the back door. Ted was already there, blocking the exit and yelling at the top of his lungs for Juan to hurry. She promptly shoved the blustering man out of the way and took his spot, swiftly assessing the situation outside.

Juan struggled to move faster under the weight of the asphalt and concrete lump he was carrying while Monica shadowed him. Keeping an eye on their surroundings, she hurriedly guided Juan out of the way of a falling zombie.

Emma ignored Ted's angry face in her periphery as he labored to sit upright on the bench he'd fallen onto, but he was too weak. She was about to jump down when Ted yanked her arm to pull himself up.

"We're going to die if he doesn't hurry up!"

Irritated, she jerked away. "Don't touch me!"

"You need to hurry!"

"Then stay out of our way, Ted!"

The reassuring sharp bark of weapon fire started again. Nerit and Kurt were positioned at the front, sniping the zombies approaching from the rest area. Nerit and Kurt were doing their jobs.

Now it was time for Emma to do hers.

Gripping a handhold outside the door, she swung herself down to the ground, landed with a thud, and drew her weapon.

The immediate area around the bus was free of shambling zombies, but there were some falling from above. The strong winds carried the zombies closer to the bus, tossing them like dolls as they fell. Luckily, most of the ones striking the ground either bashed their heads open upon impact, or were so mutilated they could barely move.

The herd that had followed the Fort crew down the hill swiftly closed in on their location. The gunfire from the front of the bus culled the numbers, but there were far more than Emma had realized. The herd must have come up the other side of the hill, drawn by the activity.

Rushing toward the cousins, she called out, "Monica, help Juan carry it! I'll cover!"

With a curt nod, Monica holstered her weapon and grabbed the edge of the heavy chunk. Arm muscles straining, she helped her cousin move at a faster pace.

Emma fell in in beside Monica and Juan. Another zombie plunged toward the road. As it fell, Emma studied its arc. It was going to miss them, so she relaxed slightly until it landed a few feet behind the trio, exploded on impact, and splattered them with guts and blood. Emma winced when a meaty chunk hit her cheek and rapidly brushed the foul-smelling thing away with one gloved hand.

"Fuck!" Juan exclaimed.

"Right on my favorite jeans. Freakin' flyin' zombies," Monica muttered.

"This apocalypse couldn't get any weirder."

Juan clucked his tongue at Emma. "Don't give it any ideas and jinx us! It's already breaking a lot of the zombie rules!"

Ted returned to the doorway despite Emma's earlier admonition. His sunburned face twisted into an angry grimace. "Keep moving! We have to get out of here! You're taking too long!"

"Shut up!" Monica snarled. "We've got this handled!" A dark shadow passed over the road.

"Nerit! Kurt! Watch out!" Emma shouted.

Another zombie landed on the roof of the bus. Nerit dodged inside while Kurt leaped out onto the road to avoid it. The zombie was older and burst apart on impact, leaving a deep dent over the entrance.

"Shit, shit, shit, shit, shit," Juan grunted.

"Dammit! The door is stuck!" Since the roof had caved, the buckled metal blocked it from closing. Nerit kicked it a few times from inside while Kurt tried to pry it loose. "Juan, get us out of here!"

"Working on it, Nerit!"

"With this door jammed like that, the bus is an all you can eat buffet," Monica said, huffing with exertion. "Maybe we should run for it."

"I trust Nerit to kill anything getting close to that door. We can do this," Juan countered.

A zombie crawled toward them. Skin and muscles tore apart, leaving its bottom half behind and dragging entrails in a bloody, gooey wake. Emma shot it in the head and aimed at another farther away trying, but failing, to walk on broken legs. Because it wasn't a direct threat, she held her fire to conserve bullets.

Juan and Monica reached the rear tire hanging over the edge of the road with Emma in their wake. She positioned herself near the rear of the bus where she could easily see down the road and also spot the falling zombies. There were figures shuffling through the trees along the top of the hill.

Working together, the cousins started to push the mass of asphalt and concrete under the wheel.

"It's a good fit," Juan announced. "Just need to shove it under a few more inches so the tire can get traction."

"You need to hurry!" Ted screamed from the open rear doorway. "They're coming!"

"Shut *up*, Ted!" Belinda appeared next to him, unsteady, her face beet red, and furious. Shoving him with both hands, she knocked him back onto the rear seat. "Now stay there!"

"Thanks, Beli," Juan called out to her.

"I know you've got this, Juan," Belinda said, positioning herself to keep Ted at bay.

"Emma, give us a little help here," Juan directed.

Holding her pistol at the ready, Emma placed her foot on the wedge and shoved as hard as she could. Juan and Monica did the same, forcing it to burrow into the dirt and lodge under the tire.

"That should do it," Monica declared.

"Try it, Arnold!" Juan shouted.

The engine roared and the beleaguered driver switched gears. The wheels spun and the short bus lurched forward toward the middle of the road.

"Yes!" Juan hooted, lifting his hands in victory.

The bus slowly rolled a few feet away, and Belinda leaned out, "Hurry! Get inside!"

Arnold brought the short bus to a stop and the trio scrambled after the vehicle.

"Let's get the hell out of here." Monica clutched the handhold near the open doorway of the bus and lifted herself inside.

Emma was about to follow when another zombie landed near her with a meaty splat and lashed out with a long, muscular arm to grab her ankle. Dressed in running shorts and a sweatshirt, it had once been a tall, athletic man. Emma jerked her leg back, but the zombie's grip was stronger than she'd anticipated despite the blackened skin on his fingers being cracked and oozing. She aimed her pistol at its head and fired, blowing a hole in its skull. She tried to yank free only to discover she was trapped by the huge hand.

"Dammit!" Holstering her gun, she leaned over and tried to wrestle her foot from her boot. The painful grip of the dead zombie pinched the leather around her ankle, preventing her from pulling free. "I can't get loose!"

"I got you, Em!"

Juan had been letting her deal with the threat while watching for other zombies. Realizing her predicament, he slung his rifle onto his back and leaned over to pry the dead creature's fingers off her ankle.

"We need to go," Kurt huffed, limping around the back of the bus to help. "There's more coming than we thought. A shit-ton of them. And we're low on ammo."

"This bastard has a good hold on her," Juan muttered.

There was a sharp snapping sound as he broke one of the

fingers.

"Can you get the boot off?" Kurt asked.

Emma shook her head. "He's got me good."

Juan broke two more fingers. "Death grip."

After a struggle, the vice-like hold released and Emma gasped with relief as she broke free. Juan's hands settled on her waist and hoisted her up into the short bus. She moved away from the doorway to give Kurt room to enter. While watching Juan climb into the bus, she became aware of a low, chest-vibrating sound hidden in the noise from the engine and the wind. She pivoted around and saw a wall of dead only a hundred feet from the vehicle.

"We're in!" Juan shouted, slamming the back door shut.

There were too many zombies for their small group to deal with and there wasn't any hope of backup. Nerit guarded the jammed front doors. Even from where Emma stood, she could see that the blood had drained out of her face. Arnold shifted gears and started to perform a distressingly slow three-point turn. Sweat beaded his face and he muttered curses under his breath as falling zombies made every second even more harrowing. Another clipped the side of the bus, metal groaning under the impact as a deep groove formed in the ceiling.

Emma wiped the perspiration from her face and forced herself to breathe. Her chest was tight with tension. Helpless to do anything other than watch and hope, she ignored Ted's screams of terror.

"Shut the fuck up!" Monica yelled at him. "Your screaming is going to rile them up more, you idiot!"

"We're going to die!"

"No, we're not," Nerit said as though she had complete authority over the situation.

It was probably the cold look in her eyes that silenced Ted. Trembling, he curled up in his seat, his hands covering his face.

The bus bounced over bodies and clipped the front edge of the herd tromping down the road. Zombies scrabbled at the vehicle, fingers skidding over the metal grates, making an awful racket. Nerit fired at one zombie trying to clamber inside and kicked another away. Monica and Kurt stood a few feet behind her, ready to assist.

Arnold at last aimed the bus toward the bottom of the hill and accelerated. Despite having a souped up engine, the bus took an agonizing amount of time to gain speed. The herd pursued, banging against the rear door, smearing the windows with viscera. Since the jammed front door faced the drop off, Nerit didn't have to deal with any more zombies attempting to board, but she remained at the entrance.

When the bus had enough distance from the herd so that it was out of sight behind the trees and hillside, Emma's shoulders started to relax. Staring out the back window at the dappled light sifting through the tree branches to dance over the cracked road, she marveled out how deceptively tranquil it appeared. The curving road would work to their advantage. Zombies often lost interest in prey when it wasn't visible.

The short bus reached the bottom of the hill and turned off the narrow road, heading back the way they had come earlier. There weren't any more falling zombies, or another herd on the main country road, but the knowledge that there was a sizable number of zombies lurking on the outskirts of town was important to the Fort.

"Okay, we're in the clear for now," Nerit said. "Good job everyone."

Juan clapped Emma on the shoulder and headed to the rear of the bus to check on Belinda. Relieved, Emma took a seat behind Monica. A tired smile flitted across the woman's lips and she gave Emma thumbs up.

"It could've gone better," Monica said softly. "Sorry about what happened with Belinda. My cousin's not always this much of an idiot."

Emma shivered at the memory of her fall into the restroom. The moment when she'd considered running for the bus would haunt her. She would have died. Yet Juan had come through for her in the end.

"Grief and guilt make people do stupid shit. I get it. But he got us out of there, right?"

"Nerit's gonna rip into his ass and he deserves it."

"We rescued everyone, and in this world, that's something to drink to."

"Damn right, it is."

While Arnold took a long, winding way home to avoid leading the zombies back to town, Emma sank back in her seat and thanked whatever power had brought her to the Fort. Her body hurt all over and she was shaken, but relief was a sweet remedy. It was nice to be among people who were willing to put themselves at risk to save each other. She was definitely in the right place for a new beginning. When her gaze drifted toward Juan where he sat talking to Belinda and Kurt, she wondered what it would look like.

CHAPTER 25

This Is Not A Love Story

Once the bus cleared the gates, Arnold pulled over to where some people holding stretchers waited. Emma didn't have to be told to stay put. The weak and wounded they had rescued were obviously a priority. The survivors were swiftly taken off, placed on stretchers, and with Nerit leading the way, were quickly transported to the small trailer with a red cross painted on the side that was the Fort's med center. There were workers already waiting in a line outside to be checked by the medical staff for infection who'd probably returned from duty outside the Fort.

Though Juan watched Belinda's removal from the bus with concern, he didn't make an attempt to follow. He remained inside the bus while Arnold drove on to the garage. Emma had detected a change in his mood after he'd spent a few minutes speaking with Belinda and Kurt. Monica appeared to notice too, for she kept glancing back at him.

When the bus rolled up to the loading bay, Greta was waiting for them with two other mechanics. Her jaw dropped when she surveyed the damage.

Arnold braked. "I'm in so much trouble. She's going to kill me."

Bounding through the jammed door, Greta said, "What the hell happened?"

"Flying zombies," Arnold replied while turning off the engine and tossing her the keys.

Greta gazed in confusion at all the deep dents in the roof. "Are you fuckin' with me?"

"No, seriously. They were coming down like cats and dogs."

The look Arnold got in response said he'd have a lot of explaining to do.

"Okay, let's do our check through." Greta started down the aisle with the two mechanics. Their exclamations of disbelief were amusing.

"Let's go, Emma," Monica said, gesturing for her to join her once Greta passed her seat.

Following Monica off the bus, Emma rubbed the back of her neck, trying to get the cricks out. Now that the adrenaline from earlier had worn off, she was feeling every bruise, scratch, and sprain. Plus, she really needed to pee.

"Fuck, I'm tired," Monica groused while checking her watch. "And it's not even lunch time."

"Time flies when you're fighting zombies. Also, it can be a little painful." One of her wrists was swollen from when she had slammed into the wall.

"I could definitely use some Advil." Monica glanced back at where her cousin and Arnold were talking to Greta. "I can't get the image out of my head of my stupid ass cousin making that crazy leap to rescue Belinda. Not that he's a bad guy. He's dealing with shit and it has him a little off center."

Emma got the impression that Monica didn't want her to think badly of Juan. Though she wished he had been a little bit more reasonable during the mission, she didn't blame him for his actions.

"It was like he needed to prove something to himself today."

"Well, he's living with a lot of guilt because he couldn't save Jenni. Plus, he has had an unrequited crush on Belinda since they were kids. You don't have to be a shrink to figure out that he wanted to save at least one person he loves."

"If it had been Billy on that roof, I don't know what the hell I would've done. I can't fault anyone for wanting to save a loved one."

"I guess you're right. If it had been Bette, I would've done anything to save her."

"We all do stupid shit, Monica. It's human nature."

"Juan can be impetuous and kinda jump before he thinks, but he's a smart guy. Usually." Monica pointed to the wall. "He didn't even hesitate to start building this. The minute the zombies appeared, he pushed everyone into action. It's just hard seeing him trying to retroactively save Jenni."

Emma had definitely noticed a change in Juan when he'd realized Belinda was at risk. She suspected he'd considered the rescue mission as some sort of second chance.

"From what I've heard, it sounds like Jenni usually did the saving."

"Which was why I was scared shitless by my cousin today. I saw that same self-sacrificial impulse in him she had."

The men jogged up to join them on their trek to the med center.

"Is Greta furious with you?" Monica asked, quickly starting a different conversation.

"Nah. She admitted that flying zombies would be hard to avoid," Arnold answered. "But she cussed a lot."

Juan looked relieved. "Belinda and the others are already inside, huh?"

"They got bumped to the front of the line since they were pretty messed up from their time up on the roof. Did you see those blisters on Kurt's face?" Monica shivered. "I will never skip sunscreen again."

"Thank God we were able to save her," Juan said.

Emma wondered if Juan realized he'd slipped and not included the two male survivors.

Monica stopped in mid-stride, whirled about, and stopped him with a hand planted firmly against his chest. "Despite you being a dumbass."

The group stuttered to a halt, standing awkwardly around the cousins.

With a frustrated sigh, Juan stared at Monica with a weary look on his handsome face. "I'm already gonna hear it from Nerit. Are you going to give me shit too?"

Arnold looked as embarrassed as Emma about the confrontation. Emma swiveled slightly to the left, pretending to stare at the sky.

"Yes, but I'm going to say this with love, Juan."

"Do we have to do this *right now*?"

"Yeah, we do. Because you pulled some seriously stupid shit."

Juan cast a desperate look at Emma, but she pretended not to see it. The image of him leaping onto the roof was too fresh in her mind. So was her escape from the zombies in the restroom. He deserved a lecture.

"Fine. Let me have it."

"Saving your childhood unrequited love is not going to make you feel better about not being able to save Jenni. There isn't a future for you in the past. You're not going to save the girl and suddenly find happiness. This is real life. This isn't a love story."

Monica's harsh words apparently registered with her cousin. "Noted."

"And you owe Emma an apology."

Emma stood with her arms folded, ill at ease with the entire conversation. It felt too personal to be having right in the middle of the busy entrance area. But she was peeved at Juan. He'd saved her in the end, but it couldn't be ignored that if he hadn't acted impetuously, she wouldn't have needed saving in the first place.

Juan turned toward her with his green eyes cast downward. "I apologize about earlier today. I acted like an asshole. I lost my damn head. Emma, you're the one who really rescued Belinda, not me."

"I did what I had to," Emma replied, embarrassed. It was awkward dealing with his guilt over his actions, but she was glad he recognized he'd fucked up.

"Again, I apologize."

"Apology accepted," Emma said, meaning it.

"I won't let you down again. I promise."

Emma smiled slightly. "Good."

"So you're not going to act like a damn fool anymore?" Monica asked, her voice slightly mocking.

"I can't promise that." Juan chuckled. "I am me after all. But I am going to do my damn best."

"Good luck with that," Arnold said with a clap on Juan's

shoulder.

Juan let out a slow, fretful sigh. "I just hope she's gonna be okay. I never should've let her leave with Ed that day."

"Cousin, I love you, but if you actually think you could've told Belinda what to do without her telling you to fuck off, you are in for a world of hurt."

With a defensive shrug, he said, "I'm just worried about her."

"Sure, cuz. Remember, I know what's up with you. Unrequited love is a bitch. I know that from personal experience. Hell, I suspect Curtis tried to kill me and Bette because I didn't love him! Not that I'm saying you're going to be a complete psychopath," Monica added quickly, observing his frown.

"I'm not that crazy and it's not unrequited love. Belinda is my *friend.* Any romantic feelings I had for her are in the past. I may have had a thought or two about picking things back up with her, but I know that ain't happening. Also, stop talking about that asshole Curtis. You're scaring Emma. She'll think we're all nuts like him."

Emma raised an eyebrow. "More like curious."

"I have stories to tell you. Reality television would've loved the shit that goes down around here," Arnold said.

Juan took off his cowboy hat to run his fingers through his sweaty locks. "I gotta agree with Arnold. A total dramafest. Cram a bunch of people into one building and shit goes down. Especially when you got a psychopath in the bunch."

Monica's upper lip curled with disgust. "Curtis was one of my biggest mistakes. I'll tell you the whole story at some point, Emma, but things are much better since that asshole got a bullet to the brain."

Arnold nodded. "The apocalypse brings out either the best or the worst in people. Usually the worst if you're already unhinged."

"It's not always easy, but at least we've got each other."

"Aw, cuz. That was sweet." Monica hugged him, grinned over his shoulder, and pulled away. The joy that lit up her face was for the blonde woman who stepped out of the med center and strode toward them. "Hey, babe, I'm back in one piece."

"I'll be the judge of that." Bette may have been relieved to see Monica safely returned, but she maintained a professional veneer as she started to thoroughly pat down Monica, searching for bites.

"I guess this is a bad time to flirt with you, huh?"

Bette remained focused on her task, but a small smile tilted the corners of her mouth. "There will be time for that later."

Monica grinned. "I do like the sound of that."

Bette finished and made a notation on the clipboard she had hooked to her belt. "You're good to go."

"I'll see you later when your shift is done."

Monica took a step back, remaining close by while Bette started her examination of Emma. It was strange having someone touching her after being alone for so long, but Emma endured it. Bette vigilantly scrutinized her swollen wrist.

"I smacked it when I fell off a roof and banged into a wall," Emma explained.

"It sounds like you've got a story to tell," Bette said, her eyes darting toward her partner.

"My cousin did a stupid thing and it got a little hairy out there."

Juan bristled. "Are you gonna let me live it down?"

"Oh, no! You were acting like you were in a damn Bruce Willis movie. That jump off the bus onto the roof of the building was epic," Monica teased.

Bette perked up at this description. "I really want to hear this story!"

Juan grimaced. "Later. After some beers."

Bette finished jotting notes on the clipboard. "Emma, go ahead into the med center. Get some ice on that wrist before gets any worse."

Emma knew she hadn't been bitten, but she was relieved to be cleared. With a nod to Juan and the others, she walked to the entrance of the med center. She wasn't surprised when Monica followed in her wake.

There was a lot of activity in the back of the portable building where the space was divided into examination nooks. While Ted was complaining loudly to Nerit, which didn't surprise Emma, Kurt hovered near Belinda, watching Charlotte treat the worst of her burns. Emma looked around, hoping for a restroom, but didn't see a sign. She really, really had to go.

A nurse's assistant, wearing an armband with a red cross, stopped the two women inside the entrance.

"Bette said to get her wrist iced," Monica quickly explained.

The older white woman with short cropped graying dark hair and piercing black eyes responded by taking Emma's wrist and examining it herself. After a few seconds, she bobbed her head as though agreeing with Bette's assessment. Without a word she walked over to a refrigerator in one corner and fished a blue ice pack out of the freezer.

"That's Anne," Monica said, her voice low. "She's one of our newer people. She doesn't talk a lot. She came in with a salvage team that was looking for medications in an old folk's home. Anne was still there with her patients. She'd barricaded them into one section of the building and took care of them after the rising. She was out of food and fuel for the generator when they found her. The last of her patients had died the previous day and she was close to checking out. I think she's traumatized by the fact that she couldn't keep them alive one more day to be rescued."

From across the room, Anne directed Emma to a metal chair pushed up against the wall. Emma took the seat and Anne carefully applied the ice pack to the swelling. Pointing to it, Anne indicated she was to keep it in that spot. Emma nodded. Satisfied, Anne returned to a small desk near the front door to make entries into a binder. Trying to relax, Emma stretched out her legs, and Monica took the seat next to her.

"So much paperwork," Emma muttered. "I thought paperwork would've gone the way of the rest of civilization. Into the shitter."

Monica laughed. "Nope. We have to keep a good eye on our supplies and keep everyone organized, so...paperwork."

Emma was struck once more by how different the Fort was

from the life she'd lived for the last year.

The door yawed open, sunlight flooding in and briefly blinding her, and two men entered. In the forefront was a tall, handsome guy with curly brown hair followed closely by another dressed in a white shirt and khakis. Though both were white, the first man had a tan that indicated he spent a lot of time in the sun while the other was pasty and looked like he was taking a break from a boring desk job.

"That's Travis," Monica whispered, indicating the man who'd entered first. "He's the mayor. The second guy is Eric. He helps with a lot of the Fort planning since he used to be an engineer."

The door swung open again, letting Juan inside. Emma expected Arnold to follow, but the door slammed shut. The three men walked toward Nerit, who broke off her conversation with Ted to join them. They huddled together, speaking in lowered tones.

Emma examined her wrist and saw that she was going to have a pretty florid bruise. Luckily it wasn't broken.

Once again, she was blinded by the sunlight flooding through the open doorway when another man entered. He was tall, black, middle-aged, and ruggedly good-looking in his camouflage.

"Kevin, just in time for the debrief!" Nerit called out.

"Is Katie coming?" Kevin asked.

"No, she's gonna be resting for a while. Maternity leave," Travis responded with what Emma suspected was the grin of a proud father. "Yolanda should be here shortly."

"This is where leave," Monica whispered.

A little bewildered by their abrupt exit, Emma followed her out the door into the hot afternoon, cradling the icepack around her wrist.

"Those are the bigwigs of the Fort. They handle most of the planning of what goes down. They're gonna want to talk to Belinda and the others about what happened to Ed's group when they left here. It's best to make ourselves scarce."

"They could use a few more women on that council," Emma

replied.

"They had more, but shit happens. It *is* the zombie apocalypse."

Emma didn't want to pry. She remembered Yolanda's sad expression when discussing the former city secretary's demise.

"That it is."

Monica gestured to Bette talking to a group of people near the gate. "But sometimes good things happen too."

"Will we be told about Ed's group? Or is that something that will be top-secret?"

"Travis is pretty transparent with what's going on, but there may be a delay between when they find out what's up and when they tell us. They usually like to have some sort of plan in place before they spring anything on the general population. Sometimes I can get Juan to tell me, but he can be an asshole and hold out just to annoy me."

The popping sound of gunfire startled Emma. A truck heavily laden with supplies was being offloaded a few feet away and no one appeared bothered by the racket. On the walls, guards were speaking into walkie-talkies. Monica didn't appear concerned about the commotion either.

Noticing Emma's worried expression, Monica said, "The guards will take care of the zombies. If they need help the siren will go off. It's fine, really. Don't worry about it." Monica patted Emma on the shoulder and strolled toward the stairs that led over the wall to the main enclosure.

Emma followed. Life really *was* different at the Fort. It would take some getting used to.

But first she needed a bathroom.

CHAPTER 26

The Legend Known as Katie

The rest of Emma's day was spent resting. With her wrist injured, she was excused from kitchen duty. So instead of working in the kitchen all afternoon, she took a long, hot shower and fell asleep for several hours. Nightmares haunted her, waking her up abruptly. Each time she fell asleep, she dreamed again and again about being trapped in the restroom with the zombies slowly advancing on her. Among the dead, as usual in her dreams, were Billy and Stan, but this time they were joined by Macy and Julian, reunited in death and decay. As they closed in on her, she pulled the trigger on her pistol only to hear it click empty, and that was when she woke up every time.

When Emma stirred, groggy and sore, it was close to dinner time, so she dressed in a blue t-shirt and jeans and headed downstairs. Hungry, she needed some food, and maybe a drink to alleviate her anxiety.

The second the elevator doors opened, she knew something big was going on. The lobby was filled with people, most of them clustered around one focal point. Emma caught snippets of the conversations around her and understood what the excitement was about. Fort legend, Katie, was making an appearance. Joyful laughter and the hum of excited discussions flowed over Emma in one big wave, overpowering her senses. Her surroundings were too loud, too bright, and too crowded. Unanticipated claustrophobia swept over her and the panic attack that followed hit hard, stealing her breath away. The need to get out of the packed lobby boiled in her gut.

Pushing her way through the gathering, she caught a glimpse of the back of the blonde woman's head at the center of the attention. Travis stood next to her, beaming with pride. From the way Katie's head was tilted downward, she was most likely showing off her newborn daughter. That was even more cause for Emma to slip out and find a quiet space to recover. After her nightmares, it was hard to see a mother and child, safe and happy together.

Emma rapidly walked along the edges of the lobby to the hallway that would take her to the hotel exit. Heart thudding, she struggled not to break into a sprint. It wasn't until she reached the memorial area outside the hotel that she realized where she was going. Sitting down on the bench facing the photos of the deceased, she set her trembling hands on her knees and took several deep breaths.

The panic attack made it feel like her chest was being pinched tight. Wiping unexpected tears away with the back of her hand, she fought to regain her composure. It would take time to get used to the sights, sounds, and aroma of so many people being around and reprogram herself not to identify unexpected movement, noise, and smells as a threat. But it wasn't just the presence of so many people that had sent her fleeing. It was the absolute joy of the people celebrating a new life. She remembered being that mother at the center of attention, holding her newborn son, showing off the tiny being who'd grown inside her for so long, and entered the world holding her heart and dreams in his eyes.

"It's not going to get easier for us," Macy said.

Emma hadn't noticed the other woman's approach and started in surprise. Macy stood a few feet away with a sad, haunted look in her eyes. Dressed in a blue button down shirt, beige chinos, and Mexican sandals, Macy looked more like someone who worked in an office than a woman who fought across several states to save her zombie son. Macy blinked back tears of her own.

Macy hesitantly approached her. "I saw the woman with the baby."

Clearing her throat so she could talk, Emma tried very hard to remain composed. "That's Katie. The mayor's wife."

Emma scooted over to let Macy join her if she wanted to and

was pleased when she took up the silent offer.

"Ah. I guess that explains the celebrity status."

"She's also the mom of the first baby in the Fort. That's what Monica told me."

"Having babies in this world..." Macy sighed.

"Life has to go on if humanity is to survive."

The two women lapsed into silence for a minute or two. Emma rubbed her pounding head while Macy plucked at the skin around her fingernails. They were both trembling. Macy raised her eyes. Staring at the photos beneath their plastic protective covering, she gestured at the memorial.

"Who are they?"

"Those who died." Emma tried hard not to focus on the photo of the woman with the black hair and eyes wearing a red sweater.

"Oh, I see. There's a lot."

"I'm not sure if it's only for the people who died in defense of the Fort, or just those who were lost when the apocalypse started."

"There are a few kids on there." Macy pointed to a photo of a teenager. "But in this world, children have to fight as well, I suppose."

Pressing a hand to her chest, Emma tried to even out her breathing. She hated having anxiety attacks. It was so ridiculous to have one now that she was in a safe place. "It's such a fucked up world."

"Bad things were always happening, but we were usually safe from the worst of it here in the States. I spent most my time worrying about making sure my son had a good home, food, clothes, a solid education, learned his manners, understood the obstacles that were going to affect him because he was black, and have the ambition to achieve all his dreams in spite of them. When I saw that first zombie, all those fears were replaced with something so much more primal. My sole purpose became his survival. And then that little girl bit him and..." Macy pressed her lips together and shook her head. "Does it get easier, Emma?"

"No," Emma answered honestly. "The pain doesn't go away. You just learn to live with it. Now I'm trying to figure out how to let all of this-" she waved at their surroundings "-into my life."

"I doubt you can ever fill the empty spot where your son once lived."

"No, we can't. Maybe we can fill in the area around it, but I don't know. I'm trying to figure it out."

Macy took Emma's hand in hers and squeezed it gently. "Me too. But thank you for convincing me to try. You're right. Every life is precious. Including our own."

Without pride, and almost as a confession, Emma said, "I nearly died today, but I saved three people."

"Did you? See! People need you, Emma. You got the skills to bring us home safely."

That brought a wide smile to Emma's face. "Thank you for saying that. That's the role I've chosen for myself here. I plan to save everyone I can."

"That's a good role to have. As for me, I'm still sorting out how I can help around here. Yolanda is giving me a few days to get my head together, which I definitely need. In the interim, I'm going to spend time with my nephew. I didn't realize how much Lewis needed me. He's a grown man, but he's got a tender spirit."

As if on cue, the skinny young man emerged from the hotel, looking around in a desperate way.

"Speaking of Lewis, I best let him know I'm okay. I suspect he's halfway convinced I'll disappear over the wall." Glancing at Emma and noticing her questioning look, she added, "I won't. I'm here to stay."

"I'm glad, Macy."

"Me too, Emma."

Emma watched Macy walk away then lowered her head into her hands. Beneath her fingers, she could feel her pulse in her temples thudding harder than normal.

With the workday over, the Fort was at peace for a little while. The sounds of the big Texas flag in front of city hall flapping in the wind and the grackles calling out to each other as the sunlight started to wane were soothing. The breeze was warm, but pushed away the heat of the day.

The scuff of a heel pulled Emma out of her reverie. Looking up through her long tresses falling over her face, she saw Katie laying a wildflower bouquet at the base of the memorial. It was her first good look at the woman the Fort occupants revered. Her shoulder length blonde hair was wavy with a slight curl at the end and it framed a face with Nordic features. Tall and slender-limbed, she had the aura of someone who had their shit together. The plaid button down shirt she wore tented over her post-pregnancy bump and hung over her hips. Instead of wearing jeans and boots like most of the Fort inhabitants, she wore compression leggings and chucks.

Katie turned her gaze in Emma's direction, catching her in the act of looking her over. Her eyes were a much brighter shade of green than Juan's and she had a slight tilt at the corners of her eyes.

"Hi, Emma," Katie said in a warm voice.

For some reason, Emma's throat tightened and it took her a second to answer. "Hello, Katie."

"Mind if I sit down? I'm a little wiped out."

"Of course! Sit down, I mean. I don't mind."

Settling down beside Emma, Katie exhaled with relief. "No one tells you how damn painful it is *after* you have a kid."

"It sucks," Emma said, commiserating. "I remember it well."

"I'm definitely going to give it some time before having a brother or sister for Bryce."

"I don't blame you one bit." Emma sat up straighter, pushing her hair back over her shoulders. "By the way, Bryce is a great name."

"Thank you. I named her after my dad. His name was Bruce." Katie's gaze returned to the memorial. "Sadly, I don't have a picture of him."

Unsure of what to say, Emma remained silent. Her panic attack was subsiding, the rough waves of emotion ebbing away and gradually calming. Katie had a comforting and eerily familiar presence. It was as if Emma had met her previously, but had forgotten the exact time and location. But that wasn't possible, so maybe Jenni had imparted more to Emma in the dream than she'd realized.

A long, but comfortable silence stretched between them. Katie leaned slightly forward, her fingers reverently brushing Jenni's picture.

"Rune told me," Katie said. "Before he left."

Emma gulped. "That Jenni sent me?"

With a sad smile, Katie nodded. "She's good at saving people. She saved me, you know, on that first day. My wife was dead, I was in shock and lost in a neighborhood I didn't know, and then I saw her standing outside of her front door in a pink bathrobe. My instantaneous instinct was to save her, so I pulled over. At first I thought I saved her, but looking back, I know she saved me too. She gave me a purpose that day. Otherwise, I'm not sure what would have happened to me. But now I'm here helping to rebuild the world."

"And a mom to the next generation." She'd caught Katie's reference to a wife, but wasn't about to ask about something so personal.

"Which I thought I'd never be." Katie laughed with delight. "I blame Jenni."

"It's good though, right?" Emma attempted not to sound annoyed, but her own loss pinched at her insides.

Katie's bittersweet smile and gentle expression said much about her as a person. "It's *very* good. It's a blessing that I am grateful for especially knowing how much has been lost. I am sad for your loss, but I am glad you came here for a new start."

Emma sensed her sincerity. It was evident Katie had realized she'd bumped a wound and was trying to soothe the smarting. Everyone was walking around with trauma triggers that could go off at the most innocuous comment. It wasn't Katie's fault that she was a new mother with a living child while Emma and Macy were mourning theirs.

"It's intense starting over after being alone for a year," Emma said, gazing at the hotel. "There are so many people..."

"It wasn't just you getting claustrophobic earlier. I got overwhelmed in the lobby too. Everyone wanted to see Bryce, so Travis took over showing her off so I could come here to see Jenni."

"I'm sorry. I should have left when you got here."

"No, no. I'm glad you're here. I wanted to meet you. I like getting to know all the new people who arrive. I completely understand how it feels to arrive here and finally be safe enough to mourn and heal from all the shit we went through." Katie glanced toward City Hall where Travis now stood on the doorstep with Yolanda. She was holding the baby, cooing with delight over the newborn. "I expected to fight to survive, but I didn't expect to fall in love and create a new family. That was a surprise."

Emma mulled over Katie's comment, remembering Rune's words. She had time to discover what the Fort could offer her. Whether that included finding love again was another matter, but she had time to find her way.

"Is it worth it? To start over? To love again? Even with the risks?" she asked.

With a wistful smile, Katie said simply, "Yes. As terrifying as this world is, it is worth it."

CHAPTER 27

The Risks

When Katie left after a few more minutes of small talk, Emma's panic attack had diminished to the point where she was starting to feel like herself again. The shakiness in her hands and her rapidly beating heart had returned to normal during her conversation with Katie. Feeling calmer, Emma watched Katie and her husband retreat back into the hotel with Yolanda in their wake.

It was dinner time, but despite her hunger, she couldn't quite bring herself to go inside the hotel. She watched the sunset while the breeze ruffled her hair and dried the remains of her tears.

The sun was just vanishing behind the horizon when Juan appeared carrying a covered tray and holding a bottle of water under his arm. She expected him to keep walking past the memorial, but he joined her.

"Hey," he said, sounding awkward.

"Hi."

Holding out the food and bottled water, he gave her a sheepish look. "You didn't make it to dinner, so I brought you a tray. It's a hamburger and fries."

Emma arched her eyebrows while taking the tray. "A real hamburger?"

"We watch over a herd of cattle on a nearby ranch, so yes, it's a real hamburger."

Pulling the foil off, Emma squealed with delight. "Oh my God! Thank you so much for bringing me this. It looks and smells amazing!"

Sitting beside her, Juan squared his shoulders beneath his clean white shirt. He had scrubbed up for dinner and smelled of soap and shampoo. "Katie said she saw you out here, so I thought I'd see if you were still here after you didn't show up in the dining hall."

"Well, I do appreciate it."

"I had some time on my hands, so it's no big deal."

Juan's tone implied that it was a bigger deal than he was admitting. He'd come here with a purpose and that made her a little uneasy. Emma set the water bottle between them, a small barrier.

"Where are your kids?"

"With my mom. Her assistant handles the night cleanup so she can spend time with them. She loves them with all her heart and they love her. Adopting them was the best thing I ever did."

Taking a bite of her hamburger, Emma savored every flavor dancing over her tongue. "Were you forgiven for forgetting to tell them goodbye this morning?"

Letting out a chuckle, Juan shook his head. "Jason reamed me out. Who would've thought a fifteen-year-old could make you feel like so much shit?"

"I hear teenagers are good at that."

A part of her heart ached at the thought that she would never know Billy at fifteen. She'd only been a mother for a short period of time in the grand scheme of things. It had been a rewarding experience. A little piece of her was envious of Juan. He had four children. Maybe they weren't his by birth, but they were his by love.

Hooking his thumb behind his belt buckle and leaning back on the bench, Juan wore a guilty expression. "The kid was *pissed*. All I could do was stand there and take it because he was right. He even had the decency to wait until the little ones were napping this afternoon and then he let me have it. Both barrels. Not holding back one bit. I know he was Jenni's stepson, but I swear I saw her fire in him."

"So what did you say?" Emma asked.

"I admitted I was an asshole, begged for forgiveness, and promised to never do it again. And I meant it. Jason was definitely right. I should've told him. Maybe the young ones didn't need to know, but as the oldest he certainly did. He's a tough kid and he deserves my respect. My mom said when I took on this role that it wasn't going to be easy, and she was definitely right. But I love those kids. I will do right by them in the future."

She couldn't help but think of her own parents abandoning her. "Honestly, that puts you ahead of a lot of asshole parents. The fact that you are willing to listen to your kids and do what needs to be done to give them assurance says a lot. I know you're new at the job, but you *are* a great dad for being willing to learn."

"Thanks, Em," Juan replied somberly. "I may have bitten off more than I can chew with Jason, but that kid is pretty awesome. I'll do my best to be a good father to him."

"That's why you *will* be a good father."

"Still, man, that hurt."

Emma ate a few more bites of the hamburger and the overly salty fries. She couldn't remember the last time she'd been in a Whataburger, but she doubted that meal had tasted this good. Juan sat beside her in silence, observing the first stars appearing overhead. She got the impression he wanted to talk to her about something, but he nervously scratched the back of his neck.

When she was down to her last fry, he twisted his body toward her so he could face her. She mentally steeled herself for what might come next and shoved a fry into her mouth.

"Emma, I don't know where to start, so I'll just babble incoherently until you tell me to shut up."

Chewing slowly, Emma nodded.

"My cousin was right earlier. I was trying to fix the past by saving Belinda. I knew I couldn't, but the compulsion was so strong. It took over me, made me stupid, and I almost got you killed. That's been bugging the shit out of me all day."

"You apologized. I forgave you."

"Yeah, but I almost got you killed because I was desperate to somehow prove myself."

"To Belinda?"

Juan shook his head.

"To Jenni?"

"No, no. To myself. Monica was right. I wanted to save Belinda to prove to myself that I could've saved Jenni if I had been there and not laid up with a gunshot wound. Instead, I proved what a dumb shit I am because I couldn't see that what I have right now is what's important."

"Your kids."

"Yeah, my kids. My friends. Travis and Katie's beautiful baby that will call me Uncle One, 'cause you know the baby will hear my kids calling me Daddy One. The damn dog and his smelly ass farts." Juan's green eyes flicked away from her face. "A chance to get to know you."

Emma deliberately took another bite.

"We don't know each other well yet, but I feel like we should…uh…maybe…uh…date."

Swallowing, Emma croaked out, "Date?"

"Yeah. That thing normal people do to figure out if they like each other enough to do…more."

The handsome man was sweating so hard one droplet was gliding down the bridge of his nose.

Remembering her earlier conversations with Macy and Katie, Emma struggled with the idea of taking a chance at allowing the emptiness inside her heart to be filled again. Yet, if she was going to live, it would have to be a life worth living.

"Okay," she said.

"Cool. Cool," Juan said, obviously relieved. "Great. Awesome. Though I'm not sure how you date in the zombie apocalypse."

"Go kill zombies together?"

"Then we already had a first date!"

"Or maybe it's just sitting here for a while."

Juan grinned at her while she took another bite of her hamburger. "Okay. That sounds great."

So that was what they did.

They were interrupted an hour later.

"Fort meeting! Lobby in five minutes!" a teenager's voice called out.

A second later, the girl appeared near the memorial. "Fort meeting! Five minutes!"

"We'll be there, Shelley," Juan called.

With a nod, the girl dashed off.

"Does this happen a lot?" Emma asked.

Looking somber, Juan nodded. "When shit's about to go down."

"So something is up?"

Nervously running his hands through his messy curls, Juan grimaced. "I knew the Fort meeting was going to happen. It was actually a big reason I wanted to talk to you at dinner. When you weren't there, I came looking for you because I wanted to have a moment of peace before shit got real. Again."

"Oh?" "After we were certain that there is a cause for concern, Travis decided to share some news with everyone tonight."

It now made sense why Travis and Katie had come downstairs with Bryce. It was a way of softening the coming blow.

"Is this about Ed's group?"

Folding his arms over his chest, Juan nodded. "There was more than one group that left. One was led by a woman named Mary. A real hellfire and brimstone type. She was convinced we were being punished with the horde because we had gay people in the Fort. When she and her people left, they formed what they called the Baptist Encampment. Though between you and me, her vision of being a Baptist ain't one I'm familiar with."

"Like those Westboro people?"

"Exactly."

"So Ed's group went to the Baptist Encampment?"

"No, Ed's group was heading northwest and got turned back by armed militia-types. Kurt said they had the road blocked off and were heavily armed with military-grade weapons. According to Belinda, who was in Ed's Durango, they wouldn't let Ed's group through the blockade. Ed told them about the horde, but the man in charge didn't give a shit. He sent them back the way they'd come, which is why they ended up running into the horde. They lost half their people right away. Ed got bit while trying to run with Belinda from his overrun vehicle to the one Kurt was driving. When they realized they were heading right for the main part of the horde, they took refuge on top of that hill."

"Shit. So why didn't they let them through the barricade?"

"This is the kicker, Em. The guy in charge was Mary's son, Jonathan. Jon was Special Ops overseas and got kicked out for killing civilians. He claimed it was an accident, but his own guys turned him in, saying he did it 'cause he liked it. Apparently, he'd been doing it on the sly and his guys had had it with him. Said Jon wanted to kill Muslims for Jesus, or some such bullshit."

Emma winced. "I'm pretty sure Jesus was a pacifist."

"That's what my bible says too, but it don't matter with Mary and her type. Worse yet, word around town was that Jon was always a sociopath. A bully at heart, power hungry. His dishonorable discharge and the local rumors are why they wouldn't hire him to be a deputy sheriff when he applied. He had a real beef about that. If I recall correctly, that's when he went off a joined some militia group out in West Texas."

A knot formed in her gut. "So Mary and her son Jon are a threat, aren't they?"

Juan shrugged. "We don't know. All we know is that when Jon turned back Ed's group, he told them they couldn't escape God's wrath. That they had to go back and pay for their sins."

"Because Mary thought the horde would destroy the Fort."

"Right."

"But it didn't."

"Exactly."

"So if the horde didn't inflict God's wrath on the Fort than maybe they'll take God's judgment into their own hands."

"That's a possibility. And since it's a possibility-"

"The Fort needs to be ready."

"Exactly."

Emma took his hand in hers to discover they were both trembling. Now it was clear why Juan had chosen to approach her. Perhaps the Fort wasn't as safe as they thought and time was of the essence. She wasn't about to lose her new chance at life and community and would fight to defend it.

"So then we'll be ready, won't we?" Emma said, her voice cold steel.

Pride lingered in Juan's eyes as he smiled at her, obviously pleased with her reaction. "Yes, we will."

"Plus, y'all got something on your side you didn't have before," Emma said, lifting her chin with confidence.

"What's that?"

"A gawddamn fearless zombie killer."

ABOUT THE AUTHOR

Rhiannon Frater is the award-winning author of the *As the World Dies* zombie trilogy (Tor) as well as independent works such as *The Last Bastion of the Living* (declared the #1 Zombie Release of 2012 by Explorations Fantasy Blog and the #1 Zombie Novel of the Decade by B&N Book Blog) and the *Pretty When She Dies* series. She was born and raised in Texas where she currently resides with her husband and furry children (a.k.a pets). She loves scary movies, sci-fi and horror shows, playing video games, cooking, dyeing her hair weird colors, and shopping for Betsey Johnson purses and shoes.

Visit her online at rhiannonfrater.com

Printed in Poland
by Amazon Fulfillment
Poland Sp. z o.o., Wrocław